SOMEBODY SHOULD HAVE SCOLDED THE GIRL

and other stories

by Paula Coomer

The following stories were originally published as noted:

"A Certain Kind of Warrior," *The Raven Chronicles,* Spring/Summer 2016.
"Cattle Need to Roam to Graze," *Knock,* Seattle, Washington, Issue 10, November 2008.
"Chemo, Then Gainesville" (in a slightly different form), *Spilt Infinitive,* Jan. 1, 2015, Vol. 1, Issue 4.
"Somebody Should Have Scolded the Girl," *Perceptions Magazine of the Arts, Spring 2014,* Portland, Oregon, May 2014.

Cover design by Michelle Fairbanks/Fresh Design
Edited by Twyla Beth Lambert

Print ISBN 978-1-945419-34-8
ePub ISBN 978-1-945419-35-5

Library of Congress Control Number 2019931075

For Daddy

TABLE OF CONTENTS

Don't compromise yourself. You are all you've got.

—Janis Joplin

BLACK OAK AND SUGAR TREE

WHEN THE WAR in Vietnam was over, Mercy Grace finally got the chance to say she'd made the right decision when she stood her ground and stayed with the family homestead instead of taking the Greyhound to Louisville like most of the women from her graduating class at Adair County high school had done. The price of housing in the city was so steep that many of them ended up living not in converted Edwardian mansions along maple-lined streets, as they had dreamed, but in the new projects across the bridge in New Albany, commuting to the meat factories or automotive plants on the Kentucky side of the Ohio, or to the government munitions manufactory on the Indiana side, instead of the downtown Louisville jewelry stores and dress shops they had once imagined, because the factories paid better.

Her cousin Amanda Sue called with the news that the last Americans had been evacuated out of Saigon and that the munitions plant—or bullet factory, as it was known—where she worked—in Clarksville, Indiana, had put all departments on notice. Two days to shut down and nobody was to report to work after Friday. One second, people had a job and the next, not.

Mercy Grace, for one, would be glad to see old friends trudging back to Adair County. She could use help. The boys returning from Vietnam over the years had proven themselves undependable, many not looking for regular work at all, lingering in the county just long enough to regroup, kiss their mothers and grandmothers, and devise a plan for getting down the road. Quite a number came back with drug habits. Others drowned themselves in the pursuit of sex or the manufacture of still liquor or shaved off trees in the middle of their granddaddy's woods to establish themselves in the marijuana trade. Rumors flew like plucked feathers. She could predict how long a hired man would stay by the stories he told, most of which had to do with earning cash enough to stake himself in his personal vision of *someplace else, someplace bigger*. The greater the vision, the longer she could count on him to occupy the old poplar cabin, her family's original homestead, down by the barn and the creek. Ray Joe Morrison, whose maple-colored eyes and muscled arms and shoulders she'd quickly grown used to, had stayed on for four months. The average she swore was two weeks, which was about how often she felt like she was swabbing the floors and bleaching out the night pot, but her records told her it was closer to a month. Otherwise, she hadn't had steady help since her folks passed, aside from Pastor Bob, the Presbyterian minister, who made a habit of hiring himself out to anybody with a nickel to spare, trying to ease the congregation's burden of his support. But his availability wavered, depending on who else needed him and which religious holiday or rite of passage lay immediately ahead. She was barely twenty-five, carrying the load that had once kept her father, her mother, herself, and her brother Donald Dale busy seven days a week.

Donald Dale, her only sibling, followed the example of their cousins, the Hadley twins, and moved out West to California. He'd come back from Vietnam missing part of his left hand, sporting a Fu Manchu mustache, long hair, and a peace sign tattooed on the web between the thumb and forefinger of his right hand. He "wasn't turning his back on her," but he "didn't jive with old-time ways anymore."

She'd thought about building a bunkhouse, providing discharged soldiers in exchange for work a place to adjust to being back in the mountains, a place to gain distance from war. Perhaps more of them would stay in the county if they had a little support. Maybe she could offer an alternative to drugs and bootleg as the hyphen between Vietnam and whatever their new lives were going to be. More and more, she saw the hyphen becoming the whole of it.

*   *   *

April was her favorite month, for all the wildflowers in bloom and the smell on her clothes from jarring the last of the sap from the sugar maples. Her hundred and nineteen acres abounded with them, and had for all of memory, as the older trees were riddled with waxed-over tap holes and the original deed called the northwest entrance to the property from the creek as being "where Petty's Fork meets Cabin Branch at the Granite Boulder betw. a Black Oak and a Sugar Tree apart from the Sugar Bush." She had a taste for the woody sweetness the trees produced, each year putting back a few jars for casual use on her biscuits at breakfast, but mostly saving it for selling to her list of longstanding customers in summer and for putting away to dress up oatmeal and hotcakes in the winter.

And for the sake of a much-loved tradition in Adair County, her family's maple-sugar candy and shortbread cookies, which she sold in ribbon-tied boxes at Attie's Drugstore on the square in Columbia and to several storefront business owners who gave them to employees as gifts at various times of the year, including Christmas: the law office, the county sheriff, the judge, both banks, *The Columbia Beacon*, and off-campus administrative offices belonging to Cumberland Basin College, not to mention a tier of Kentucky state offices, including the local parole officer, Wade Elvin Locklear, whose job it was to keep track of men returning to the county after their time in prison at LaGrange. Wade Elvin mailed her a check each July for the coming season's shipment, a dozen boxes of candy and a dozen of cookies, making quick work of his Christmas list, which consisted of every parolee on his docket and his mother in South Carolina. Every year Mercy Grace made enough cash from her Christmas sales to keep herself in flour and sugar and lard for the ensuing months, pay her telephone and electricity bills, and fund the next year's round of production. Even if she was at times curious about the greater world, she was proud that she so far had been able to continue this tradition, as the women of her mother's family had been handing down those two recipes since the Murrells had settled the section of Kentucky known as Petty Fork Creek, before Kentucky was a state, before Adair was a county, and before Lewis and Clark made their famed journey west—more than a hundred and seventy-five years.

She started tapping the trees in late January or early February, as soon as the daytime temperatures got above freezing, and the boil down took up most of her time during the ensuing otherwise quiet weeks of the year, but the cutting and topping and stripping and grinding and cooking down of sugar cane to molasses began in the cool of the autumn, after the stalks yellowed and grew striped with red. Ripe cane looked like a field of corn, and the tops made good stock feed. The work was exhausting, hot, and messy, but it made high-profit money for the farm. Not only was molasses a component of both time-proven recipes, but Mercy Grace sold quart jars of the dark-sweet stuff alongside her maple syrup. She'd just secured holiday orders from Goodin's Market and several other spots around Adair County. Over and over she heard it said that her family's traditional "Black Gold"—*Since before Kentucky was a state!*—label was a called-for favorite by all manner of local baker.

The transformation from cane to molasses was a lengthy, energy-consuming process, in part because it required harnessing one of the mules—usually old Danny, as he was less apt to balk at the task—to turn the grindstone, plus steam-washing and sanitizing the boiling vat afterwards and the long, skinny separating chute—nearly twice as long as she was tall—with its many strainer fins. As a youngster she was instructed by her father to climb in and scrub the still-warm copper vat with buckets of water and rags that subsequently had to be chugged clean in her mother's Kelvinator, its side-by-side zinc tubs filled with even more buckets of water for first the soap cycle, then the rinse, all of which had to be heated on the wood cookstove that sat on the summer porch. The cloths then had to be fed one at a time through arm-eating rollers to press out the rinse water. Today, it was a matter of hoses and spray nozzles. Then and now it was also Mercy Grace's job to keep the fire under the vat stable and the temperature of the molasses cooking at a steady boil, which required her to feed the firebox underneath. Oak worked best, because it burned hot and long, but oak was getting harder and harder to come by, which was part of why she was planting a new grove of black oak out beyond the barn. At two to three feet of growth per year, she should easily be able to harvest a thinning crop in four or five years. Life, to Mercy Grace, was nothing if not about looking ahead and being prepared.

When she was young, her father climbed on a box to stir a five-foot long paddle hard and fast enough to keep the foam down. Now she does it, wearing the same leather apron and shoulder-high gloves that had served as his and his father's protection against hot splatters. With the new tiltable platform built and installed, Mercy Grace had arrived at the next level of engineering in the history of her family's molasses production. She was able to accomplish an hour's worth of cleaning in a matter of minutes merely because she could rotate the vat and lock it into a perpendicular position instead of risking a fall to climb a ladder. If she dispensed with the grindstone and installed a wringer apparatus similar to the clothes washer, she could make operations even more efficient, but she advertised old-timey goodness. How could she guarantee old-timey goodness without old-timey process? Even the tilt mechanism was a concession.

In her spare minutes she was sketching plans for the bunkhouse. If she had eight men, she could build a milking barn, keep more dairy cows, raise dozens more acres in cane. She could quadruple the amount of molasses she sold, expand to surrounding counties. She still wasn't growing her entire allotment of tobacco, because the government was paying her to do otherwise, but she could, and more, if allotments were increased, which was the talk. With the country full of bored ex-soldiers standing in unemployment lines, discharge bonuses burning a hole, tobacco use was expected to increase, even without federal contracts for the tens of thousands of filter-less pre-rolled cigarettes being shipped overseas with C-rations. Only a few choice friend-distributors knew, but already she was selling bootleg tobacco: instead of carting it to the warehouse to auction, she dried and chopped and processed it herself and sold unprinted muslin bags of it for half the cost of store-bought rolling tobacco. Her profit was more than ten times what the government paid her for not growing during price controls. Since nobody was looking over her shoulder, she didn't have to report what she didn't sell to the big wig corporate buyers. Revenuers so far hadn't come hunting bootleg tobacco, and if they did, being as young as she was, she'd claim ignorance, and that would be the end of it. Wouldn't make the money she earned meantime go away. Money she kept buried in the ground at the back of the old stone room and not in the bank. If she were smart, she'd be into what the law did come looking for, however, and that was still liquor. Everybody in the U.S. was having a romance with shine, which she expected to grow more pronounced now that Vietnam was over. Ever since *Deliverance* was at the movie houses, it wasn't just locals living in a dry county looking for Saturday fun. People came from all over to whisper about shine. She could have acres of money buried in the ground. She could fill the old stone house. Mercy Grace would never do such a thing, of course, but it did make her think about how gullible people were, and how much money could be made off of gullibility. In her mind, if she used tobacco to build a bunkhouse and could keep a half-dozen or more boys off the booze, her crime would be in balance. Call it her war effort. Part of her felt guilty anyway that she didn't sign on for one of the factory jobs or one of the women's branches of the military. She could have joined the medical corps, travelled the world. Done a bit of good.

She was thinking about how the first job she was going to hand over to the next person she hired was walking old Danny to turn the grindstone, plus saw-dusting and scooping his plops, when it occurred to her that she could get Albert Goodin, whose brother owned the grocery market in Columbia, to smith her a stout set of tongs with locking clamps on the pincers so she could hoist the grindstone up and out into a vat of soapy water, then hose it down while it hung mid-air. Obviously, some expense, but she'd reached an impasse with the health board. If she was going to insist on using traditional practices, she was going to have to continue to update her cleaning and hygiene procedures, which was how she arrived at the point of using sawdust to sanitize Danny's pile before she scooped it, as was using a galvanized shovel so it could endure a brief soaking in sanitizer afterward.

Then she thought about how no one save the long line of the Murrell side of her family had ever walked a mule around that grinding stone, until the Murrell women started marrying Hadley men. Even if it was fifteen miles of dirt road and a half-mile of slate creek bottom to get to the main road, and until recently by mule and wagon, since the time they settled this original sixteen-hundred-acre section of Kentucky, Murrells had grown cane and cooked molasses and sold it to whomever wanted it. At one time, they'd had a dozen vats going and shipped it by buckboard from holler to holler and into the flatwoods west of Petty's Fork Creek. Midway into the nineteenth century, before the Civil War, when the first Murrell married the first Hadley, the land got split into half-sections of eight hundred acres each and the easternmost half-section was given to the bride and groom. It was from this marriage that her father, Jonah Bryant Hadley, was descended. By the time her parents were in the ground, they still owned two hundred acres, including the original homestead. They left eighty-one acres to her brother Donald Dale, which he promptly sold off to a couple by the last name of King, whose cute, tawny-haired, wide-eyed kids Mercy Grace would see waiting by the gravel road cut-off for the school bus in the early morning as she waited for the Farm Fresh truck to pick up her carefully sterilized stainless steel cans full of the day's gallons of what her father called, "white gold." He long insisted that he should be milking more cows not growing more cane, as the profits were steeper.

She was left with a hundred and nineteen acres, and by county zoning, no further splitting was allowed, not that she wanted to, but at times when she had no extra, when she thought she was going to have to haul out some of the cash she had buried in the old stone room, she fantasized about breaking the place into twenty acre lots, keeping only nine for herself. She could move into the cabin or the old stone room and live out her life on the dollars she had sealed in half-gallon jars and covered with earth. Of course, she wasn't the only one to do the burying. The Murrells long had been keepers of stories and keepers of the copper penny. She would have no idea how much usable molasses and maple syrup money was in the ground on her place, except that a handed-down map in her mother's diary told the tale. A map that had been kept up to date since the last decades of the eighteenth century, when her mother's ancestors, John and Sarah Murrell, Scottish immigrants, had claimed their section of Kentucky. John was a Presbyterian cleric and trained as a physician, and, as a consequence, was allowed into the country at a time when the Scottish had little station in the eyes of the New World.

A bit of her father's advice, too, was that she should never trust a bank—one of the many things her mother and father had in common, she supposed. Some of what was underground was so old it was no longer worth its printed value, of that she was certain, but some of it was worth much more to a collector. That was her Plan B. Selling pre-Civil War confederate banknotes. If she ever found herself in financial trouble or decided to turn her back on the notion of family continuity. Part of the reason she remained single was that she couldn't think of even one suitor, save her high school boyfriend Torrence, who didn't have dollar signs in his eyes. Every deer season, when she went hunting to refill the meat freezer, she'd find earth disturbed where some likely-drunk yokel had gone looking for her family's treasure. She figured the Kings, the extended Murrell and Hadley clans, and other families living up and down Petty's Fork Creek experienced similar intrusions. The secret of buried money in the mountains of Adair County was an alluring tale and so old it had taken on the essence of folklore. Of course, none of those treasure seekers knew about the old stone room.

It was her Grandpa Hadley, her father's father, who started transitioning cane fields to tobacco beds and even more to hemp stands during the second world war. Church people thought tobacco was a sin, but it brought in more money than molasses at the time, which was before the government stepped in after the Depression and tried to solve the problem of farmers going bankrupt by imposing price controls and paying people not to grow certain crops while subsidizing others. Mercy Grace got twelve hundred dollars a year for not growing her full base of tobacco, which had the added benefit of freeing ground for cane, not to mention a bunkhouse.

* * *

The first one from her graduating class to arrive at her place after the fall of Saigon was Ezarene Campbell. Mercy Grace was driving her garden tractor along the narrow gravel lane from the southeast sugar bush, her largest grove of sugar maples, hauling boxes of in-the-jar syrup, rounding the corner to see Ezarene in plaid culottes and a white polo shirt, looking mature and very modish, leaning against what from the distance appeared to be an older Fairlane, tan-color. The noise of the tractor had kept Mercy Grace from hearing the car coming up the creek. Ezarene had always styled herself after what was popular in magazines, in ways not instinctive to other girls in the county. The Campbells had lived in town during their daughter's high school years, as they had gotten to the point where they could afford to, after oil had been discovered on their land in the east part of the county. Ezarene came from the hills, but unlike some, didn't turn to snobbery to make herself forget it. She brought patterns and fabric swatches to school and consulted Mercy Grace and others about what she would sew for herself next, which could have been construed as boastful, but Mercy Grace saw it as sharing and the chance to imagine something fancy for herself, too. At graduation, Ezarene surprised a half-dozen girls she wasn't even close to with handmade, tie-dyed halter tops.

"Well if it isn't you," Mercy Grace said. "Can't say I'm sorry to see you, E-Z."

E-Z was what school kids had called Ezarene, from the time they were riding mules bareback through autumn leaves and winter snow and the occasional cry of wildcats to the one-room school up McCluskey Holler, where Mercy Grace's aunt Meredith had been headmistress going back to before the Great Depression. E-Z suffered some for the nickname at the hands of boys in their class once they reached puberty, but as she was well capable of pulling a left punch, she didn't suffer for long.

"Goody for you," Ezarene said.

"Got tea and a porch swing."

"You don't look to me like you got time for tea and a porch swing. Any shine?"

"Nope."

"You never were any fun."

"Nope. You want to help? I got a shovel." Mercy Grace pulled her drawings for the bunkhouse out of her hip pocket and handed them to Ezarene. "I've got to have help. I want to build a bunkhouse."

Ezarene smoothed the notepaper drawing out over the hood of the Fairlane and said, "Huh. Well, welcome home, I reckon."

"At first I thought I'd do it for hired hands, for the boys who right now are coming back from overseas in droves, but just about the moment I saw you had driven up, I decided I want women to build it."

"What's the big deal about that? It's not like no women in this county never built a building. How many chicken coops you build in your life? How many you seen built?"

"Now, just listen. It hit me what it would be like to live with people just coming back and with drugs and booze calling at them all the time. I've seen it already. It makes things tense when your worker is thinking about nothing but quitting time so he can open that first bottle of bootleg beer. Or worse, smuggle in a flask. I don't want to deal with drug and booze problems, and particularly I don't want any shine trouble. I really don't feel I'm qualified, for one. I've been assuming a certain level of guilt over not having gone off and done my part for Vietnam, but guilt is not a qualification, is it? Women can build a bunkhouse, can't they? I thought, what if I build a bunkhouse by women for women coming back from the war. The women who'll live there can help me build it."

"Lord, let me catch a breath," Ezarene said. "I swear I've walked into a tornado."

"All right. Well, help me or not, welcome back, and trust me, I'm glad to see you whole for more than one reason."

"Well, I could say the same for you, I guess. I thought you'd be married with a couple of brats by now. So, here it is, Mercy Grace: I *could* use a place to stay for a spell. Pa's on the jar again. He doesn't get to do to me what he used to do. I'll kill him first. I may kill him anyway."

Mercy Grace put her arms around Ezarene, and the two of them held there for a long moment. She'd forgotten what it felt like to hug an old friend, a woman friend, the way the time and space between them immediately filled with feelings and history such that the two no longer felt like separate people and like they'd just seen each other yesterday. Hugging a man did not feel like that. Hugging a man either made her feel drained and vaguely frightened or like royalty with a dash of helplessness. She couldn't explain that last part. The first part was obvious. Some men sucked the energy from her, and she was scared to death of falling for somebody like that. But the last part was harder to describe. Some men, and Ray Joe had been one of them, made her feel like a damsel in distress, like a princess suited for a golden carriage, and she liked it. She liked feeling that fleet sense of need, the need for rescue, even though alone and by daylight rescue was the last word anybody in Adair County would use to describe her. Half the time she'd just as soon drop a man off a cliff as look at him. She supposed that what she experienced was a certain sense of vulnerability and maybe inevitability, since she and Ray Joe had slept together that first night and every night thereafter until he moved on.

"I don't know what got into your daddy, E-Z," Mercy Grace said.

"Well, it was oil, I reckon," Ezarene said. "Turned him to the jar and my mother to the Bible. Oil turned our house into a place of worry. Then you grow up and figure out the whole world is a place of worry. Once in a while you get to pluck a rose off a bush, and even so you got to be smart enough to dodge thorns. Pisses me off that I didn't get to put off learning the dark side of life until I was good and done with the fun of being a kid."

"Which is why you need to think about something else," Mercy Grace said, releasing the embrace. "We can teach each other. I have it in mind to get along without a man. I'm saying for life. A firm decision. This last one, well, you weren't here, but it burned me pretty bad. My own doing for getting caught up, but anyway, listen. It's fortunate that you drove in just now. And there's plenty more like you, just coming back from wherever the war sucked them to. There's also Ruth and Martha Abrell. They went to nurse training after you left and both worked in MASH units overseas. It messed them up, but they're not beyond help. I talked to Ruth at the harvest fair last fall, and she says Martha has nightmares. It was that conversation that gave me the idea of somehow helping people who are coming back lost. Bootleg is a good business right now, especially running beer over the county line. I'm seeing drunks in the town square in Columbia and Hodgenville sitting on benches in front of the courthouse and inside the counter at Loy's Merc, and when have you ever seen that before? Ruth and Martha both work at the hospital in Greensburg, but I ran into Clarice Baxter, and she said she saw in *The Columbia Beacon* where Ruth had been pulled over by the law for trying to cross the county line with a case of beer in her trunk. She's in jail! Ruth Abrell! She'll never lift a finger as a nurse again. I don't know. I want to help, but I don't want to see the molasses business go down. I feel like if I could do more, I could make more, and maybe make life easier on a few people in the process."

"Lord!" Ezarene said. "You're chattering like a June bug. It been awhile since you seen another human being, Mercy Grace?" The two laughed, hugged again, briefly, and Mercy Grace motioned for help with the syrup.

"I heard you was at one of the big automotive plants," Mercy Grace said. "That doesn't really sound like you. What kind of work were you doing?"

Ezarene shook her head, "Not fitting people for suits and dresses like I'd hoped. Not designing clothes for a big fashion magazine. Guess I shouldn't have gone to Louisville if that's what I wanted to do. Those jobs belong to glam girls, not hill transplants. I could have gotten hired as a seamstress in a laundry, but—ugh. Soon as the last flight left Saigon, they laid a bunch of us off. Not two weeks after I'd been promoted from engine mounts to ratcheting door panels onto pickups. No more hanging inside the hood by my belt and more pay. Eight o'clock shift instead of six a.m. Bankers' hours. Two weeks of vacation went up to three."

"After six years," Mercy Grace said.

"After six years. But it was a hell of a lot better than some women were doing up there. I've heard stories about the meat plants. I'd rather shovel hog manure than turn hog dongs into phony baloney and call it meat."

"No kidding."

"No kidding. I'll never in my life eat another sausage that didn't come off the farm."

Mercy Grace couldn't imagine laboring according to another person's idea of what work hours might be. Her clock was in time with the animals. Her father and mother had arisen at four in the morning every day of the year, and she had hated more than anything being pulled day after day from a warm bed when it was still dark and having to go with her father to the milking barn before she had breakfast. When Mercy Grace took control of the farm after her father's death, she pushed feeding and milking time back fifteen minutes a day, suffering through the bawling of a half-dozen milk cows, until eventually it was the roosters who awakened the entire population of Cabin Branch Holler at Petty's Fork Creek at the first rosy shimmer of dawn. Everybody ate early in summer. Everybody ate late in winter. It meant she had to race through the creek to meet the Grade A dairy truck by seven-thirty in the dark time of year, but she didn't care. A new thing called Daylight Savings Time helped, as did the four-thirteen engine in her pickup truck.

Nor could she imagine a boss handing her a paycheck for *doing*. Work and cash were not two things that often connected themselves to each other in her life. Work was its own reward. Cash-in-hand came and went with the seasons, excluding what she had buried.

Christmas two years prior, Mercy Grace had taken some of that buried cash and bought herself a telescope from a mail-order catalog. In the summer, to help keep kids out of trouble, the high school had some kind of function every Saturday night. Once a month it was a star-gazing party, and the science department at Cumberland Basin College brought the astronomy program's big telescopes out on the playground and taught people how to use them. Mercy Grace was so completely taken in by what she saw through the lenses, the way those shining spots in the galaxy made her feel small but lucky and, in a single glimpse, helped her to see her worries as just about the same size in the span of a life, that she wanted to make certain the star party became a tradition. She felt it gave people context and at the same time let them off the hook. She read all she could find, refreshed herself on what her grandparents had taught her about the constellations and the planets, and they had taught her much, because they farmed by the moon, as did most people in Adair County. That next year, on the third Saturday of every month, starting in June when school was out, she hauled her telescope to the high school, to loan it to the night, and joined the group of professors and science teachers to share with those young people what she knew. Weeknights, she studied the sky from her porch. Often on those Saturday evenings she'd talk to somebody just back from 'Nam. People happy to be alive. Boys tipping their grandpas' flat glass flasks. Boys who four years ago or three or two or even one had been sneaking behind the family barn to dip chewing tobacco or roll a cigarette.

All of this she explained to Ezarene, who had tripped over the telescope as she came from the front room to the porch.

"If I didn't get you before, I sure don't get you now, Mercy Grace. I really don't," Ezarene said, stirring a sugar cube into her tea. "You could have any man you want to help you maintain this place, if you lost a few pounds and washed the manure off your boots more often than twice a year, but you settle for squinting at the sky with a bunch of kids."

Mercy Grace did her best not to grit her teeth, which resulted in her hand tremoring enough to splash tea into her saucer. *Judge not lest ye be judged,* her mother's favorite saying. "Ezarene Joanna Campbell. It's the 1970s. Even in Adair County, Kentucky, I have a right to do as I please. As I just told you, I'm not after a man, and I like the size of myself just fine. You're pissed off because you don't want to be back here. You got a taste for town, that's clear. Ain't nobody blaming you for it, but don't take it out on us poor little ol' unschooled hillbillies."

Ezarene turned her head and stared off in the direction of the barn. The humidity rose visibly from the rows of a checkerboard patch of young tobacco growing in Cabin Branch's flood bottom between the house and the creek. The big black oak had held a tire swing since the invention of tires. Three generations had launched themselves into the summer blue Kentucky sky. Mercy Grace at night would sit on the porch and imagine the parents and grands and great-grands who had pushed her and Donald Dale and decades of cousins squealing with delight and freedom.

"Suppose that tire's dry-rotted, don't you reckon?" Ezarene asked.

"E-Z, you think I don't know enough to switch out a dry-rotted tire from a rope swing every now and again? You think I don't care enough about my young second cousins than to put them at risk out of laziness?"

"Well, what do you want from me, Mercy Grace? It's not you who's out of a job. It's not you who kissed dead goodbyes to every single one of your high school boyfriends. Goddam war screwed up life for us all and for good."

"Huh. Well, let me remind you that, first-off, I had better things to do in high school than to chase after buckets of boys. Second, E-Z, let me further remind you that this is my porch swing you are sitting on and my hand-grown and hand-picked mint tea you are drinking. You showed up at my homestead for the first time *ever* in your adult life, not the other way around. Not that I'm not glad to see you, because I am, but I still as yet have no idea why you are here, beyond needing a room. Why are you *really* here? I mean, I know you must have gotten a bit of severance pay. Enough, I'm guessing, to set you up in all kinds of places your daddy can't get to. I'm only fifteen miles of dirt road and a half-mile of slate-bottomed creek bed away from him."

Ezarene turned to face Mercy Grace, reached a hand to forearm.

"And for your information," Mercy Grace continued, "I went to every damned funeral there was and kept a scrapbook of obituaries out of *The Columbia Beacon* and the little folded funeral home programs with their little gold praying hands on front. Every. One. And sometimes I was just about the only person there. Nobody goes to a poor man's funeral. But I said goodbye to every dead boy from this county. And there were plenty of them, let me tell you. One and two and sometimes three funerals a week. All colors, shapes, and sizes, and all of them practically babies. I hugged people I've never seen before and wept and broke bread in houses tucked into parts of this county I didn't know had places to tuck. I wore out half a dozen church dresses."

"What happened with you and Torrence anyway? Your daddy didn't skip a beat, did he, about you going with negroes," Ezarene said.

"Watch your tongue, woman. Don't forget yourself. One. I loved one boy in my life—*period*," Mercy Grace said, "and he was not a so-called *negro*. You say it like he was a breed of houseplant. He was smart and funny and he made it okay for me to dream and have plans. He made me see the value in books. He was a person, flesh and blood, a man but still also a boy, and at least I didn't go around hiding it the way you and your mother did. Honey, I love you, and your mama is fine people, she is *fine* people, and she and me have shared many meals, and everybody in the county loves her, but she does her best to stay covered up and out of the sun, and you know it. That fact alone should have taught you better than to talk about a person according to the hue of their skin. I said that to Pastor Bob the other day. He said he had no prejudice against me and my actions, but that people still bring it up from time to time. I said bring what up? He said, 'The fact that you dated a negro.' He told me like he was proud of himself because he said he puts people 'kindly and gently in their place' about the subject."

"I said, 'Pastor Bob, you don't see where you're being every bit a racist, same as those people are being?' He said, 'No,' and I let him have it. I said, 'There is no kind and gentle about it. You tell people in no uncertain terms that Torrence Harlan was a young *man*. Now he's a dead young man, and he died in a war that you and your conservative bunch kept voting in. You tell them that, Pastor Bob, and if you do, on every Murrell and Hadley grave in this county, I will start coming to church.'"

"All right, all right. Enough with the lecture. I don't see what's wrong with the word. It's a step up from what I've been hearing all my life about my mother. But I hear you. But what did Pastor Bob say?"

"He said, 'Mercy Grace, God and Torrence both would show up for supper if you ever came to church,'" and the two laughed.

"I saw him in the ground, E-Z," Mercy Grace said. "He was drafted in July just after our graduation and dead by November. You and the others were long gone. Torrence. I'll never forget him. I still have a stack of books he gave me. But I'll tell you something else you don't know. Standing by that coffin with that flag on top, I had his baby in me. That baby left my body before I could get back home from the graveside service. I started cramping during the gun salute. Little boy. Came out of me in the creek. I had to stop the truck and get out. No bigger than that teacup. Came falling out from under my dress onto a gravel bar. I didn't wear any underwear to the funeral. It was my secret way of flipping the bird at all the machine-people who bring war about. I hope to goodness I never again feel that kind of pain, in my gut or between my legs or in my heart. Guess the little boy didn't want to be born into a world that kept him from having a daddy."

"Law, Mercy Grace. I'm sorry to hell. I couldn't have known. I'm sorry, Hon. Something in the water down here sometimes, I swear. Makes people say stupid, do stupid. Maybe it's the hollers. Maybe people don't get enough sun."

"Get enough sun in Louisville, do you? Because you ain't been home long enough to get Adair County stupid."

Ezarene laughed. "No," she said. "No, I guess I haven't. People talked about it, you know, how many boys came from backwoods counties when compared to the number from cities. Poor people fight wars, they said. People said that's just the way it is."

"Folks around here said the same thing. We tried to get the newspaper interested in investigating, but they never did. A reporter from one of the Louisville papers told me it was just the law of averages. I asked him what kind of math he took in school that thirty-eight dead boys out of thirteen thousand people in this county is the same ratio as a few hundred out of three hundred thousand, which is the case in Louisville and Jefferson County. I looked it up. Maybe it's true, all those city boys sidestepping the draft on account of being in college. Or leaving for Canada." Mercy Grace wiped tears from her face. "Ezarene, you can sling a hammer. I know you can. You want to build a bunkhouse?"

Ezarene stared off again in the direction of the barn. "You'll have to put plumbing in," she said. "County won't stand for open-pit shitters anymore. How you going to hoist trusses?"

"Block and tackle, Brainiac," Mercy Grace said. "Old Danny will help us. He's smart enough to know how and when to stand still. I can rent a backhoe. Put in a septic. Might decide to hook it up to my house, too. Can you believe it? It is 1975, and I have lived my entire life with a two-seater."

Ezarene shook her head and began to laugh again. "Yeah, but you at least buy toilet paper now, don't you? No more catalog pages? Mercy Grace, behind your back in school people were calling you 'The Girl Most Likely to Stay the Same.' Of course, I can believe it."

"Well, I'll be," Mercy Grace said. "Trust me, behind my back is a gross exaggeration, but I'm taking that as yes. So, you'll help me? I'll give you a bed and feed you. I believe I told you a fib. It just hit me that I've got a touch of Wesley McCluskey's apple cordial left over from last Christmas in the old stone room. Seal it with a toast?"

"I hate Wesley's apple cordial, but yes. It's five o'clock somewhere, Miss Hadley."

"E-Z," Mercy Grace said, "I'll grant you the point."

"You know you could convert molasses into shine, don't you?" Ezarene said. "They do it down in Jamaica. You can make your own bootleg rum. And maple syrup. They make it out of maple syrup. People make liquor out of just about anything, I've learned. I knew a boy in Louisville who made it out of ripe cherries. You'd be rich enough for indoor plumbing."

"I'm already rich enough for indoor plumbing," Mercy Grace said. "Haven't you heard the stories? But if I spent it, I wouldn't have the money anymore, now would I?"

Mercy Grace gave Ezarene a bit of instruction on the telescope, pointing out the risen half-moon, a faded scrap of image framed by the young black oak and sugar tree, which she had planted when her parents each died, a kind of repetition, an echo, to remind herself how long her people had been working this place, and how much of their capability lived in her bones. The black oak sent a deep tap root. It could survive difficult times. The sugar maple made its own sustenance, like a mother.

Mercy Grace admonished Ezarene not to look at the sun, then hiked west down the hill beyond the barn to the old stone room, which was a really a large limestone cave situated in a short bluff near Cabin Branch. Before the arrival of the Europeans, Cherokee people had dug out and deepened the space into a cavern, shoring it with yellow poplar timbers, mud brick, and stone and lived there in winters since before time. According to her great, great, great, great-grandfather Murrell's 1838 diary, dozens of people, stragglers from the Cree and Cherokee and Seminole nations arrived, apparently hoping to hide from the coming wave of soldiers when President Jackson gave orders to for the final round up during the Great Removal.

Later, escaping slaves knew it as a stop on the Underground Railroad. On the stones again and again were dozens and sometimes hundreds of hashmarks where people tallied the days spent hidden. Walking through Cabin Branch, the slate-bottomed creek, was a way to put dogs off human scent, although treacherous, as the stream was inhabited by water moccasins, the bite of which caused a world of grievous pain, sometimes led to amputation, and sometimes death. According to the old diaries, of which she possessed an extensive library as her family had long seen themselves as recordkeepers, her great-great-great-great grandfather Hatcher Ezra Murrell was forced to remove the leg of a Cherokee man who was bitten *en route* to the old stone room. He got better quickly once the leg was off, but prior to that he grew sicker and sicker, gesturing and pleading in his own language for something to be done. Women kept trying to hold him down, speaking in a way that required no translation. They were trying to treat him, to administer a poultice from a sack of dried leaves and tea from another. In Hatcher's account of the story, the women finally threw up their hands and backed away and gestured toward him and the saw he had brought with him. He described the room as becoming "filled with the smell of human blood and the hot stench of saw blade on bone." People were afraid to leave the stone room, so it came about that two dozen of the man's extended family and fellow refugees, children among them, were crammed in, watching what took place. Hatcher wrote that he had feared misinterpreting the request, but an older woman took him by the shoulders and shook him, pointed to the saw, then gave him also a sharp blade. Afterward, several people spoke and gave him bits of tobacco, pemmican, and dried fruit. The group remained for many weeks, and Mercy Grace's great-great-great-great grandmother cooked for them and learned enough language to get everyone fed and their needs met. Hatcher climbed onto the roof every morning, where he could see west, through the oak and maple and scrub cedar, to the entrance to Cabin Branch Holler and east to where the waters of Cabin Branch met Petty's Fork Creek. In this way, people could emerge from the stone room, take care of necessaries, move about. At night, Hatcher carved a beautiful crutch for the wounded man, who was called Adahee, engraved it with birds and suns and the word *craic*, old country language for sovereignty and the promise of freedom. Adahee and his people stayed living in that stone room for nearly two years, until the government's focus shifted west. During this time, Hatcher's trips to town were rare, but enough that he heard the whispered stories of a forced march out of the Kentucky and Tennessee hills and the thousands who died of cold and starvation. Sadness descended on Cabin Branch Holler as people began making decisions about what to do. Some stayed on, permanently, including Adahee and his family, living in that limestone room, sharing the work and the harvest, happy days and hard days, several marrying members of Mercy Grace's extended family, including her great-great-great-grandmother Jessica. Up on the rise behind the house sat the graveyard where eleven of the original group were buried, including Adahee, alongside the generations of Murrells with whom they had intermarried. Hatcher's diaries were full of his love for his adopted family, as he called them, and he lamented the fact that he was an extension of the wrong-doing that resulted in the land's original people being driven into desolation and death. He shamed and cursed the notion of progress and his European ancestors who in their discontent and greed had thought it their right to possess land long stewarded by Adahee's people. According to his diary, in his will, he returned the sixteen hundred acres back to its first inhabitants. Why nothing came of that, Mercy Grace did not know. Perhaps because shortly thereafter, the first Murrell married the first Hadley, and the land was divided, and time marched on.

Her grandmother Murrell also occasionally told the story of the stone room becoming part of the underground railroad, and of history repeating itself: a young man wading high spring waters with a group of other fleeing slaves, bitten by a water moccasin, or cottonmouth, as they were also known. Mercy Grace's great-great grandfather Joseph Hadley, who was half-Cherokee, and still pretty young himself, tried all the old medicine first, then finally sawed off the man's leg. The former slave's name was also Joseph, and he inherited Adahee's beautiful crutch. Because there were many "stations," as their place was called, among people who were part of helping slaves escape the south, they didn't stay as long as her Cherokee ancestors, just long enough to heal Joseph's wounds and get him accustomed to the crutch, but one of the other men did end up coming back after Emancipation and married her great-Grandmother Murrell. Not on paper, because it wasn't until the 1960s that such a pair could marry in Kentucky, but Mercy Grace had a framed, handwritten piece of paper on which they pledged themselves to each other and a small daguerreotype of them taken some years later, after they were old and gray and had born a number of children, one of whom would become her great-grandfather, Joseph Hadley, Jr.

She thought briefly about how the various wars had framed the lives of her people, those who refused to fight in the Civil War, as the state of Kentucky did not secede, and how that for a time turned her family into pariahs, until her great-uncle Hadley redeemed them by volunteering for the Army during the Spanish-American War, rising to the rank of captain, the photo of him in his uniform framed and sitting on the mantle next to both sets of her great-grandparents, above her bedstead in the room where she had been conceived, as well as Donald Dale, and babies going all the way back to when her mother's side of the family had claimed the original sixteen hundred acres along Petty's Fork Creek, after Daniel Boone and his bunch had finished their carnage, before Kentucky was a state, before Adair County was a county. She thought about the places where her pedigree crisscrossed, second cousins marrying, and sometimes even first cousins. Every time she occasioned down to the old stone room and laid open the thick door built of black oak beams, she drew the earthy limestone air into her lungs, along with the ancient traces of family members who had built it and the succor provided there. She had made love to Torrence in the old stone room, on the night her baby boy had started his physical journey, but not Ray Joe. Ray Joe was just fine for the old poplar cabin, all that fun and sensation. But Torrence was joined to her soul in ways she couldn't describe. Perhaps that was why the child hadn't lived, being conceived as he was in a place of worry.

A CERTAIN KIND OF WARRIOR

DANNY WASN'T KRISTIN'S biological father, but he'd stayed by her mother's pregnant side. Sixteen years later he was still there, trying his best to be a father to Kristin. Out of a sense of worth and value, Danny's decision. To his credit, he had not lit up in relief or anticipation when she put forth her proposal to move out of the family home, drop out of high school, listen to her own urges rather than prescribed ones. Nor did he call her hippy or commie or moron or slut or any of the names a stepfather might have. Rather, he acted concerned, saying he truly got where she was coming from but could see a bigger picture also.

In the end, something quite rare for 1973 in Southern Indiana, the judge allowed her to exit school as an emancipated juvenile, a process that required her, her mother, and Danny to stand before a great wooden bench surrounded by men in suits and uniforms. Judge Rasmussen, who scolded her for the choice she was making, declaring it an absolute that she continue to abide at home until she had a GED in hand, a job, and a few months of practice keeping a budget and a checkbook.

"You'll thank us. You'll thank him," her mother said as they walked from the courtroom.

Buildings in downtown New Albany near the lunch counter where she found work still had the feel and look of the old steamboat days. Victorian mansions on the waterfront, painted ladies radiating in long, maple-lined blocks from the central business district. The town took up the north bank of the Ohio, a bridge away from Louisville. New Albany was workaday industry; Louisville was genteel with shops and tall, glass buildings. Louisville meant good fish restaurants and *The Courier Journal*. Of course, being a city, it had its seedy side, the West End. Worse was the dogfood plant and the soap factory with its giant clock, not to mention distilleries, which had to be passed to get to downtown with its dress and shoe shops. Window shopping was free. She had grown up holding her nose against that parade of smelly chemistries every time she and her mother crossed the K & I bridge to do just that.

The Culbertson Mansion was the biggest house in town, built from pinkish sandstone. The Scribner House, two-story and whitewashed, was once home to New Albany's founders. Both were open for tours. McConnell Mansion, technically a giant duplex, with four-story Edwardian bays front and rear, gold filigree embedded in the doors, on the staircase landing, and the stairwell wainscoting between each floor, housed offices for doctors, dentists, and lawyers. Falls City Printing took up the entire first floor of the southeast corner of the building. *Wedding Invitations to Business Catalogs!* the neon above the window said. Kristin stopped by afternoons to talk to the craftsmen. They acted happy to share trade knowledge, letting her watch them graph mockups on big grids, load paper into the gargantuan camera machine, stand quietly in the weird un-light of the darkroom. When she told them about her plans and the GED, they gave her the job of dusting piece by piece trays of old typeset, telling her to be careful of the years of hardened ink clogging the inner corners of letters like B and P. That was *patina* one of the men told her, and *patina* made antiques more valuable. They paid her in grid paper and use of the pre-press room and she was just fine with that. One day she wanted to run a newspaper, she told them, staffed by nothing but girls who were trying to figure things out for themselves, who could write about the mixed-up truth about all people, because she felt like the news was about nothing but men, to which they nodded, smiled, looked at each other, and patted her on the shoulder, telling her to *go for it*, that a newspaper written by girls would certainly be unique. "Find some real, true stories, about real, true people, and we'll help print them." She saw these afternoons as her substitute for college, putting tireless effort and energy into learning all she could.

Tate was the real reason she wanted to move out on her own. He and Kristin were "doing the deed," as Uncle Gerald called it. Tate wanted to make it respectable. He told her this each time. In the woods at Community Park wasn't appropriate to him. He was from down in Kentucky in the mountains, just like her family, but he grew up in an actual shack, where her family had lived in the flatwoods, had dozens of head of Grade A milk cows and made good money off selling milk and cream to Farm Fresh for pasteurizing and bottling for the retail market. Tate was short for Potato Head. He got a yardstick to the shins once for being so hungry he ate a seed potato raw before it got to the garden. That was the story *he* told. According to his mother, however, he was barely toddling and trying to say "brother" when they brought baby Van Keith from the hospital in Campbellsville to bury in the family gravesite. Van Keith's backbone was born outside his body, which happens sometimes, according to Aunt Amanda Faye's big medical book. Tate cried so hard he couldn't speak the word right and the word *brother* came out "tater."

Amanda Faye was Uncle Gerald's wife, and she came from the Kentucky mountains, too, in fact was probably a distant relative of Tate's. She was so upset after falling down the rickety staircase caused her to miscarry that she tried to shoot herself in the belly. Luckily the gun was heavy and her aim terrible, so she only shot herself through a little roll of fat. The doctor told her this was one time being overweight was good for a woman. They all lived up rickety staircases like that, since the cheapest apartments were always on the upper floors. At Gerald and Amanda Faye's sometimes a woman in a hoopskirt wisped across a doorway. Every room smelled like two hundred years of people smoking tobacco, and just as dingy, high up where nobody could reach to clean.

How she could do that—put a gun to her stomach, feel the stiffness of a trigger, and not give up on the idea was something Kristin couldn't make sense of. It was hard enough plinking cans or shooting the noise out of a blackbird.

Amanda Faye's breakup with Uncle Gerald came on a Saturday morning, at the breakfast table. Kristin was spending the weekend as she did most weeks, because listening to their arguments gave her interesting things to write in her stories. Uncle Gerald said, "You can't rape the willing," holding the Louisville newspaper bent-arms in front of his face, then turning it around to show a photo of a woman in a short skirt being arrested and a caption, "West-End Call Girls Busted." They always ate breakfast that way—reading sections of the paper between bites of toast and sips of black coffee, Amanda Faye taking hers with sugar.

Right after "You can't rape the willing," Uncle Gerald stood, grabbed his crotch, walked over to Amanda Faye and started moving his pelvis against her, telling about the girl he liked to visit. It took one very, very long second for Amanda Faye to start screaming, quickly escalating to the point that she and Gerald were both slapping and scratching and hollering like panthers. Uncle Gerald fell to laughing, bellowing, saying he'd won a shitload of money from buying pull-tabs and rubbing them for luck between the girl's cleavage. That Amanda Faye ought to feel glad about it. He'd bought her plenty of burgers with that money, not that she needed them, either, but those burgers very likely saved her life. Then he got up, ripped the article out of the paper, and shoved it between Amanda Faye's breasts.

*   *   *

Lying on her back now, months later, in her free-rent apartment, after she'd finished the GED with a near perfect score, on her raspberry-red bedspread, chenille she'd dyed herself with packaged dye and vinegar, Kristin thought about the situation, watching the rise and flat fall of her belly. *It all works out or it doesn't or it will.* She thought sometimes about pregnancy, had read the women's section in Amanda Faye's big medical book cover to cover a dozen times, so she'd know the drill in case she ever did get that way. The free rent part, well. Danny and his ideas about what was good for her. He found the deal by talking to their dentist. Kristin had gotten a room with a hotplate and shower in the top level of the south rear bay of McConnell Mansion in exchange for cleaning his offices. The plan was meant to teach her how to work hard for what mattered to her. Out of protest, she bought a pair of Nancy Sinatra boots and wore them to clean in. It irked her that she didn't get to find the deal herself. So, she went from her job at the diner to Falls City Printing to Dr. Ruby's and swept up fragments of people's teeth.

After a while, the telephone jingled—the new pink princess phone she'd bought with Big Value Stamps, which she'd collected for more than two years, stealing the last few from her mother, just so she'd have something that she had struggled and saved for herself. It was Tate, calling from Madison. "Honeybun, two more days, and this misery is done," he said from what sounded like inside yards-thick prison walls instead of the flimsy cement-block dayroom across from his dormitory at the Indiana state mental hospital.

A thirty-day lockup. One way to pass time was to spread her stack of brochures across the chenille bedspread, read headlines and pictures, imagine configuring them into a newspaper. "To recognize how far understanding of mental disease has come," the mental hospital one read, "remember in bygone days treatment for criminal madness included hanging." She guessed the electric shocks and ice baths and drugs Tate told about were nothing compared to that.

Kristin loved pamphlets, and Tate did, too. She kept them in her chest-of-drawers, their subjects of focus ranging like an encyclopedia. They had one for every cave in the Kentuckiana area, hitchhiking once down to Mammoth Caves to ride the glass-bottom boat and gather the free brochures about different national parks, including The Great Smoky Mountains, not to mention Cherokee Village in North Carolina, plus education pamphlets on bears, panthers, birds, and one on wildflowers.

She thought Tate did not belong in Madison. Rather, that Judge Rasmussen—the same judge who emancipated her—didn't like him. The man had demonstrated this thoroughly after Tate's most recent offense—making a pair of pants from the American flag—saying he'd had enough. Shoplifting, vagrancy, petit theft. Nothing worked, not Juvie, not The Farm, not the fines Tate's mother paid. Tate argued, calling the pants *art*, said he was making a statement about Vietnam and Wounded Knee, at which point Judge Rasmussen said he was tempted to declare Tate incorrigible, lock him away for life.

Tate replied, right in court, "You can't do that to an Indian anymore. Not these days."

"Boy, I'm sure the original people of this land would take great offense at you claiming to be Hiawatha."

"Hey, my granny is bonafide. She's got papers, and pictures of our family going all the way back. Just 'cause I look one way doesn't mean I can't be something else. Looks is deceivin'," Tate said. "You can't deny my heritage on account of the way I look."

The day of sentencing, Judge Rasmussen said it had occurred to him that Tate might not be criminal. Said he awoke so hard he sat up in bed with the words on his forebrain loud and clear: *Tate Goodin might be a mental.* He decided to send the boy upriver to Madison. Let them pump him full of antipsychotics, see what Mr. Rules-Don't-Apply-to-Me thought of standing out against society. "Look at it this way. You no longer have to worry about being drafted. Hard-brained Kentucky backwoods transplants," he said. "Save the people of Indiana a boatload if we'd vote to drop every one of you into the blue Ohio at the first offense. Look, kid. This is your last time around as a juvenile. Make a choice about yourself. Next birthday, life drops you into a rougher playing field."

* * *

Pearl Street, where McConnell Mansion stood, spanned
the length of New Albany, parallel to the Ohio River,
except where warehouses and the box factory interrupted
it. The railroad formed a continuous third route of
transport, right through the industrial district. State Street
dead-ended at the river, and at the corner of State and
Pearl was the New Albany Bowl, where Tate told Kristin
she might catch a glimpse of him boarding the
Greyhound for the ride to Madison.

She ran up as they were boarding, could tell by the
way the deputy acted he admired that she made the
effort. He uncuffed Tate to let him hug her. Tate kissed
her cheek, said it was too bad she couldn't ride along,
which sent her running back into the New Albany Bowl
to hand the clerk a wadded fist of bills in exchange for a
one-way ticket to Madison. She figured to hitchhike home
or call Danny and her mother, ask them to fetch her.
"Run," the clerk said, "run!" Which she did, shouting as
the bus pulled from the curb.

The driver squeezed the door open and said, "Get on
up, Hollywood." A small, elderly woman smiled, moved
next to the window, gesturing to offer Kristin the seat
across the aisle from Tate and the deputy. The bus smelled
like gas and cigarettes and whatever was used to disinfect
the vinyl seats, which were sleek like they'd just been
scrubbed and squeaked against her bare thighs as she
scooted into the spot where the grandma had been.

"Hey now, metal to metal," the deputy said indicating
handcuffs to belt buckle when Tate reached for her hand.
"This ain't no meetin' of magpies."

Kristin noticed the deputy had an empty sleeve. Uncle
Gerald swore he'd once been arrested by an armless cop,

but nobody believed it because he told many stories that weren't true.

"Did you lose your arm in the Army?" Kristin said, too late recognizing the pun.

"I was in the Coast Guard," the deputy said, finally, "but I lost the arm cleaning a shotgun. Dog, too, sad to say. Nice collie. Ladybug. Never wanted to own another dog, but the department gave me the duty to keep the dope dog. Let's hope we never have to use it on you."

I love you, Honeybun, Tate said in her direction, moving his lips without sound. The motion and smell of the bus made Kristin drowsy. She leaned her head to where she could see Tate's reflection in the window across the aisle. They'd buzzcut his long hair. The one little patch of white looked like a polka dot among the black.

The little grandma jumped and so did Kristin a while later when Tate suddenly said, "Hey, I got to tell you all a story," just at the moment the bus slowed, pulling in front of Freddie's Diner, the red and blue greyhound dog painted in the right-hand corner of a big plate glass window where it was easy to see. Families hunched over their meals in diner booths turned to stare. "Wait, we're stopping already?" Tate said.

"You stay," the deputy said, taking keys from his shirt pocket to unlatch his part of the handcuffs, climbing across Tate to the aisle before closing it on the handhold of the seatback in front of them. "Reckon now's the time to smooch, if that's what you want to do," he said to Tate. "I can't stop you if I'm not here. Mr. Goodin, I need to whiz and get a bite. Union. You're low security. I'm on overtime. The driver has instructions to take a wood bat to your skull if you try anything goofy. I'll take you to the head soon as I return. Soft drink and sammich if you want. Sorry I can't do for the lady. Rules." The deputy walked to the front of the bus, spoke to the driver, who handed him a wooden Louisville Slugger, which the deputy waved and pointed at Tate.

"Well sir," Tate said. "Bring me a cola and a burger and I'll give it to the girl."

"Ain't buying for girlfriends," the deputy said, bowing in her direction. "No offense."

"Bummer," Kristin said, scooting over to touch her knees against the edge of Tate's seat. A soft cluck coming from the grandmother: *Jesusjesus*.

After his break, the officer led Tate to the toilet in the back of the bus, Tate's butt leaving a bowl in the vinyl that didn't completely fill in before they returned. The deputy had Tate by the elbow with his good arm. Nobody spoke. Kristin could feel all eyes on Tate's movements. "I'd like as you'd be quiet now," the deputy said, once they got settled.

"Let me tell my story," Tate said. "Won't take a minute, and you'll see why I'm telling it."

"Let him," the grandmother said. "We need to hear the younger generation speak. I find them interesting, myself."

The deputy pushed out a breath, fidgeted. "Get it over with, I reckon. But then no sound 'til Madison. This is my last nerve."

Tate explained about a certain kind of warrior ant from Africa he had read about in an insect book at The Farm. The little grandma tightened her grip on her purse and said, "Jesus, Jesus," under her breath.

Tate said, "Amen, Sister," then described how this breed of ant is ugly with oversized parts and moves into a village to scare to death the local ants who are gnawing the same sugar cane crop as the warrior ants want. Fear kills the local ants.

"The warrior ants then eat the dead ants, which makes them too full to eat the crops. Eating the dead ants is like eating candy, so the warrior ants don't get the right kind of nourishment. They die from malnutrition. So, the warrior ants save the sugar cane crop. Every bug dies, but the cane, the village's livelihood, survives. Nature's bug killer. Bugs die from killing bugs. Don't make sense, but it protects the cane. It's a mystery to scientists who study it."

"I reckon they all lived happier ever after," the deputy said.

"Don't you see," said Tate. "It's philosophy. Don't be in a hurry to change circumstances. Let what is be. If you don't do nothing, life takes care of life. Don't go to battle 'til you see what happens next. You should learn something from it."

The deputy said. "You sound like a goddamned dope-smokin' hippy flower child to me. You smoke dope, boy?"

* * *

They let Tate out on the first of October, a month to the day after they put him in. He didn't want anything to do with Kristin under the dyed-raspberry bedspread at first.

Twin Ferries Park over in Louisville interested him, though. It was the first place he asked to go after she picked him up from the Greyhound. He wanted a job running the Ferris wheel. He thought it suited him, maintaining a big machine, one that made people laugh and have fun. They sat on a bench watching the overgrown cog with its red, white, and blue swinging buckets full of waving hands going skyward then rotating around again over and over.

When he finally did want her, months after his release, he held her afterwards, back to belly in his arms, telling about a girl named Ladonna who was only eighteen and in Madison to get over her miscarriage and the death of her sister. Ladonna sat in her room and sobbed most of the time.

The day before Tate was released, she left the chow line at a hard run, escaped one burly orderly after another, made it to the kitchen, grabbed a knife from the block, jabbed herself in the chest and thighs, hitting major veins and arteries. "She knew right where to jab, too. She had clearly studied this. Bled out in seconds. Those drugs they gave us," Tate said, "they are true the Antichrist. They made me imagine that I didn't deserve to exist because I was the devil. By my own will, I overpowered the circumstances by making myself remember that it was the drug that was the demon." Poor Ladonna was married to a man twice her age named Dirk, who originally was engaged to her sister Katrina. Dirk, with Ladonna's approval, pushed Katrina off the waterfall at some big nature park because he decided he preferred Ladonna. He went to the state pen at Henryville, Ladonna to the state hospital at Madison. Once Ladonna discovered she was pregnant, they were married by the very judge who sentenced them, between their two trials, who told them he was only marrying them because they deserved each other, Tate getting that part of the story second hand from one of the security officers.

Once he gave up on the idea of working at Twin Ferries and got his job at Mr. Freeze, which required him to wear a white apron, a white hat, and to serve cones of vanilla ice cream to all the many types of people who lived in New Albany, Tate's conversations turned away from his concerns about his family's heritage and to other meaningful things, like how life was not the same as television. Kristin had enough stories for her newspaper just from being around Tate, except that he wasn't a girl. She decided she might have to once in a while include a story about a boy, if it were interesting enough. They were driving across the Ohio River on the K & I bridge on the last day of the season for Twin Ferries, when Tate told her his grandpa once had been in prison—for what, he didn't know—and helped build the K & I, and that there was a man who fell into the wet cement still buried between the twelfth and thirteenth joists, pointing to a small, bronze plaque on one of the bridge's rusty beams. Kristin involuntarily started counting the bumps the tires made as they crossed the metal section joists.

"My mother took me to live down in the holler at my grandma and grandpa's when I was born. Van Keith was Grandma and Grandpa's. Not my brother. He didn't come from my mother. He was my uncle. They were too old to be making babies was why his backbone was born outside his body. I touched it. Did I ever tell you that? His backbone. True for a fact. It was like the grizzle end of a chicken bone. She never once came to see me, Ma didn't, and then on the day I turned four, she showed up. We lived there on the mountain with grandma and grandpa after he came home from prison. They were Cherokee, my grandma and grandpa, but not the Oklahoma branch. Their kin escaped all that somehow. Honest to Pete, I don't remember much after that until I got to New Albany. I don't think a person ever gets over a situation like that, do you? Leaving a kid behind or having one die in your arms the way Van Keith did in Grandma's. That's why Ma paid all those fines and bought all those attorneys for me, don't you reckon? Her way of apologizing for abandoning me. You make your bed when you make a baby. Why don't people know that?"

Kristin noticed the lights and traffic of the Louisville night, wavering, twinkly jewels. "Your grandma told me your mother had lost her way, said she forgot she had Indian in her." The sounds of the bridge in between her words and his were metallic, quick and choppy, in time with the river beneath, which was just visible in her peripheral vision.

After a time of silence, during which they exited the bridge and turned toward downtown Louisville, he said, "Open the glove box."

For a flash second, she thought he was going to give her a ring, a plum-sized diamond like Uncle Gerald had once given to Amanda Faye, and for a flash second, she knew she'd say yes. Instead, pamphlets, a stack, with a red rubber band around the middle. "What?" she said.

"Don't know. They were at Mr. Freeze. Nobody said who dropped them by."

Each pamphlet, more than a dozen, was for a branch of the military, including the Coast Guard, Army, Navy, the reserve branches, plus the Merchant Marines. Some were duplicates—there were three copies of the same Army medic training program. Some were full-color. Some featured photographs, some cartoonish with line drawings of soldiers, officers, tanks, battleships, the American flag. The Coast Guard one was plastered with men in white suits with gold buttons, saluting. Gold like stars, like little galaxies. On the back, written by hand in black marker, bold strokes, all capitals—*Tate: Plot a course. Look for home.*

"You reckon it was that deputy?" Kristin said.

"Don't know. Don't know why he'd care," Tate said.

"I guess you don't have to care about another person in order to have good intentions toward him."

"I reckon. Maybe. I don't know, really. I'd hate to have to go to Vietnam, I know that."

"Uncle Gerald says Vietnam is almost over."

"Well," Tate said, "your Uncle Gerald, now ain't he a case?"

"Yes," Kristin said, "that's a known fact. But I don't think they'll let you go to war if you've been in a mental hospital."

"No," Tate said, "I reckon not."

SOLES OF OUR FEET

DAMNED FINE TOBACCO! Since the world arrived at the seventies, his mother's plan to keep him sheltered from violent communication, which is what she called cursing, had been foiled by television and movies and magazines. This was an ad in *Locker Room Magazine*, on loan from his buddy Toby, where vile language advertised various products from cigarettes to booze to curious personal paraphernalia. Three years to the day after the murder of Dr. Martin Luther King, Jr., when his father was shot and killed, and crisp-suited policemen arrived at their door to deliver the news, his mother herself had said, "Fuck! Fuck! Fuck! Fuck!" with her hands over her face, after which she cursed almost daily, in all situations, while continuing to admonish him to do otherwise. The years of training had fixed in him an urge for civilized modes of expression, such that the word *damned* jarred his sensibilities. Damning, his mother had taught him, was a thing earned by ill will and poor intentions and best left to fate.

His parents named him Leroy Martin Grube at birth. Not only his middle name but his nickname Chipper came from Dr. King, who, greeting the family after church one blustery day in 1965 in Montgomery, Alabama, rubbed Leroy's six-year-old head and said, "I notice you are very chipper, young man. You remain chipper. It's an attitude that will serve you. You follow your mother and daddy's example. Honor your parents in all things. Pay full attention to your school work. And remember: the best we can do is a life of service to our fellow man."

From that moment on, Leroy's mother and father called him Chipper as a form of teasing—especially when cajoling him into getting to his homework. It gradually became his adopted name, settling into his family's household without further consideration. Leroy practiced his penmanship by writing "Chipper M. Grube" on the chalkboard in his room and on his school assignments. His teacher insisted on addressing him by his given name, but classmates quickly switched to Chipper. "It's like being knighted," Toby had said. "Knights always get a secret name." Leroy found this to be a comforting and astonishing change. Over a matter of weeks, at the age of six, a reimagined version of himself was born. Drawings of his family now featured large yellow suns, backgrounds full of grass and blooming flowers, and a boy wearing a coat of armor, connected by a penciled arrow to the word Chipper.

The smell of Dr. King's shaving lotion hung on Chipper's head until his mother forced him to bathe. The same fragrance in a fainter form accompanied his father when he came home from meetings when Dr. King was in Louisville. Chipper's parents were both peace marchers. Beth, his mother, who was born in New Albany, wore tie-dyed skirts with fringed, knee-high moccasins. His father, Marquis, who was called Mark, had grown up in New York City, in Harlem, and had spent his teenaged years trying not to get sucked into the brash ways of ghetto life, at which he succeeded, he said, thanks to his decision to pursue an education and to *step up and get involved*. "Life," he said, "begins and ends at the library. Anybody can find his way to a good future at a library." He wore his turtlenecks high, his afro long, regularly admonishing Chipper never to forget how blessed he was to have witnessed the greatness of Dr. King. To be so privileged as to travel from New Albany to Montgomery not once but four times as part of the man's personal caravan was something most boys would never get to experience. Chipper also should be proud of his parents' inter-racial marriage, and particularly of his mother. It was brave in the 1970s to marry someone from another race in the United States, especially since some states had only recently made it legal.

Chipper marveled in essays he later wrote in junior high and high school about the coincidence of having two of the people he admired most afflicted by a bullet. He wrote about the way their bodies were tunneled by the force of metal and velocity and about the way he imagined their dismay at the heat of impact, wondering how long it took the terror to reach their brains on such an occasion, how long Dr. King was aware that he'd never see his wife and children again before he slipped into the ever-after. How long his father. He wrote about their grief, his and his mother's, about how he felt imbued with the responsibility to stand for the same brand of righteousness as Dr. King and his father. Those essays earned him A-pluses. Once, a boy accused him of "playing Daddy's race card for an easy A." Chipper told him and everyone listening that he wrote as he thought, and he felt passionate about his subject matter, and, as their English teachers had always told them, with those two things, half the job is done.

* * *

Around the time he should have been practicing driving the family sedan with the man who'd sired him, the world turned surly for Chipper, which was the phrase his mother used—"The world seems to have turned surly for you, Chipper." She said this in response to his dark criticism of the nightly news report about the county not prosecuting a member of the KKK for inciting a riot that killed three police officers and two civilians.

"I hate political white men," Chipper said.

"Is that your own thought or an opinion you've adopted?" his mother said. "It's a pretty racist statement."

"I don't know," he said. "What's racist about it? That's all you see on the news."

He listened with one ear as she continued to say, in her pay-attention voice, "When you've formulated a view, you can spout all the angry rhetoric you please, but until then, keep quiet. Don't be ignorant. Don't base an opinion off a single news report."

What she didn't know was that he was processing the day's events. His venom came from the fact that he'd lost his job at the library that afternoon, and he felt certain it had to do with who his father had been. Despite his fair skin, to honor his father, he always checked black on job applications and other forms. He could tell the director was uneasy with him from the beginning. When he challenged her about possibly harboring some prejudice against him, she had said, "We're shortening after-school hours, Chipper. That's it. Nothing sinister. We sent notice with last week's payroll."

He got himself escorted out of the building by saying, "Here's my last pay envelope. I hadn't picked it up yet. Nothing but a check. Which I appreciate. I appreciate quite a lot, ma'am, but which I also earned. I'm never late, and I'm never sick. If it's not the way I look and who my father was, then I'll do my job for free. You can pay me when you're flush again."

The library director checked her hands, clicked her nails as if testing their durability. "You're wrong, but maybe you should watch the way you're dressing," she said.

Chipper had taken to wearing his father's ankh on its bulky gold chain against a black turtleneck over which he wore a fringed, brown suede vest. He thought his style represented the two sides of his parentage. He let his hair grow long and woolly, touching it off with a dose of Afro-Sheen and planting a large pick-comb, both of which he purchased at The Nickel and Dime Store under the arched-brow scrutiny of the owner, Mr. Flock, whose daughter, Tara, also attended City High School, along with him and two thousand other mostly white kids. Tara was fair as a dove but had joined the illegal Black Student Union along with several of the more civic-minded white kids and others who were clearly of mixed ethnicity. Chipper doubted Mr. Flock knew. He doubted any of the fair-skinned kids' parents knew their sons and daughters had passion for what was happening racially in their country. What the *Huntley-Brinkley Report* and *Life* magazine called The Civil Rights Movement, as if it were something foreign trying to will itself through the great bowels of the United States, which, Chipper supposed, for some people was exactly the case. Even with widespread support from other student groups and the student senate, faculty were still refusing to allow legitimate meetings on campus, or to endorse the BSU as an extracurricular activity, which would have meant school district funding to participate in greater events in support of the Black Cause, to take bus trips to listen to people like Julian Bond or Angela Davis. In his mind, it should be called the Civil Rights It's-About-Time *Arrival*. Everybody talked about waiting for Jesus to come back when what they really were waiting for, he thought, in agreement with what his father had always said, was the arrival of America at a state of human equality and the peaceful exploration of individual potential. Chipper agreed with his mother when she said she thought they should all be concerned about growing backyard gardens for their families, not stockpiling C-rations in hollowed-out hills, like the one down Hwy. 111 near the Ohio River town of Leavenworth.

His idea was to take over the school, to make his philosophies, which he saw as consistent with those of the BSU, public. The group met at the city library on his day off to mull possibilities and had argued amongst themselves. Some said Chipper was too pale-skinned and too middle-class to be in charge, but he asserted that he came from a family of activists, that he had the most experience with such things. In the end, the group voted him out of leadership, and Devron Jordan, who was president of the debate club, was voted in as chair and as head of a potentially less-volatile lunchtime march on the school. Chipper saw that it wasn't a stretch to think a librarian overheard the conversations. When he argued with the group about a meeting spot, his defense in support of the library had been that it was, as his father had taught him, a place of intellectual freedom. A committee seeking to promote freedom surely could count on being well-supported by those great limestone walls and black-and-white checkered marble floors.

He shared all this with his mother, who cradled him in her arms and let him cry until he couldn't catch a breath. His grief had pushed him outside his body, where he often had retreated in the weeks and months after his father's murder. He'd watched his mother comfort his father similarly on the day Dr. King was shot and wondered whether in the depths of their bedroom, she ever had needed such comfort. The only time she cried out in the open was after his father had taken his own bullet, shot from within a mob of segregationists.

She got up and made Chipper a cup of valerian tea, her solution to all ills. The earthy scent calmed him long before the tea was cool enough to sip. She once confided that she used valerian tea to relax herself before nursing him, spoke proudly of having breastfed even when store-bought baby formula was all the rage and people chastised her for being bold enough to bare her milk-laden breast in public. She loved telling the story of a woman walking up to express her negative opinions on the subject, only to have Chipper pull loose from the nipple and release a spray across the front of the woman's dress.

"You are not made of skin, Marcus," she said. "You have a brain and hands and feet. No doubt life is going to get hard for you. You are sensitive to injustice, so I know you can handle yourself, but you tend to have a temper around it, don't you?"

"Yes, ma'am," he said. "I reach boiling point."

"Your father and I cultivated your talents. We saw to it you were exposed to many sides of life. Your father was proud. He believed we must work to subdue the abuse of power and that informed his and my decisions about child-rearing. Understand? Like you, he had a predilection to what's right. And, yes, he had a temper."

Chipper told her a story he knew she didn't know, how he had once watched his father argue after school with another parent. One whose kid had called Chipper a white nigger. His mother remained silent for a moment, cleared her throat.

"School is necessary," she said. "You can't re-mold a world you don't understand. None of us gets to start from scratch. We pick up where the last person left off. Your father believed in public schools, believed you could learn from whatever struggles you found there."

They talked about him having taken on his father's mode of dress. His mother thought it was a way of honoring his father that might not be serving him as well as he liked. Chipper needed to understand the impact of personal appearance. "It's not about black power for you," she said. "You always will be a mix of dark and light. We all are, no matter our race or ethnic origins. Nobody can knock you off feet planted in self-knowledge. Figure out how you can help the world from there."

He made her cry when he told her he just wanted to be a person, not an intersection or a hybrid, as if he were grafted like a rosebush or an apple tree. He told her how ugly the library situation made him feel.

"It's not groovy," he said. "Now I have one less place where I don't have to be self-conscious. Why do people treat me like it's my fault that I look the way I look? Nobody asks what I know about books. Nobody asks what I know about history. In fact, nobody asks me a damned thing. They look at my hair and my facial features and assume something. I'm supposed to groove on that? I want to stop it. I want to educate the motherfuckers with my fist."

The look on his mother's face told him exactly how far he had over-stepped.

"We each get a puzzle, Chipper," she said, once she had regained composure. "We get one gigantic puzzle to solve. Life is crazy. It is mean. It is cruel. People are angry and tired and hungry for relief. But the rule is simple: always be the better person. Strive to set the bar."

He was so moved by his mother's last comment that he went directly upstairs, pulled a new notebook from the shelf, and labeled it across the front in black marker, "Autobiography Notes—please return to Chipper Grube, 1433 Marianne Drive, New Albany, Indiana." He put carbon paper between two pages and wrote down her exact words:

Strive to set the bar. Then he trimmed the original to fit into his wallet behind his still-crisp driver's license.

* * *

Chipper walked through the aftermath of his firing by going to his father's mosque. He used his mother's bobby pins to secure his *taqiyeh* to his head, said prayers on an antique Turkish prayer rug he had received for his twelfth birthday, when he began fasting for part of Ramadan with his father. He positioned himself toward Mecca between classes at least once or twice a day, far short of the prescribed five, in the boys' upstairs restroom, until his mother pointed out that a bathroom floor would be considered too unclean for prayers. When he shared his problem with his English teacher, she began allowing him to use her classroom at lunchtime and later during her grading period, which happened to coincide with his study hall. He also went to Mass with his mother and drove alone in her blue hatchback to the gospel church on Broadway in Louisville, where the sound of slave-time gospel rolled through him like a boulder, served an internal place nothing else reached. After the service, hearty-bodied older women hugged him and called him Sugar. Then he'd walk a few blocks west to a place where one of the deacons early on had whispered that he could pass three dollars through a window and take away a plate of ribs and cornbread. The men would say, "Good to see you in church, Son," as they leaned with one shoe heel against the building's asphalt-shingled wall and one against the green grass, eating in relaxed confidence their own brand of communion meal.

He took an after-school job at the Sunoco filling station. Gene's, everybody called it. He was hired to pump gas and wash windshields, but when he didn't have customers, he helped the mechanics, trying to learn what he could. Even though he had his eyes on a college degree, he thought trade skills would serve him as much if not better than Dr. King's admonition to keep a chipper attitude. Having a degree would not make him impervious to poverty as he had learned from the Unemployment Bureau training sessions he attended after his library job ended. He liked working at Gene's, the red grease rags, the petroleum smells, the music of the signal bell customers drove across as they pulled to the pump. He liked treating customers in a friendly manner, erasing the evidence of their buggy travels by rendering their windshields sparkling.

His big mistake was complaining when one of the mechanics called him Thirty Weight. One day several months into his employment, tired of the way it made him feel, Chipper tried explaining to the man that such a nickname was a form of ignorance, of racism. Quoting his mother from a discussion about stereotypes, he said, "It indicates political naivete." The mechanic, who was called Doc, for the way he expected to be handed tools while under a hood, was a husky, big-handed man. He had been amenable to Chipper handing him tools, emptying oil pans into the big barrel, greasing nuts and bearings. Almost immediately, however, he began referencing Chipper by the name Thirty Weight. When Chipper explained the connotations, Doc, clearly entertained, started broadcasting from across the station lot when Chipper was on the pumps. "Hey, Thirty Weight, where's your spout, Dude?" or "Hey, Thirty Weight, rub some oil on this, would ya?"

Doc defended himself by saying the nickname came from the oil dumping, nothing more, and that Chipper needed to learn a thing or two, and to lighten up.

Gene said, "Don't go picking fights, Grube. Doc deserves a raise, not some twig like you stirring trouble.

Take your pay and go. I'm not having an ounce of crap in my place." He handed Chipper a twenty and said, "The rest will come in the mail."

From Gene's, he tried flipping burgers at a brand-new joint called McDonald's with twin yellow arches horseshoeing the building. Daily they had to be hosed off to keep the soot from the steel mill knocked down. He worked his way to assistant shift supervisor in a matter of weeks. McDonald's philosophy was to help high school students break into the work world, moving them into management training as soon as they showed promise. He did his job with a smile, keeping an eye on grill production and fryer temperatures, making certain the ice cream machine didn't freeze during runs on milkshakes, and inspecting the burger patties for signs of taint.

One day the franchise owner called him on the phone in the middle of a Saturday lunch rush and said he was starting to hear rumors about trouble with forced busing across the river in Louisville. "What does that have to do with me? I'm not involved in that," Chipper said.

"Well, nothing, Chipper. Not really. But you'd have a better time over at one of the pizza joints maybe. Give it a chance. You might make manager there."

When Chipper started to protest, the owner said, "Welcome to the world of adults. Fair is where you spend your money on the merry-go-round."

*   *   *

The night of his high school graduation, Chipper made a spontaneous decision to ride out west with Toby, who had heard good money could be made picking grapefruit and cherries. They planned to leave in two weeks. Toby had a dependable station wagon, which they could fill to the brim with gear, boxes of food, and a big, zinc-lined cooler loaded with ice and various brands of soda. It would be an adventure and educational. Chipper's mother cried. She thought it was unsafe, offered to pay for a summer in Europe after his junior year, instead. In the end, she heard his argument: he needed to see the land. He and Toby wanted to drive through the West, see the Grand Canyon, Yosemite. He was headed to Berkeley in the fall anyway. This way he'd at least be in the right part of the country. It would be a good experience to see the sights. A lesson in geology and sociology. She could fly out and help him settle into his dorm.

Instead of an answer, his mother handed him an envelope of cash.

"Mom," he said, "I've got saved money. If I need help, I'll ask."

On the car ride out, he watched the United States zipping past, just as he had imagined. The misty, fertile green bolls of Missouri and Arkansas and charbroiled oil fields of Texas. Toby, red-haired, and freckled, said, "Jesus, I didn't think about Texas," insisting Chipper wear a big cowboy hat and sunglasses. While Toby drove, Chipper took notes, wrote long passages in his notebook about the changing landscapes, read Kerouac's *On the Road* aloud.

They took their meals at car hop drive-ins, slept zipped into sleeping bags in the far reaches of truck stop parking lots between idling eighteen-wheelers on the Falcon's bench seats. Toby in the front, Chipper in the back. Chipper, at Toby's suggestion, slept in a knit cap.

He realized he'd had it relatively easy in New Albany. The one time he was assaulted was during the lunchtime picket-line his fellow Black Student Union advocates launched in lieu of a school takeover. A pair of male students in letterman jackets pushed and tripped him, bloodying his nose, in response to which eight picketers dropped their signs and bodily carried both boys into the principal's office with the entire picket line following. The principal thought it was a takeover and locked himself in his office, calling first the police and then warning the other teachers over the P.A. The resulting chaos sent the teachers hiding in the faculty lounge. Although it was the two letterman boys who wrestled the door keys off of one of the janitors and locked down the building, other students were accused and suspended from school for a week. Devron Jordan was initially expelled, but when his attorney father filed suit against the school district, the expulsion was rescinded and the letterman boys were suspended for ten days, after which the school held an assembly to formally recognize the BSU.

Despite the minor bullies he'd faced during his years in New Albany public schools, no one had otherwise physically threatened him. Even during that awful summer of 1976, after he was fired from the burger stand, when forced busing across the Ohio River in Louisville brought masses of screaming parents into the streets, burning cars and forcing authorities to call in the National Guard, who dragged struggling bodies by the hair and belts and handcuffs into paddy wagons borrowed from neighboring Cincinnati, Lexington, and as far north as Indianapolis.

* * *

Anxiety eased as they crossed into New Mexico and then Arizona, where they met people from all over the world, such that Chipper stopped wearing both the cowboy hat and the knit cap at night. And because it was too hot even to zip his sleeping bag.

He daydreamed about working a job where the only measure of worth was how fast and for how long he could pull grapefruit off a tree. Toby said the branches had large thorns, so you wore leather gloves, like golf gloves, and denim shirts with long sleeves, dropping the fruit into a canvas bag slung across the chest. He said the bags weighed more than fifty pounds full. They'd be ripped as longshoremen in no time.

Toby had an address for an orchard in Lodi, California. The sun there was higher in the sky than Chipper had ever seen it, the smell of hot pavement permeated, and the grapefruit trees looked pained, as if begrudging of their fates. Getting hired was easy. Toby's buddy had vouched for them ahead of time. The foreman, a dark-haired woman wearing a spotless white shirt and jeans with ironed creases checked off their names on a clipboard. They were taken to a patch of ground where they could pitch a tent and leave the station wagon. Absent a tent, could they sleep in the car? They could. Provided they kept a tidy camp. Showers were near the bunkhouses, the beds of which were spoken for. They were a few days late for the start of harvest, but the foreman would take them no matter. Lucky for them they'd had a referral. They were not to sample the fruit. Quickest way to find themselves kissing their asses in the unemployment line was to peel a grapefruit on the ladders. The foreman's minions were watching.

Chipper couldn't imagine peeling a grapefruit and biting into it raw like an apple.

For the first few days and nights, he ached from scalp to toenails from the constant effort to balance on the ladders with the ever-increasing weight of the canvas bag threatening to throw him askance. Part of it had to do with his slow pace as he adapted to the twist-snap movement required to leave behind the stem and calyx and careful placement in the bags to prevent damage. Eventually Chipper learned to lean into his effort, wedging his body between a limb and the ladder once a few of the green-yellow orbs gave the bag enough weight to balance on a rung. In this way, he could pick a branch with both hands, work his way through a cluster and get a rhythm going. The gloves and heavy shirts they'd purchased turned out to be useless and unnecessary, as the thorns were fairly supple. If he leaned too hard, he'd bruise the fruit he'd already picked or break the limb supporting his back and likely fall and kill himself, which he did not want to do. It took a few moments each time he reset the ladder, but he always found what he and Toby started calling "The Zone."

His mother loved grapefruit. She once told him they were called the Forbidden Fruit originally, but she didn't know why. He wished to ship her a crate of them. She would cut one in half, sprinkle it with honey, then score the halves and scoop the pulp with a special corrugated spoon. Chipper never developed a taste for them—too sour, despite the honey—but in the orchards, the citrusy smell of the leaves and oils from the disturbed fruit reminded him of home and his mother and the mornings spent over breakfast sharing coffee and talking out the details of their daily routines. She often came to the table puffy-eyed, clearly from crying, and Chipper was always struck by how hard she worked to conjure a happy smile and a transfer of joy to him. He understood his father would have wanted her to continue this way, that his priority was that Chipper's start in the world not be interrupted no matter what calamity befell their little family. This awareness, among many others, came to him on the ladders in the grapefruit trees near the arid village of Lodi.

Once it became clear that Chipper and Toby both were capable, quick workers, the men around them made it obvious through smiles and vague gestures that competition was the game. How many bags of grapefruit and how fast.

Each canvas sack was emptied into a bin, each of which held fifty pounds of fruit. A pound less and the unlucky picker was scrambling up a tree to grab another piece of fruit. A cold, rainy spring in the region had produced a late but heavy crop, so the boxes filled quickly.

He knew he had made some kind of impression when at the end of the first week the foreman clapped him on the back and said, "Good week's work, Grube. Here's your pay. You earned it." He and Toby were standing by the station wagon staring at their checks when a woman walked over and said, "Eat," took hold of his and Toby's hands with each of hers, and pulled them toward her family's camp. Thus began a pattern. At night they ate tortillas patted out by hand and cooked on an iron griddle over a campfire grill. One night one of the men tried to make a point of Chipper's height. He pulled Chipper to his feet and stood head to back with him. The man was at least a foot shorter. "*Muy alto. Pero, no grande. El otro gringo es un poco grande, un poco,*" the man said, patting his belly, then pointing at Toby, who always seemed to carry a layer of excess. The rest of the group laughed. The woman who had invited them to the first meal jumped up and pinched both boys on their cheeks, saying, "*Muy buenos chicos!*" At which, again, people laughed. Chipper felt embarrassed by the attention.

On the opposite side of the creek camped a family with shaved heads. Toby said on account of lice. Each evening, one of the women crossed the footbridge to take plates of tortillas and beans. Chipper felt sorry for them, as did Toby, and they both tried to no avail to give money to help pay for not only the meals being shared with the headlice family, but for what he and Toby ate each evening. The shaved-head family wasn't allowed to work or move on until the Health Department came and cleared them, so they couldn't earn money, but at least the grower was letting them stay.

Chipper hated the way it made him feel his lack of courage, but, like most everybody else, he stayed clear of their side of the creek. He thought they looked exactly like the family in the movie version of *Grapes of Wrath*. Only bald.

The grapefruit ran out the third week of June, weeks behind a normal year. By then, the shaved-head family had pulled out. Toby decided he was ready to head back to New Albany even though, as Chipper argued, it was Toby's idea for them to be out there in the first place, and they had sworn to stick it out for two months. All in all, they'd been gone just shy of five weeks.

"What about looking like a longshoreman? The girls you were going to get? What about Charles Atlas and all that?" Chipper asked.

Toby rubbed his scruff of red hair, admitted he wasn't as adventurous as he originally thought. "Jesus, Chip. I'm sick of farting beans, for one. I want to sleep in my own bed. I'm tired. I feel like an old man." He preferred to spend his summer boating the Ohio until check-in at Indiana State, figuring to sling a hammer or twist a wrench or flip burgers for the summer's entertainment. "Plus, I need dependable money. We're spending everything we make on gas and restaurant food and stupid stuff."

"What stupid stuff?" Chipper said. "I've already saved more than a hundred dollars. We're only halfway through. I get it. You miss your mama, don't you?"

Toby laughed. It had been the mutual joke throughout the trip, as neither of them had ever been away from home for such a period of time. They manufactured a country song about being a lonely traveling man and missing a woman, down to Chipper writing the words, adapted to the tune of Hank Williams' "I'm So Lonesome I Could Cry," Toby at night around the campfire playing backup on the harmonica to Chipper's vocal talents. They called it, "Missing Mama."

Chipper put the song in his wallet, where his mother's speech had originally been: I'm a lonely old bluesman/blue from tired feet/I'm a lonely old bluesman/miss my hotdog mama/She's so sweet.

"Well, I don't have a hundred dollars," Toby said.

"That's because you smoke cigarettes. You go to town every day when the rest of us are still picking. You buy junk. Buy an apple instead of chips and hamburgers and soft drinks and candy bars. No wonder you're tired. You barely eat the Mexican food. Food we can't even make them let us pay for," Chipper said.

"I told you those beans make me fart. I don't want to go around smelling like a fart."

"You do anyway, Tobs," Chipper said, to which Toby squared off and feigned a punch.

*   *   *

From his berth in the back of the station wagon that night, Chipper came to a decision: he'd continue traveling on his own. Berkeley campus wouldn't accept dorm residents for six more weeks. He'd heard the large cherry groves near Stockton needed pickers. Cherries took more care in the picking, so the pay was better. Perhaps he could earn enough to buy a vehicle. He always wanted an old round-nosed pickup like his mother's father had had. Toby agreed to drop him at the Lodi Greyhound station before turning the Falcon back east. "Careful riding the Dog, my friend," he said, waving and driving off.

Chipper took a piece of advice from his mother, went to a bank and turned his bills into traveler's checks. He explained the situation, charming the teller with his opinion of the West's landscapes. She assured him he'd have no trouble cashing the checks at any other bank, so long as he kept his carbon copies, which he later folded longways and stashed under his right shoe's insert. The other shoe held his transcription of his mother's speech, similarly folded, which he had transferred from his wallet in case he was robbed or was intercepted by a pickpocket. The traveler's checks he wrapped in plastic wrap, taped the bundle with adhesive tape to his side—all but twenty-five dollars in getting-by cash, which he tucked into the front pockets of his jeans. He still had his original one-hundred-dollar traveler's check stored with the carbons. He'd learned that a bus ticket to New Albany was eighty-four dollars, from just about any place in California. Another option was an Ameripass if he wanted to spend the entire bill while also expanding his options. Regardless, he could finance his way home—the travelers check was good for a year.

* * *

The bus hit Missoula, Montana, just as threads of light began appearing along a purplish eastern horizon. "Hey, Bud!" a uniformed man with a grey buzz cut, clearly the driver, said. "You been sleeping! End of the line!" Chipper surveyed the staring faces, people gathering belongings, preparing to get off the bus. He was thirsty, disoriented, his stomach twisted and sour, his clothes vaguely damp, as if he'd overcome a fever. His bladder lit like a dynamite fuse.

"Excuse me," Chipper said, launching himself up and out of his seat, through the sleepy throng, the smell of an idling engine, and into a pine grove to take the longest piss of his life. His urine hit a tree trunk, spattering back against his pant legs. Memory was a closed door. Why was he in Montana and not Stockton? He pulled his bus ticket from his pocket, squinted in the spare light extending from the bus station-diner. It wasn't a ticket but more like a thin passbook. The backdrop was a muted color photograph of an empty road lined by trees in full-green summer leaf. Red and blue-shadowed letters next to a mid-leap greyhound dog read: *Welcome to Ameripass! 30 Days of Travel! One Low Fare!*

Then he remembered. The cherries. Nobody in Stockton would hire him. He hitchhiked around the region for days, mostly walking, since rarely did anyone stop to give him a ride. "Colored and wetbacks don't mix, and I don't hire college types," one orchard boss had said, even though Chipper tried to argue that "colored," alongside "wetbacks," was a completely racist way of referring to people, plus he wasn't yet in college, so he wasn't a "college type," but the man turned his back and walked away.

In his disappointment and fatigue, he had slept across three states.

Eggs and toast at the diner. Coffee. He watched another patron scoop grapefruit pulp into his mouth.

Since he'd slept enough to last a week, the bus travel that day gave him long stretches to think, to piece together the time since Stockton, to admire the western states' topography. He saw bonafide cowboys urging long clots of cattle along barbed wire fence rows. Scattered groups of pronghorn antelope, white-sugar bellies and throats contrasting with brown-sugar backs, nearly invisible in the higher elevations where small drifts of snow, white and fluorescent, lingered even as the calendar neared July. The vastness made him lonely, and he felt the tug of his mother's worry. He had not called her to explain his decision to tour the west for a few weeks before school. *Ameripass!* He'd take stop-offs here and there to see the sights, then circle back to California and Berkeley to find employment before orientation. He meant to work alongside his studies, was prepared even to wash dishes. Anything to make the money taped to his side go further, to stave off the day he would need his mother's assistance.

During a long break in Billings, Montana, cruising downtown sidewalks stuttering with cracks and upheavals from a tough winter, it occurred to him that he liked this new sense of disconnectedness. He liked being footloose. He had packed a paperback-sized dictionary with him, as he figured the best college prep would be to expand his vocabulary, and had run across the word *misanthrope*, recognizing something about himself in its definition. He was not a pure misanthrope, but he did glimpse a truth he'd never been able to express before: it was actually hard to be around people at times. At times, he thought, a person needs space.

As much as he had compassion for other humans, he'd started to notice how so-called failure arguably could be a matter of choice. For example, if he kept himself ignorant, he was choosing to disqualify himself from what gains come with an education—even if that education was self-directed. In the case where a person couldn't afford college, couldn't he go to the library and read books? Thousands of years of wisdom and knowledge was housed in the library, free and for all. Chipper started to notice himself not having equal levels of empathy. If a man was dirty, was it so hard for him to wash his face? Was use of all the various forms of tobacco necessary? Particularly smoking cigarettes, a stinking habit that made its rank existence known by leaving traces on bystanders' clothing and caused congestion? He listened to crude language, angry language, useless babbling, small talk, and people holding forth on subjects about which they sounded clearly unschooled, even to someone as young as Chipper. At which point was luck to blame? Did anger draw bad luck? Did the failure to take sufficient care of oneself? How long did it take bad luck to render a person listless, barely existing, half-lidded in the middle of the day, glossed over as if bored to death by the effort to breathe? He saw people with no teeth, reliant on coffee and cigarettes to get through the hours of daylight, cigarettes and dollar-a-bottle wine to get through the night. It was a curiosity to him, how people had money for booze and tobacco but not food. Money for MD 20/20 but not for toothpaste or even a toothbrush. He thought if he were rich, he'd use his wealth to buy dentist visits for all the sad people roaming the country with rotten or missing teeth. If they felt better about themselves, might they decide to improve their circumstances?

He saw women with infants and young children who smelled of urine and cigarettes. Women at milk-run bus stations who would ask any grandmotherly stranger to watch their babies while they "took a little smoke break." Babies who sucked on bottles of juice and nibbled Fritos from the snack bar. A conversation with his mother about reproduction put an unforgettable image in his mind of these children's futures—"Get into trouble. Have the baby. That's what women do," she said, "then fifteen or sixteen or eighteen years later the mother ends up trying to talk sense into a daughter who is fooling around with boys just like she was. You turn into a broken record, trying to make your child understand that getting a foothold first has got to be the number one strategy and priority. You want to prevent them from making irreversible mistakes."

He wondered if his mother could truly perceive what it was like for the kind of people he'd been seeing since he left Indiana. She was born to money. His father was also middle class. No one in the bus stations looked to be very well off— no one who was riding the Dog. A majority of them looked similar to people he'd seen in the fruit camps—disheveled, disconnected from the present, lacking hope, tamped down. Some even without suitcases, their belongings in brown grocery bags. Others clean and pressed, from the world of workers, trying to save a buck by using cheap travel.

Almost right away he realized he didn't feel self-conscious on the buses. Rather, he felt somewhat at home. He especially liked the older women drivers as they were no-nonsense and made it clear from the start that this was public transportation, and they were public transportation professionals, and by public, they meant, as one woman said, "open and for use by *any*body who's got the cash to pay for a ticket and maybe buy me a soda pop," at which everybody laughed, and at the first stop just about everybody brought her back a pop-top can of some kind of soft drink, which she turned around and shared with anybody who wanted one. He was surrounded by many sorts of people, much more varied than high school had been: tall, short, middle height, gaunt, hefty, proportionate, long arms, short arms, big hands, gnarled knuckles, calloused fingers, soft feminine hands, chewed nails, polished nails, cut and trimmed nails, smooth arms, hairy arms, tattooed arms, missing arms or fingers, tiny feet in too-big sneakers, big feet in cowboy boots and flat-soled oxfords, chubby knees, bony knees, fuzzy hair, straight hair, blonde, brown-haired, red-headed, blue-eyed, brown-eyed, hazel, big ears, small ears, pierced ears, one guy with no ear at all. Women in dresses, shorts, or slacks, men in overalls, denim jeans, non-descript dark or pale fabrics. Plaid shirts, denim shirts, sweatshirts, jackets, yellow rain slickers.

He also quickly came to understand that what people saw in cigarettes, dime store paperbacks, cheap wine, candy bars, and lousy snack bar food was an impermanent form of joy. He could detect it on their faces, their lightened expressions as they walked back to the bus. The drink, tobacco, sack of burgers, the cheap novel—all were treats. It was the act of consumption that mattered more than the substance. For that few moments, the person knew satisfaction. It disgusted him to realize that advertisements worked on people's need for joy. He'd previously thought of ads and television commercials only as part of the entertainment.

Inside the Billings bus station, he learned that a mechanical problem was going to delay departure for at least two hours beyond the scheduled forty-five-minute break. An older man came past him a second time, asking for change. He looked like a black and white photo from the Great Depression—lonely, ragged, worn out. His pants were tucked and cinched at the waist with a length of cord. He wore an oversized, dark-green wool military coat, despite the fact that it was nearly July, with epaulets and tabs at the cuffs, his brown leather work boots scuffed, bootlaces frayed. Immediately Chipper wished for a coat and boots just like them. He thought the man seemed familiar, and a memory flitted through his mind, his mother talking late one Friday night after the television had stopped broadcasting, its snowy drone providing an otherworldly backdrop as she spoke. She was telling him about the phenomenon of "familiars," about bad spirits that roamed looking to snare us off our paths. The snapshot vanished as Chipper, in a surge of unplanned generosity, handed him a pair of fives.

"No!" the old man said. "Now, you shouldn't have done that. I'll drink myself to sleep tonight with them bills, and I have other business to be about."

"Buy us breakfast, then," Chipper said. "I can see open seats across the street."

The look on the man's face stayed with Chipper until he was much older himself. In a letter to his mother he later described it as "elation, recognition, gratitude, and deep longing all curled up inside a stone of need."

His fellow traveler broke into a smile, then a deep laugh and a little dance, then clapped Chipper on the back and said, "Now that, youngster, would be an honor." Chipper ate eggs and toast with coffee for the second time that day, and the old man ordered a double bloody Mary "with eyes," meaning fortified with a pair of raw eggs. The lines on his face advertised each joy and hardship. He was trying to get to Alaska to work the pipeline, make his fortune. He meant to be in Seattle by now but had hit a jackpot on pull-tabs in Reno, decided to take a "wowie route," as he called it, to see his ex in Sheridan, Wyoming, try to get her to reunite and head north with him. He had had his run of wild oats. Now he felt ready to shack up with a woman again.

"Thanks to you," he said, "I'll see her not at the bad end of a bender, but with food and friendship in my gut. God helps those who help themselves."

*   *   *

Chipper came back inside the bus terminal with a few minutes to spare. Long enough to use the toilet, wash, and return to the passenger waiting area to rescue his pack from one of the twenty-five-cent lockers. Bus terminal was too big a phrase. It was designated benches in the train depot. He wondered about the price of a train from Billings to Indiana, whether it would be unmanly to admit, as Toby had, that he was ready for a real bed.

Then out of the women's restroom walked Tara Flock's older sister Debbie and another girl from high school, Betsy Sonntag, with a child who looked to be barely a toddler.

Debbie had been valedictorian of her class at New Albany High, a year ahead of Chipper, who missed being valedictorian by one-tenth of a percentage point, the honor instead going to Devron Jordan. Chipper's quest for gainful employment was partially to blame, but fault mostly fell on nights spent writing essays instead of doing geometry homework. He did not relish spheres. He did not appreciate radii and circumference. He did not care for obtuseness in people or angles. He understood dimension, perspective, relationship, and infinity. He simply was not interested in calculating those things.

Chipper had made out with Debbie at a party once, one of those random make-out sessions that had no permanent bearing but were a requisite part of high school parties, along with bootleg beer and drams of moonshine from someone's Kentucky grandfather's still. He remembered the sensation of her smooth blonde hair and the sweet of her lips. He hadn't seen her since, other than across campus and at graduation festivities.

They were travelling from where they'd been picking cherries outside Sacramento, Debbie explained. Not for a lark, not to educate themselves about the world, but because after high school they'd discovered heroin and LSD together, fell in with people hitchhiking to San Francisco, Debbie forfeiting her free ride to Sarah Lawrence. "One hell of a year. We've had ourselves a shit-ton of fun. Anti-establishment, you dig? Nobody's going to light your fire. You gotta do it yourself," Debbie said. "This is the age of Aquarius, baby. Make love, not war. School's out forever, Chipper Grube. Life happens on the playground."

Chipper figured every boy in his class always would remember Betsy Sonntag. They were to a one as in love with her as a teenager can be, meaning they were hormonally fixated—at least this was his mother's explanation. Betsy played golf and tennis, was on the cheer squad. Toby had cut her photo out of the school newspaper and replaced Linda Ronstadt's head with Betsy's on a poster tacked to his bedroom ceiling. Linda Ronstadt was a dream for certain; Betsy was at least in the same universal quadrant. After nearly a year of travelling with Debbie, she was mildly ragged-looking and just as surprised to see him as he was the two of them.

"Well, look at us," Debbie said. "Didn't we turn out fine."

Chipper subdued the urge to detail his circumstances, instead climbing on the bus behind them, listening to Debbie go on about how they ought to get off for a few days in Steele, North Dakota. "Steele's a real party spot. I'll buy a kit and you can make Betsy and me look like Marilyn Monroe. Then we'll go partying in Steele. I'm serious. Only a few hundred people live there, but I've made lifelong friends in Steele who'll put us up. My friend Roach owns the trailer park. Plus, we can take pictures next to the future site of the world's tallest sandhill crane. People are trying to raise money to have this famous artist build it."

Betsy smoked outdoors at every stop, even in the rain, leaving her little boy with him and Debbie. People stared as if the three of them were from outer space. One woman with few teeth and dyed black hair walked up and told Debbie she ought to be ashamed.

"Didn't ask you, did I, Witch?" Debbie said, and the woman, as if cued, hissed, and spat.

Chipper heard the words "fucking hippies" whispered back and forth.

Betsy in high school was one of those girls from a poor family who tried to make up for it with ambition. She was on the speech team. The business club. She participated in every group and program that did not require cash to join. Probably nobody but Chipper noticed that part. Certainly, he'd never heard it mentioned in the hallways. Apparently, however, she possessed ambition to carry herself only so far. She told him she'd always wanted to be a ballet dancer, but her father wouldn't let her take lessons, because of money and also because of the skimpy outfits and form-fitting tights dancers wore. A maiden aunt, her father's sister, insisted Betsy deserved more opportunities, offering to pay for ballet classes and to help her choose modest apparel.

Still, her father refused, threatening to withdraw permission for her many after-school obligations. When the letter arrived announcing her academic scholarship, he dug in his heels again. Betsy dialed up Debbie, and off they went to seek a more random form of education.

Debbie, on the other hand, the Debbie Chipper had grown up with, belonged with a rich crowd—all Hollywood and shiny and put together. Even road- and drug-worn, with stale make-up and pony-tailed hair falling out of its pins, she was joyful, pretty. He felt he should be able to fix things for these two friends, but they were bent on continuing as they had been.

Chipper accompanied Betsy and Debbie through Sheridan, Wyoming, with its big rodeo billboards and cattle baron mansions, along droning miles to the parched landscapes of Steele, during which they took turns playing with Bean, Betsy's son, at times loaning him out to fellow passengers who offered soda pop sips or bites of homemade peanut butter and jelly sandwiches or to let him play with sets of keys, especially grandmother types who found the boy's curiosity hard to resist. Chipper said goodbye outside the smoky bowling alley and restaurant that doubled as Steele's Greyhound station, posing so a stranger could take snapshots of them holding Bean across three sets of arms. When he looked at the photo later, he analyzed those forty-eight hours. How the hell *did* Betsy Sonntag and Debbie Flock happen to be in Billings, Montana, on the same night as he? What did it mean? Was it an omen? A caution? Could he spiral downward as they had?

He also realized that, except for crude instances where others cursed him, he hadn't felt self-conscious around Betsy and Debbie and certainly not Bean, who sported a pale, fried-brown afro of his own. If signs from the heavens were meant to guide us, perhaps running into girls from high school meant he should thank the stars nothing bad had happened to him so far and turn his attention home. No sin in returning back out west with his mother. It would be a suiting end to his carefully-constructed childhood.

Always he would question his next choice. Without premeditation, instead of staying with the bus all the way to the New Albany Bowl and the Greyhound station, he decided to get off in Louisville and, via a series of City Transit buses, to make his way to the freight yards. Reasoning became a chess match between two possibilities: going home or hopping a freight train. Just for a short while. Just for the experience. The entire trip from Chicago, where he had found in a wall rack a shipping schedule for the freight trains, he had battled himself. Ten years in the future, what would it matter whether he took an extra week for a blood and guts adventure? He never truly would be unsafe, not in the way of Debbie and Betsy or the old man in Billings, or those who made a life of the trains. He had money enough to eat well and rent a room if it didn't work out and enough to get home by any number of means. He called his mother, endured her worry, explaining that he'd decided to continue using the Ameripass until it expired and how he happened to be calling from a tiny town in North Dakota. He'd later have some explaining to do if she noticed the Louisville exchange for this date and time on the phone bill, but by then he would have survived the journey, and he would make her understand that he lied to protect her from worry.

He arrived at the freight yard at dusk, just as a B&O train with open car doors was starting to move. The smell of brake exhaust, coal burning, and rusted metal reminded him of the field trip his eighth-grade science class had taken to Louisville Industrial Works, where coal was turned into electricity. A group of clearly practiced men strong-armed their way aboard. They were mostly clean shaven, although several sported untamed beards. One man had a ponytail in back and one at his chin. It looked easy enough, scrambling aboard, and it was, almost. In the end, several of them had to claw his backpack to hoist him. "Throw your pack first," one said. But Chipper was worried he'd wind up on the ground, his pack on the train headed to Cincinnati.

Once the train was fully rolling, the men started talking about how easy it was to get out of Louisville, more so than other cities, which is what the old man in Billings had said when Chipper asked about his rail experience. He had also said that watchmen turned their backs for a bottle or a few bills, and that railroad bosses and personnel were decent, world-weary, but accommodating, mostly professional. The car was loaded with barrels marked LARD. The other men, eight of them, recognized their situation at once, began to laugh. A tall rangy fellow with gnarled hands said, "Reckon we in the piano car. Lard's white'n we all black."

Another said, "E-bon-y and i-vo-ry. Except him," pointing at Chipper. "What are you anyway, boy? Parts of you is nigra, but you ain't nigra."

Chipper took out his notebook. He hadn't thought of his genetic combination as a purveyor of music.

One older man, with white hair and no teeth said to Chipper, "Boy what in Hades are you doing here? Some kinda cop? Do what your mama say and get yo' ass off dis train. A rail habit is not a life. See that right here?" He rolled up his sleeves. "Needle marks. Tracks. They is needle tracks and they is train tracks. Both dead ends to the devil. Get your checkerboard ass home, son. You ain't old enough to get laid. Although, bet ol' Charlie here be happy to help with that."

Chipper was stunned when another man dropped his pants to reveal feminine anatomy.

"I looks like a Charles on account I don't gots titties. But I take you on. I don't mind me some of that sweet, young onion," Charlie said.

The smell inside the car was of hot dust and wood, nauseating Chipper. He didn't want to be the subject of such discussion, which came to a halt when he told them he'd had his privates blown off in Vietnam. Charlie said, "You sho'nuff older than you look, then, boy. You 'got your balls blown off in 'Nam,' my ass. I got my balls blown off in 'Nam. Got 'em soaking in juice in a jar in my pack." The men howled in laughter, repeating the woman's words, slapping thighs and stomping feet to accentuate their glee.

Eventually, they turned away, fell into discussing their various circumstances.

Chipper left them fairly quickly, in Cincinnati, an hour down the line, for a westbound car full of pallets loaded with white-labeled industrial-sized cans lettered in black that read, "Beef Stew. U.S. Government Commodities." No one was in sight, so he tossed up his pack and easily vaulted into the plank floor. He dozed, then wrote descriptions of the group of the seven men and one woman, the physical experience of vaulting into a car, deciding it might be in his interest to create a persona for himself, to tell people he was writing a book he hoped to sell to pay his way to college.

Across the country, most drifters and watchmen expressed doubt about him getting ahead enough to go to school. A few called him uppity. Mostly he kept to himself, made a point of talking to the watchman at each new station: Chicago, Minneapolis, Fargo, Omaha, down into Denver, Albuquerque, Amarillo, Phoenix. He slipped each a couple of dollars, hinted that he was conducting research for a book, which led to a few sharing their stories. He exchanged addresses and promised to send copies of his published book. When he finally reunited with his mother, she brought a bundle of letters full of the details of their loves and lives and losses. Some were back from Vietnam. He felt a bit guilty about the fact that he was going to skip all that. By the time of his graduation, the war was over. He could have been recused from military service as an only male child, but he would have served, even if he was, as he had now concluded, a pacifist. There must be some job in the military that didn't require killing.

For every decent human, Chipper met two or three con men around the trains. People who would pick a man's pocket while buying him a barbeque sandwich. The number one rule of the rails was don't cozy up and don't let yourself be cozied up to. Keep a distance. If you feel your sex, keep a further distance. Act like somebody hard of hearing. At times Chipper wasn't sure what the raspier men were looking for—whatever money he might have or to join with him in base acts, and they were always white. Did black con men exist but they did not approach him because they perceived him as a "brother"? Or did only white men let themselves be reduced to relying on the art of cunning to get by?

*   *   *

A toothache finally inspired him to face the direction of home. It was the last week of July. Time was dwindling. He was sitting around a scrap fire with a trio of hobos who were drinking from a can of Instant Fire, a type of alcohol fuel the consistency of jelly. You could light it and heat your can of beans with it. You could also drink it. Hobo gin, the men called it. He'd thus far avoided alcohol, but his tooth hurt so badly he was willing to explore. Each had a different remedy: clamp down on a chaw of tobacco with the offending tooth; do the same with pine resin, according to a toothless, scrawny man who called himself Mountain Joe. "Or you can make yourself some mullein tea. You've seen mullein," he said. "Tall, fuzzy stalks. Yellow flowers. Like taking a dose of penicillin. Never eat the seeds, though. Make you bleed from your ass, the seeds will." Chipper envisioned himself hungry enough to chew on poisonous seeds, falling dead at the side of the road.

"What you need is a little horse," the black-bearded man named Sam said. "Horse will make you forget a tooth."

Chipper thought of Debbie and Betsy, wondering how things had gone for them in Steele. The warmed camp fuel tasted like paint remover smelled, but combined with the wad of tobacco clenched between his jaws, he was less consumed by the pain. They were near a siding called Clancy northwest of Walla Walla, Washington. The desert sage smelled like his mother's herb garden. The moon ascended full and rose-hued from summer wildfires. Coyotes yelped to the north. His head spun. He had eaten little in recent days. Wondered if the body could digest sage. Sam, swayed, walked past Chipper and wandered into the brush. Chipper could smell the musk of a long untended body, the dark filth, stale excrement. After a long while, the third man, bald but for a few strands like weeds sprouting from his pale head, said, "I don't think we'll see old Sammy until sunup." This one's name was Cletus. He claimed to hail from Oklahoma, from people who survived the Dustbowl. Chipper wasn't good at telling the difference between a subtle lie and an enormous lie, but he always got an odd twist in his gut when a person spoke an untruth. He felt the same sensation when he was being insulted, a feeling akin to jealousy, and he had learned to detect from body language when he was about to be assaulted. Immediately, he knew what Cletus had in mind. Sure enough, an enormous hard-on erupted through the zipper region of the man's trousers. A rimmed sore peered from the side of it, reflected moist in the firelight. Chipper had never seen a penis extended except his own mostly involuntary blooming. Masturbation was a subject Toby was fond of, but Chipper was so prone to sleep afterward that he rationed the activity. He had seen boys in the shower room and men in a magazine Toby had found under his mother's mattress, but all were flaccid. Healthy. Clean.

He had recognized the propensities of certain men. He had no judgment, but he knew where he stood. His mother taught him that sex, as skin, was formulated in all hues, and his was not of the man-to-man variety. He expected to come out of this part of his life, find a smart, strong girl with a book habit, and establish a shared life. Once they had their educations.

Cletus moved closer, lined up with Chipper's face. "I got a cure for a tooth," he said.

Chipper noticed the shifting breeze, the dimming moon as a cloud passed, the click of a switchblade. None of the other men moved.

"Are you atremble, whitenigaboy? No daddies out here to save you now, is they?" The man reeked of cigarettes, the combined odors of unwashed skin and smoke akin to fried pork.

Cletus swayed and stumbled, dropped the knife. The clatter of steel echoed, but barely. Chipper took the moment to spring up and shove him in the chest, knocking him to the ground. Cletus landed with a thud and a groan, shocked enough that he lay disoriented, rubbing his forehead, his member still exposed and visible in the firelight. Chipper stared briefly, then ran, sprinting harder than he had ever been capable of before, his body's adrenaline turning normal functions into hyper-capability. Initially, he stumbled headlong over sage and cheat, disrupting tumbleweeds, then his eyes adjusted to the darkness, a thing he did not know they would do, and he hit a welcome stride, glad for the days on ladders hefting bags of grapefruit, hours of staying himself against the sway of railcars, pulling himself and a pack up onto platforms over his head.

Each pound of a foot became a rock pick hammering his tooth. He first ran north, flanked by the milk-pale slit of light at the horizon, Cletus hopefully a good distance behind him, then veered west as the morning brightened.

The light grew quickly once the sun breached the far reaches of the eastern landscape. After perhaps ninety minutes of running, he stopped to piss and to vomit, heaving the Instant Fire, the swallowed tobacco juice, the partially-eaten burgers pilfered from a dumpster in Walla Walla. He had not dared pull dollars from his jeans pocket, not even for food, not in front of Cletus and his band. The group had been pleasant and conversant when he hooked up with them, thinking to collect more stories, then grew moody and vulgar once the Instant Fire hit their empty stomachs.

Once he was certain Cletus hadn't followed, he slowed to a walk and continued hiking away from the sun, which was nearing mid-morning, cloaking the day in a yellowish haze, predictive of more heat. Eventually he came to a great confluence of rivers he assumed to be the Columbia and the Snake, more than two thousand miles from where he'd hopped the first train in Louisville. He had run and hiked dozens of miles along the river, sleeping away the worst of the stifling weather inside a weathered old building from which he first had to roust a very angry pair of chipmunks. A robin and raven duet woke him just before dawn the next morning, and he resumed hiking, not stopping until, once again, midday heat became unbearable. He came upon scattered farmsteads near the unincorporated village of Burbank, which, according to his map, meant the larger town of Pasco wasn't far.

The water below made him think of his hippie-leaning mother who had birthed him in a water bath, caused him to wonder what it was like for her. The quality of the pain of childbirth. More than a sore tooth, certainly. He had discomfited her in his arrival and now in his departure into adulthood. He scrambled down the riprap, removed his shoes, sunk his feet into the liquid current. They were markedly changed from when he left home, now marred with thick calluses and blisters. Chipper looked at the skin on the tops of his feet, sun-darkened from wearing shorts and going barefoot as much as he could, considering his circumstances this summer, white soles luminous under the water. Weeks of crusty skin soaked loose, such that he decided to remove his clothes and give them a rinse, using his undershirt as a cloth to scrub the rest of himself, being careful of the traveler's checks taped to his side. He admired the now-tan color of his arms and torso, as he had spent much of the past two months minus a shirt, his thighs and calves, the pale soles of his feet, calloused around the edges and wider than he remembered. He'd once read that before shoes, humans bore a horn-tough layer over their soles, which is why even dark-skinned people have no pigment there. The part of himself that carried him through life was what his mother and father had in common. What all humans have in common. *All souls have pale soles.* He remembered a ceremony from the slave-gospel church. Foot washing. In the Bible, Jesus washed the feet of his disciples to show servitude toward them.

He wished he could do something about the world, take the love his mother and father held for each other and turn it into a pill to distribute among the races. He laid his clothing on boulders to dry, then lounged back on the stones. looking to the western horizon, which was punctuated by mountains, the whiteness of their snowcaps blazing and surreal against an egg-blue sky. In the West, the sky was voluminous, as if the atmosphere were humped higher east of the Mississippi. He'd seen signs in Montana for Big Sky Country, and he understood what that meant. The east was close in. The sky paler. Sky blue now was more than a color in his Crayola box. It was a way of distinguishing east from west. He caught himself several times dozing, startled awake over and over, but eventually gave in. Almost immediately he began dreaming of that morning in Montgomery, of Dr. King on a balcony before a crowd of people chanting, "You have a dream. You have a dream." Dr. King pointed to a man in the crowd who was crying like a baby. It was Chipper, watching a black-skinned twin of himself standing there bawling next to Cletus, who was sipping Instant Fire, poking Chipper in the thigh with his penis, saying "You're a zebra. You got stripes like a barber pole," at which point Cletus took out a whip and slashed at Chipper until, indeed, he was striped red, white, and blue. Only his hair remained black.

The blunt stab of a billy stick and a boot to his hip pulled him out of slumber, although initially he couldn't be certain he wasn't still dreaming. His head felt like it was being squeezed between two boulders, a Sisyphus pushing from either side. If he wasn't dreaming, this was the worst waking experience of his life. Two dark-suited police officers in polished boots and complicated-looking gun belts stood over him. "Son, you come out here intoxicated and decide to set up house?" the taller one said.

Chipper had never known such fear and panic. The taste in his mouth was of copper, as if he might have sucked on a penny. His nose filled with the smell of ammonia. His hands tingled, heart rushed into his throat as he broke into a sweat. His larynx felt constricted and red, voice replicating its preadolescent squeak. "No sir, I'm sorry, sir. I don't drink. I had a toothache. I'm in the wrong. I'll be going. My ID is in my bag."

"You want to get that ID for us, son?" the second officer said.

"Yes, sir," Chipper said. "It's in my pack. May I get dressed, sir?"

"You got dry clothes in that pack? Anything else we should know about before I pick that pack up? Weed? Firearms?" the tall officer spoke again. The name on his tag was Rodriguez.

"No, sir," Chipper said. "Well, yes. A Swiss Army knife and a compass. They belonged to my father. He gave them to me when I was young. Younger. A boy. He died. I was headed to the bus station. I've got a change of clothes, a notebook, my wallet, a few books."

"No bus stations out here, son. What's with the tape? You're wrapped up like leftover Thanksgiving turkey." Officer Rodriguez said. "Are you wounded?"

"No, sir. I was working in California with my friend from high school. I was worried about getting robbed. It's my earnings."

"You're a long way from California, son."

"Sir, I, well, I thought I would write a book. I was travelling. On Ameripass. It's a—"

"I know what a damned Ameripass is. You're not the first out-of-place high school kid I've had to haul to the bus station," Officer Rodriguez said.

The second officer pulled Chipper's extra jeans and a shirt from his pack and handed them to him, along with his wallet. Chipper passed his driver's license and high school ID card back to the officer, along with the emergency medical card his mother had filled out. It included her name, address, and their home phone number plus hers at the district court in Louisville, where she now worked, having just passed her bar exam in the spring. The officer—Evans on his tag—radioed in Chipper's name and date of birth while Chipper dressed and told his story. When he got to the part about the trains, Officer Rodriguez said, "Now son, don't go telling me about trains. I like you and I don't want to have to arrest you but telling me you've been trespassing means I have to rethink my perceptions." Chipper's stomach stopped clutching, and his heart and breathing slowed as he increasingly understood that these men were just going about their work day, doing their duty, making sure he was first, alive, and second, not a threat to anyone or himself. His father had seen law enforcement as the enemy of black people. But he wasn't feeling threatened, rather a sense of concern, of being cared for, of being supported. Perhaps his mother's white skin was serving him.

Eventually Officer Evans came back saying that no warrants existed for Leroy Martin Grube. "Looks like it's your lucky day, Mr. Grube. We're going to give you a ride clear into Pasco to the bus station. Greyhound comes just about ninety minutes from now. Time in between to get a bite at the café next door. I'm guessing I don't have to tell you find a more private place to take a bath next time. Especially if you're planning to dry out by sunbathing."

"Yes, sir," Chipper said, beginning to tremble and struggling to hold back a spontaneous giggle plus the sudden need to piss. He had not known that great relief had such a tremendous impact on the body.

Gathering his damp clothes, Chipper followed the officers up the riprap to the patrol car. Officer Rodriguez stopped, scanned the sky and the rivers and said, "Although I will say you picked a damned fine day for it."

Dedicated to Albert D. Coomer d. 12/04/2015 and James F. Coomer d. 11/28/2016

CUP FULL OF NICKELS

HE WEARS A cowboy hat. Maybe a Stetson. Her heart pounds like a cartoon. Big, red Looney Tunes thumping straight out of her chest, so bad she wonders if he can see it. He is older, dark-haired, tight-muscled like he wears a hard hat for a job. Here she is, all by her lonesome on the Greyhound, just-about-to-turn-eighteen, riding across the map.

Riding the Dog.

"Is this seat taken?"

Could be worse. She could be hitchhiking, which is her number one fantasy, one she hasn't yet the nerve to manifest: a movie of a daydream where she wears faded jeans tucked into knee boots and a flowy gauze shirt hanging loose from big boobs, the full, round variety, not her pointy, more-than-a-mouthful-is-wasted version, and her baked-brown hair is dyed blonde with the roots showing in that sleazy-sexy way call girls on television sometimes have, her mama's full lips painted full-on red, summer tan peeking from worn-through denim knees. The truck driver looks like Robert Redford. Some days he *is* Robert Redford.

Either way, it's love at first sight, and they have sweet horn-dog sex in the sleeper. Cosmic love. This is the fantasy that made her hit the road. She has a list of experiences she wants to put herself into, to create a resume, an adventurer's resume, and getting picked up by a good-looking trucker like girls do on TV is A-number-one top-of-the-list. It's nineteen-seventy-six, the damned national bicentennial, and she's a few days from eighteen, which means she can do every shit thing her mama begged her not to do. Her dead mama who fell on the ice and hit her head two years back on Christmas Day while they were visiting Uncle Peter and his wife Christine in New Albany, Indiana. New Albania, Uncle Peter calls it. *Uncle* Pee-*ter*. Pee-*ter with a* pee-*ter*.

She searches the ground at every stop for dropped change and dollar bills. Morning two and still no *dinero* for food. The Greyhound. Smokers in back. Non-smokers in front. Everybody shares what they've got, even food, but she's too shy to ask, especially since Stetson got on. She doesn't want to come across as poor. A hippie group travelling the country preaching about tofu and bean burgers got on in St. Paul, the smells of their food cooking on backpack stoves during breaks in Steele and Laramie nearly causing her to overcome her timidity. "Skin is a color? What color? Weed is the great equalizer," she hears one of them say. Toking takes place in the toilet. People sip their soft drinks down by an inch, top off with whiskey. The bus drivers whistle to Top 40 radio during the day, turn it up so it's a great big rolling party in the afternoon, through all of which a handful of babies and toddlers doze, cry, and beg to run the aisles. Night coach drivers turn down the sound, and in response, everybody moans. "I like to think of myself as the Guardian of the Sleeping," the first night driver says. "I promise a smooth ride and safe so you can stretch out and get some shut-eye. Come tell me now if it's too cool or too warm in here."

Late into the second night, she hears the stifled exit of a pair, listens to the huffing sounds of their two bodies against the john walls, imagines them inside a bullet. She dozes without knowing it, surprised that the next thing she's aware of is the honey-in-blue streaks of dawn out her window on the left side of the bus, which means they've turned south. Now it's the third day, and she couldn't care less about Las Vegas. She feels like she's seen enough of it in magazines and on TV, worries she'll be bored by it. Uncle *Pee*-ter loves the Vegas crooners. Idolizes their records. Memorizes the dialogue to their films.

Three hours. The layover in Vegas is three lousy hours.

He stands. Yawns big. He's going to play the nickels. He'll give her money to play if she wants to hang. Buy her breakfast. Hell, he'll give her an entire cup full of nickels, pay for a motel, if they decide to keep on having a good time. All on her decision. He wasn't the kind to force the issue. No matter what, she looked like she needed breakfast in a bad way. "What say? Promise I am not a letch, just an admirer. Good time guaranteed. Double guaranteed. Monday bus goes to Reno. You can finish her up then to Sacramento."

Oh, and pardon him being so forward.

Her brain is a tornado. She reads Aunt Christine's magazines. She's supposed to hump if she feels like it. Free sex. Free love. Hippies, peace, and flower children. And she reads her books: *The Feminine Mystique. Masters and Johnson. Sex and the Single Girl.* Uncle *Pee*-ter snuck her into the drive-in to see films about sex and films with naked people in them. She considers herself something of a pro, thanks to him. *See this palm tree? Now put your palm on the palm tree.* Does she feel like it? An ache low in her belly rises in an instant, tries to tell her that what she feels is small, inferior, like she's a blank page and Stetson's a walking dictionary. Like he's the white marble statue and she's just the dusting cloth. She feels him sucking power from her like a car wash vacuum, her whole body one big hickey. If she goes with him, does it mean she likes feeling that way? What if she does?

She snuffs out the flicker just as quick. She is a female lion. She is bionic. She is a cat burglar. What those magazines don't say right out, what is between the lines, is what her Aunt Christine told her and what she had already started to suspect on her own: the true business of life is that the world belongs to men. Her mother and Aunt Christine both told her to skip the assholes altogether and go for a good career to pay her own way. Then, both of them, out of the sides of their mouths: "Save yourself for a guy with a decent job. Get one who reads library books, not girly magazines. Learn from my mistakes. But if a man ever hits you, leave. Keep a bank account back just for that. Save a quarter from every dollar you earn."

Out of the next breath her mother had said, "Most of us go with the first one who will have us. That's the reason for divorce. Women aren't taught to have the confidence to wait."

Motherly advice. You either push the mower or you are the mower. She was going to be the rake. The one who got rid of shit that didn't belong.

*   *   *

In the Las Vegas bus station, he hands her a foam cup overrunning with nickels. She drops one after another into the machine, the grapes and apples and cherries and lemons spinning and spinning but never lining up. She loses one hundred percent.

"Hell," he says, "at this rate, we'll be too broke to buy booze."

Stetson pays for breakfast. She hasn't eaten since New Albany. Nearly three full days. "Eggs, toast, yes to coffee, no to juice," he says to the waitress, and "Give my daughter here whatever she wants."

"*Daughter?* What, you some kind of pervert?" she says.

"No point being a question mark," he says.

Blue jeans. Long, muscled legs spread beneath the little diner table. His hand resting on a thigh, near his crotch, flicking a nail against his inseam. *Clean nails. The good ones clean the dirt from under their nails.* He turns to watch the waitress walk away, and she involuntarily stares after the woman, too, hearing Stetson's thought: *Don't you wish you had an ass like that?* But instead she's thinking—bow on the white apron tied at the waist, Nancy Sinatra boots, almost-glimpse of butt cheeks, *wetwetwet makes me wetwetwet.* Girls back home were into jumpsuits and maxi-dresses. She's the only one who stayed with mini-skirts and hot pants. Trouble. Trouble is what the good people at Aunt Christine and Uncle Pee-ter's church think she is. Trouble. She feels fresh tension between her thighs. Stetson turns back, sees where her gaze is, her shift in the seat. "Ooh," he says. "You like?"

The question makes her feel short of breath. There's more than one reason she's thinking twice about Stetson. She asks him to pass the cream.

He doesn't talk, so she doesn't talk. They eat. He pays the tab. Slot machine bells ring in the background. The diner counter is lined with little tabletop models people play as they eat.

She breaks the silence. "I can go with you, but I want to write a story on you," she says. "Plus, you have to feed me and give me money enough to get to Sacramento. You dig? Ain't no whore. Just underfunded. And I get to write a story on you. That's a fair trade, considering you're practically getting a virgin bargain. I can pretend to be a daughter, if that's your turn-on."

"Hell no, it ain't no turn on," Stetson says. "As for the rest, it depends on what you mean by *on me*. You talking with ink? Is that what hippie types do these days?"

"I'm not a hippie, but, yes," she says, "I want to write on you. On your body. I want to write your story right on your skin. It's on my list of bizarro fantasies. That's why I'm on this trip. I'm working through my bizarro fantasy list. You tell me your long tale, and I'll write it."

"Good god. Are you escaped from somewhere? Never heard of nothing like that before." Stetson stops for a moment and then says, "But there's a first time for everything."

He thinks it sounds kind of kinky.

In the motel, she straddles him like the back of a mule. "Guess I shouldn't have believed the virgin story," he says, "holy shit." She likes the top. Uncle Peter always holds her face down.

When they've finished, she takes out a pen. Pink. She has pink, teal, magenta, orange, and violet. The ink is black. She likes the thick barrel and bright colors, easy to grip and easy to press deep, and ballpoint, so they're cheap, refills ten to a pack.

"Who travels with a bag of writing pens?" he says. "Are you still in school?

She does. This time, anyway. Just in case. A fantasy she imagines at home when she works magic on herself in the bathroom.

"Do I look like I'm still in school? Shut up. You came along for the ride, now let me do my thing."

Turns out the hat *is* a Stetson. Says so on the label. She wears it and prances around the room. Feels the movement in her breasts. Makes him lie still, watching her gyrating, standing over his face playing with her own pussy. Takes her hairbrush, drives the handle deep inside, fucks herself right over his face so he can see. Then she straddles him again and fucks his dick. "Shit," he says, and she goes at him, and he thrusts his hips to meet her time and again until the sweat is rolling off them both. She doesn't come, which makes her bored. She never comes when the dick is in. She thinks she must still be too young. Lucky for her, a woman can't get pregnant if she doesn't orgasm, or so Uncle *Pee*-ter told her. She can make herself come. So could Uncle Peter, if he took the time to put his face between her legs, which he did in the beginning. She does it for Stetson. She moves up high on his chest so he can see and moves her clit until she explodes into eagle feathers and sunlight, flying.

She chooses to write on him with the orange ballpoint, for no reason whatsoever. His entire story. Stetson moves his lips, narrates and cusses at his wrong turns and screw ups and once even cries, while she moves her pen. First on him, until she runs out of room, then on herself. It begins at his neck with his daddy fucking his mama, long sentences down his arms, across his chest, his ripped belly, his muscled thighs. One word after another. Cursive. No periods. No quotation marks. No commas. She slowly and gently draws a palm tree on his dick, then one on her open hand—"Get it?" she asks. "Palm to palm"—then makes him turn over, continues writing his story on his back, hamstrings, and calves.

Once in a while she takes a break and gives Stetson sips of whiskey through a straw. She pours whiskey on the words and licks it off. They don't fade, but the cold elicits a sound from Stetson, a *wooo* or a *whooo*. Sometimes she slips or presses too hard with the pen. "Fuck," he says, when that happens. "What the fuck you doing to me?"

"Flesh is fleshy. Blood is bloody," she says. "I could fuck you with my hairbrush instead. Do you want me to fuck you in the ass with my hairbrush?"

"No," he says. "Crazy bitch. Get on with it."

His story winds through his traveling years and his attempts at college. It follows him to Montana and a wife and baby and a divorce and custody nightmare, followed by a bonafide cowboying job. It works its way through a drug phase and a booze phase and a fuck-anything-that-moves phase. It buys a house and loses a house and buys property and builds a log cabin in the mountains of Idaho. It hunts big game in Alaska and learns to fly an airplane. It buys a houseboat with a bad motor and shoots it full of holes until it sinks. It lands in jail briefly on possession of cocaine charges in Oregon. It finds Jesus, loses Jesus, then finds Buddha. It ends at her belly button with him on a bus coming back from a construction job installing elevators in a new Indianapolis high-rise to a middle-grade Las Vegas motel with practically a school girl sucking his balls, a fact he's sorry and not sorry and a little freaked out about.

"It's the story of your life," she says. "It looks cool. It's art. We ought to be in a movie."

"There's an Instamatic in my pack," he says. "Take some fucking snapshots if you want."

Which she does. Some from a few steps back, and some up close, so the only thing visible is words.

"Maybe I'll go get us some codeine," she says. "I'll go get us some codeine, and then I'll fuck you with the brush."

This next part she doesn't plan on. She's imagined it with Uncle *Pee*-ter, part of her bizarro fantasy list, but never thought she'd have the nerve to act on it. Life has switched to TV slow-motion, reflected on the screen and visible out of the corner of her eye as she picks up the lamp, a see-through brown-globed Monkey Ward piece of junk that breaks in pieces and causes Stetson's head to bleed all over the pillow. Fast. Head wounds bleed hard and fast, heal quick. That's what her mother once told her. *A little mercurochrome and you're all good.*

Either he's a wimp or she's built a few muscles somewhere along the way, maybe from trying to push Uncle

Peter off her back. She watches Stetson's eyes get big and round and moves in close to as they roll back into his head. They are blue, but more than blue, with gold ringing the pupil. She leans over and whispers, "I'm fucking legal, asshole. Today's my birthday."

She trembles, tries to light a cigarette, wondering over what she has done. It was easy, actually, easier than she might have imagined when making her bizarro fantasy list. Since he was going to front her anyway, she figures it's due her, so she takes his cash, all of it, more than a hundred and fifty dollars, writes a little note to say goodbye. If she wants, since it's legal in Nevada, she can buy another bottle of whiskey to stash for topping off her soft drink the rest of the way to Sacramento. She puts on her shorts and a tank top and grabs her pack, steps out the door into the parking lot, into the early evening and the neon, sees a liquor sign at the market across the street. The codeine cough syrup she can get at the drugstore kitty-corner from where she stands, its windows daytime bright and full of movement and stacks of all the crap people buy. The building with a large, goosenecked lamp on the parking lot side over a painted sign that says, "No Loitering." Where girls in raccoon make-up and beads and bangles with their cleavage showing above flat bellies and tight mini-skirts and high heels stand around. Girls with dyed blonde hair and a little bit of roots showing. Girls who whistle and yell, "Oooh, look at that honey. Gal, you come on upstairs and play a while with me."

MY FATHER'S HYPNOTHERAPY

WHEN I WAS young, my father's life was dominated by two things: his habit of cigarette smoking and his hood of terrifically red hair. My mother berated him to his face for smoking "in front of the child," behind his back whispering to me that red hair had made him the center of attention in his youth, an atmosphere from which he'd never recovered. Smoking was his method of securing the focus of others, she said, the way it made people fan and wave and cough and engage in guilt-inducing diatribes about the newly-discovered dangers of nicotine. "When you grow up," she said, "you are never to take that first puff. Not that first one."

His arms were covered in freckles. So were his chest and back. I only know this because sometimes, when he and my mother were giggling and whispering in their bedroom on Saturday mornings, he'd come running down the hall in his underwear. I would be sprawled out playing on the wood floor of our dining room reading vampire comic books or watching cartoons in the living room, pretending not to notice, out of the corner of my eye stealing glimpses of the carved-muscle shape of his pale back and calves sprinting down the hallway, the sound of his feet an intersection of *squeak* and *splat* against the polished boards my mother scrubbed and buffed on Wednesdays.

His favorite chair, the Morris, sat in Mission-style wood and studded-leather glory near the south end of the enormous living room picture window, facing northeast, toward the big catalpa, with its summery green elephant-ear leaves and foot-long bean pods framed by blue and white Indiana skies. He must have begun telling me the story of the chair's builder, Gustav Stickley, early in my youth, because at no time do I recall not knowing the details. "This chair is an art deco relic," my father would say, followed by "Son, listen to me. If you've got a craft, follow it. I'll understand. Just as much honor in being a furniture builder as a doctor or a lawyer. Shoot, you could turn out to be the world's best potter, and I'd be just as proud. You've got to become expert at whatever you do. That's what will make you happy in this life." The ashy tang of his cigarette smoke flitted through and around the sound of the words. Later, once I was older, I realized those Saturday-morning cigarettes had been his post-coital reward.

He was thirty-five when he began trying to quit tobacco. Keep in mind this was 1974—smoking was popular, ads were pasted on gigantic highway billboards, filled the backs of magazine covers, and reporters smoked live on the nightly news. I considered trying them myself. One night when my father had fallen asleep in the Morris, reclined back, which was one of the features he admired most and had explained and re-explained to me, turning the Morris on its side while pinpointing the greased, gear-toothed minutia of Stickley's craft, I slipped a cigarette out of his red and white pack only to take one whiff and quickly return it to its position next to the rest of its machine-rolled brothers. This was maybe a month before I tried to tell him the first time that I was beginning to suspect something about myself, that I might not be completely what he expected me to be. He ranted about the magazine ads and television commercials taunting him with images of savvy men hoisting lit cigarettes as they bantered with beautiful women, meanwhile giving cigarettes up for a few days or weeks or months. Eventually, the familiar square shape would once again bulge from his shirt pocket. Mother and I reached the point that we both began cutting out magazine and newspaper articles about the Surgeon General's statements concerning cigarette smoking and cancer and taping them to the various mirrors around the house.

Finally, he approached Mother at dinner one night, over oven-fried chicken and potato salad, about paying a hypnotherapist to jumpstart the quitting-smoking effort in a more sincere fashion. "For good," he said. "For good and for all." I had just turned fifteen, living day in and day out with the need to talk to my parents about my situation before I got too old to do anything about it. I had heard about programs, much like the smoking hypnosis clinic, where a hypnotherapist could swing a watch in front of a person's face and make him stop thinking the thoughts that had made him want to be hypnotized in the first place. In my case, what I was *not* thinking about, which was girls. Mother was angry at my father over the smoking hypnotist fee, even if she never told him. She only told me. She didn't see why he couldn't simply quit. I was afraid she'd hurl the same worry about money in my direction, so I never brought up the idea relative to my condition.

Hypnosis not only worked for my father—Daddy, as I called him at the time—it worked in a flash. Except for once, as far as I know, he never touched another cigarette after that. We'd drive past the usual cigarette billboards, but his eyes failed to vary from the road in front of him. None of us knew how the spell had been carried out because he refused to talk about the session. Eventually Mother and I got tired of asking. Now, when he sat in the Morris, he drank a glass of tea, in the summer with a leaf of mint from the creek in our backyard, in the winter with a lemon slice from the box of lemons his sister sent every year from Florida. No more stories. Rather, he drank the tea, sip by sip, looking out at the grass, the catalpa. Once or twice I tried to bring up the subject of my problem, but between his daze and my panic, the words remained immoveable as big iron hinges, rusted closed by the passing seasons.

In place of the Stickley discussions, my father wanted to joust broomsticks in the front yard, teach me football at City Park, insisted we swim laps in the lake there when it got hot. He took me fishing on the banks of the Ohio at Leavenworth, on a small beach near his favorite fish sandwich place, where we could smell deep-fried catfish while I learned to spin the clasp ten times to secure a hook to a leader. Explained the difference between a crappie and a bass. One night right before I was to get my driver's permit, he took me camping at the county forestry, at the edge of Leavenworth, finally showing me the Rebel Yell, leaning backward with his red hair tipped golden in moonlight. He had dropped exaggerated hints about the Rebel Yell for as long as he had been narrating bits and pieces of Gustav Stickley's biography. This built an excessive measure of tension in my young imagination for something as unexciting as arching the spine and screaming to the Milky Way after spotting a shooting star.

"What about making a wish?" I asked.

"Girls make wishes," he said. "Men do the Rebel Yell."

* * *

He was smoke-free for the better part of two years before the relapse. Once again, the square package in his shirt pocket appeared. Immediately we demanded the cigarettes, convinced him with tears and screaming that tobacco would kill him. Our southern Indiana brick bungalow bloated and heaved under the weight of Mother's and my fury. What could he do but turn them over. "For good," he said, "and I'm sorry," after which he immediately scheduled a booster visit with the hypnotist.

"I hope you are paying attention," Mother said to me. "What you are witnessing is love in all its dimensions."

Instead of Daddy, I started calling him Father, turned my attention toward college and getting good grades. Saturday tea in the Morris fell by the wayside altogether, as did his efforts at arranging manly activities for us. He took up carving relics—whistles and figurines—from old wood he pulled off people's barns, yellow poplar being his favorite "because it would hold up to time," spent his spare moments at his workbench in the garage, chipping with tiny scythe-shaped tools at bits of wood in a vise, the smells coming from him now of sawdust and shellac.

He and my mother bought an annual membership at the public golf course in Harrison County. They went on Saturdays with two brown leather bags of clubs tucked into our car's trunk, came home with descriptions of their game that included trudging across greens beribboned with hardwoods, sand traps, and small lagoons. My father mused over buying a golf cart. My mother argued that walking and carrying clubs was good for them.

"Did Stickley ever play golf?" I asked him once, early on, for which he cuffed me about the ears, calling me impertinent.

One night we were sitting around the long, pine harvest table, a family heirloom from the generation prior to the

Morris purchasers, finishing off the most memorable of Mother's pecan pies, with its caramel drizzle and scatter of toffee chunks. Father shared a possibility. He and Mother wanted to take up formal dancing, the sort that required proficiency with a partner and a significant time commitment. I was growing up, old enough to drive and even earn a paycheck, which meant their jobs were nearly done. They thought it would behoove us all if they were to demonstrate what healthy adults do when their children reach my age.

What choice did I have but to respond as if they had won the lottery?

Mother and Father began lessons, soon enough winning prizes, which was hard to do, as New Albany, Indiana, at the time, didn't have a dance studio. They drove across the river to Louisville, to a studio at the fringe of the city's seedier west end, a neighborhood that grated at my mother's gentle sensibilities. When they learned about master classes and a regional competition in Evansville, downriver on the Indiana side, they signed themselves up, and our weekends became trips on the Greyhound bus and bottles of soft drinks sipped through paper straws, an hour and fifteen minutes of holding my breath against people's cigarette smoke as we headed west, the same on the return trip east. My father cursed about being forced to breathe other people's tar-filled exhalations, even if they were restricted to the back seat, worried about the effects on his and my mother's lung capacity, commented loudly about how it made him so glad he had quit.

*   *   *

When they were together dancing, Mother and Father were clearly in a world apart from the rest of us, orbiting as a single organism. They made the audience feel the wonder of being alive, a judge once told me. I took it as a personal compliment.

Had it not been for the depth with which the dancing captivated me otherwise, I would have been happy staying home, pondering my problem and looking for solutions in medical books from the library, leaving them to their marital bliss. Had it not been for the fact that I could attend to the quick, controlled movements of men as they waltzed or did the mambo or merengue, no one suspecting that I wasn't keeping tabs on the entire couple.

Plus, to experience my mother, beautiful, effervescent even, in a swirl of peach or aqua or lavender skirt, tight bodice revealing arms and cleavage, her sweet, graceful neck, and blonde, Princess Grace hairdo, my father, poised and confident in shoes and clothing I never would have previously expected to see on him—flat oxfords and pleated black pants, white pressed shirt appearing to contain his physique rather than passively adorning it. Red hair shorn high on the sides with a shock of it falling over his left eye. Around him, the dancing motions of other men, some in tuxedos, elegant but understated, some fancy—exotic, even—in skin-toned tights with sequined bolero jackets, some open-necked, with a silk scarf at the throat in a loose knot.

This image was an irrevocable gift, reminding me of the love I'd been born to, love that might one day translate to acceptance, if I ever got the nerve to share my secrets. I suspect he knew and chose not to question it. Mother figured it out on her own when I told her I wasn't interested in going to the prom. We were sitting in the living room, I in the Morris chair, she on the vinyl sofa for which she'd begged my father because it was easy to clean. Dancing had cut into her housework time, she had told him.

"Toby, I know why you don't want to go to the prom. It's perfectly fine. The regionals are that weekend. You'll come with us. Who knows what happiness you might find there."

I fell in love with my mother twenty times over in that moment, wondering if she had always known.

After that, it was never discussed, a point which left me feeling both lonely and loved.

CATTLE NEED TO ROAM TO GRAZE

I LIKE TO think of myself as a vegetarian. I eat the pickles on my restaurant plate and the lettuce and the orange slice. Plus, of course, the parsley, which is good for digestion and sweetens the palate. At least that is what I've been told. Funny how the tiny lessons are the ones that stick. Might have something to do with the fact my mother would rather watch cowboys play with ponies and ring-nosed bulls than stay home coaching her sons or cutting yard goods into shirts or baking beans for potlucks. Not that my brother or I held it against her. Quite the opposite. We were proud of our trailblazing mother. She never roped or rode herself. She spent our growing up years working as a rodeo doc. Patched torn elbows and bruised shins when such remedies were needed. But that has little to do with me. Other than to explain what I did not become.

It's a mercy I missed inheriting certain family characteristics, but an equal mercy to be born with the habits I have, lucky to be born with a trade. My cousin Perry, who moved from our home town of New Albany, Indiana, to

Kearney, Nebraska, when we were kids, is not so lucky. He did not take to mechanicking the way I did. Too much smell of axle grease, cigarettes, and concrete over dirt for him. But he did make himself a name as a television sportscaster specializing in all things related to water—swimming, skiing, jet boats, crewing, sailing—you name it. Perry likes the smell of water and to gaze upon a liquid, open landscape. Says it makes him feel heroic to stare across a sun-glittered lake or to watch snowmelt burst from slate-colored to white through a bottlenecked riverbank. Can barely swim enough to save himself and never could pull himself to stand, even on two skis, let alone one or barefoot like the rest of us can; can't row a lick. Nearly drowned himself outright trying to do a can opener off the high dive into the Colonial Club swimming pool in New Albany when we were kids. But by god, he knows water and can tell the temperature of the air just by smelling the rain and says it wakes him up at night, dreams of jet-fueled hydrofoil and skin coated in glycerin. Might even find his way one day to the sportscaster hall of fame. Who knows. Right now, he's just glad as beans to be free of his daddy, my mother's brother, my Uncle Jessup McClure and *his* daddy's idea that a human being is *born* to a family trade and has obligation to stick to it. Before automobiles came to be, his family were blacksmiths, all of them whale-shouldered from mechanicking in the horse and buggy days. Except that one fellow nobody could name who moved to the treed green of West Virginia to be a miner. Jessup has his own ideas about that boy anyway. He says blacksmithing is in the next category to coal mining—one ferries up to the other in hardness of labor and in the clarity of mind it requires, and men in both fields start a work shift clean as a new hay mower and end it black as a pitch knot. Besides, he says, that relative was just a little brain-addled is all, and prone to spontaneous changes of heart, as the brain-addled often are.

As if more proof were needed, one Sunday afternoon the man was said to have washed down a plate of corn grits with a decanter of still-liquor. A man who before that moment had never licked a drop. The way Uncle Jessup tells it, that cousin called his wife to come sit by him on the davenport. She was at her kitchen table where she'd been keeping a steady watch on him. "It'll kill ya," she is reported to have said as she walked over. "Dead as a hard-rode mule, it'll kill ya."

The relative sat himself up and said, "I believe you was right," then dropped back to the davenport dead. Uncle Jessup blamed it on a diffused spirit. Had the man only known, he could have warded off death by decades just by lighting himself a ring of coal fire and commencing to blacksmith. It was awful, Uncle Jessup said, to have that mar on the family, since the rest of us, for as far back as anybody can remember, lived to be ninety and beyond, this black sheep fellow having succumbed just shy of fifty.

* * *

The women on Uncle Jessup's side of the family always made doctors. People doctors or horse doctors or "closet" doctors, the kind who, as he termed it, kept the spark to a household's eight cylinders, curing the aches and pains of body and soul for all who lived in the confines of the woman's jurisdiction. Jessup had no use for the notion of liberation when it came to the sexes. It took both, plain and simple, and he mocked images on TV of women marching for "equality," expressed frank consternation at the constant discussion of it. "Can't ever say, 'hits a no news day.' Either gotta go looking for it or make something up. What say, camera people close their eyes for a week. Then, hallo! Wake up! Look at how this wheat has grown, and this corn! Look at how this hill *has not changed*. Women's lib, my hairy backside. Women was born liberated. Anybody's slave to anybody, it's men to the women. Gotta work to keep shoes on them *and* the kids *and* on theyselves. No woman in my line ever complained about being set free. Gosh and howdy, I've a mind to rid us all of that television set, I swear to God. I swear to God and Moses and all the rest."

Sometimes I think it was Jessup who penned the commandment: *thou shalt love the Lord thy God with all thine heart*. He thought if men and women "put their time into blooming where they was planted and the Divine that grows inside each and every being," there'd be no room for other thought. "Take the sticks you've been given and build a raft," he was known to say. "Let the river lift you on its swells, baby you along still water. Cattle need to roam to graze, that is a fact. A philosopher or teacher needs to roam to furrow insight and harmonize new ideas. But for the rest, roaming gets to be a bad habit. Roaming for average folk just stirs up bad memories and creates malformities in the mind, various types of discontent, don't you see. Leave roaming to the ones what need it. Consider it the other feller's luck of the draw, is what I say. He's got his bundle of sticks, and we got ours."

It never dawned on Uncle Jessup, then, to question my mother's attitudes about kitchens and dustrags. "She's got the mechanicking attitude. Ain't nothing can be done about it, Jesse Lee," Uncle Jessup told my father. "You're going to have to find a way to see it as one of the sticks of your bundle and go about building your raft of it." Bad part about it was that there weren't many rodeos in southern Indiana, but there were some, and fewer rodeo docs, still, so my mother's expertise was in high demand. She earned her wings out West when she was younger, before Dad, before my brother and me, and loved the life too much to give it up, and my father knew it from the start. Much as she loved him, rodeoing came natural to her long before he did. I can't see my father telling Uncle Jessup about the red-hot fire it made in him, thinking about my mother straddling in the flimsy dust a downed cowboy's stripped torso, the rodeo crowd hushed in the stands with cups of beer amidst smells of tobacco juice, manure, and hot dogs, to force a shoulder back into joint or leaning into his good-looking face to listen and watch for his tight, young chest to rise, hoping he's just got the air knocked out and not something worse. Thinking about her examining their groins for swollen lymph nodes a week or two after a night of unprotected lust. My father hated that part more than any and came to live with it by sitting on the back step during rodeo weekends slivering a pile of birch branches into spiny, pointed sticks. Sweat would collect at his hatband until a dark ring circled his head, and the muscles in his forearms and under his beard became small, furred hills. After a while, my baby brother Alva, whose arms were like twigs themselves, puny from birth, started calling those sticks "arrows," at which point my father started teaching him to carve. The lessons seemed to calm my father until Alva cut his finger bad enough he bled all over the porch boards, a stain you can see still yet, and my mother had to give him stitches. I heard her and my father talking about it late into the night, voices through the flocked wallpaper of my room mixed with words hard to make out. *Loretta. Support. Direction. Condition.* Or at least some of them sounded like it.

*   *   *

One Christmas Uncle Jessup and Perry drove up from Kearney back to New Albany. Jessup had this idea about bringing the Christmas tree with them. He claimed to like the irony of bringing a Nebraska pine all the way to Indiana, which was, to his way of thinking, altogether way too boastful of its piney woods and hills called "knobs" and slate-bottom creeks its inhabitants were prone to calling rivers. "You might construe Nebraska land less favorable for its plainness," he said, "but I'd dare any tree in Indiana to bear likeness to the scent and green of a Norfolk pine bred and nursed of a Nebraska tree farm. Not a wild evergreen in any state compares. Nebraska tree farmers know their evergreens. Know its needles and seed cones. Know to confer with their conifers, pardon the pun. Know it as partner with the sun and moon."

By this time, I began to suspect Uncle Jessup's brain was addled, and Perry seemed to suspect it, too, which made Perry twitchy and restless. Part of it also may have been that our Indiana homestead was landlocked, and Perry knew the mighty Ohio River was less than thirty minutes away. Jessup and my father had barely shaken hands and given Alva's hair a tousle before Jessup went inside to look for Mom. Perry went back to the car and unroped the Norfolk to pull it from its plastic sheath. Mother sent me back out to help Perry and to ask about Jessup's declining mental condition. "I wouldn't ask such a thing of a child your age, Jerry, but Jessup's tearing the house apart looking for a Christmas tree skirt I don't believe ever existed. Talk to Perry. Ask him outright if your Uncle Jessup is taking any kind of medication."

My mother was beautiful to me at that moment. I think it was fear of the unexpected that made her that way. The same look she must have had standing over a downed rodeo jock: the humidity from her own body heat causing her dark hair to curl a bit around her face and cheeks, and her lips to redden, her chest to push quietly against the insides of her shirt. It's the memory I've always held, as if it were the only snapshot ever taken of her, and that a quick-develop.

Whatever truly was eating Jessup remained to be seen, however, because when I questioned Perry about him, he said, "Tell your mother Daddy claims my mother came in a dream, telling him to drag the Norfolk up here because Alva needs the spirit medicine this particular tree has to offer and that the spell will only be complete if you encircle the trunk with that red Jacquard tree skirt she made for your mother and daddy's first Christmas as a married couple. In the dream, she told Daddy specifically that the tree skirt is still full of her and Jessup's young love. She sent it to Indiana from Nebraska that year in a box with your daddy's share of the family's childhood Christmas ornaments. You know your Uncle Jessup holds to signs and omens. Tell your mother to please just humor him."

If anybody had asked, I'd have said Perry and Jessup were the same kind of crazy, but I was just the court reporter, so to speak. I walked back to the house and told my mother Jessup wasn't sick, he'd had a dream, which made her recall the box of ornaments and pull down the disappearing ladder from the attic. "Get up there and get it, Jerry," she whispered, "big, square box in satin paper. I was mad at your daddy that Christmas, if I'm remembering correctly. I don't even know what for. I think he got drunk and tore down the Christmas tree. I think the box arrived that day from Jessup and Stella, and I decorated the tree, and your father threw a fit. I put the stuff away and never took it out again."

That Stella Jean, Uncle Jessup's wife and Perry's mother, never came home from midnight mass that Christmas was never mentioned in my family. That Jessup was supposed to have picked her up and forgot and that she froze to death sitting on a bus stop bench never was either. Nor was the fact that he didn't go looking for her until the next morning, and even then, only because baby Perry cried so long and hard he woke the neighbors, who first came over and banged on the front door, and when Jessup still didn't wake up, they decided to call the police. In his defense, Jessup said he was used to Stella Jean getting up to breastfeed Perry, and equally used to sleeping through his cries.

* * *

The night we take Alva to the hospital for the last time, it is raining. Paoli is distant from Evansville where the hospital is, and the road is mostly a windy downgrade through pines and scrub cedars. Sometimes a bear, like a big, black, jellybean will plop in front of us across the dirt and gravel of our isolated lane. The doctors in town don't know much about Alva's leukemia, but my mother does her research and educates them along the way. The effects of Alva's last visit to St. Jude's in Memphis have worn off and my mother won't let me give any more bone marrow. Only a brother or sister can give bone marrow, and the St. Jude's doctor told me Alva was lucky to have me. It hurt, truth told. Hurt a bunch. But I didn't say so. They only take maybe two tablespoons. It was actually more painful when Alva hugged me and thanked me for trying to save his life. But we got a good story out of it. For weeks afterward I told over and over about my plane ride home from Memphis, when I got upgraded to first class thanks to Danny Thomas and The Children's Hospital and sat across the aisle from Roy Rogers and Dale Evans, and some guy ran up front to the bathroom and puked just as Roy was coming out the tiny door and the way he calmly opened the service cart and took a ginger ale and poured some into a clear glass and gave it to the guy, then took a towel and cleaned up that guy's vomit while the stewards and stewardesses stood watching with their mouths open.

"What more proof do you need?" Uncle Jessup said when he heard me telling Alva the story. "One more stick in old Roy's bundle. And what did he do? Leave it in the pile? No sir. He lashed it to his raft. Didn't give it a thought, just lashed it to his raft. Now that's confidence, boys. That's confidence."

My mother still contends, all these years later, that one more trip to The Children's Hospital might have done it, that a few more tablespoons of my bone marrow might have grown a rodeo in Alva's bones. My father lets her use up all the words she needs to, then softly reminds her it was Alva's choice. He was twelve and he'd been courageous long enough. The time was right: end of rodeo season, end of the school quarter, end of gardening and canning season for my father. Time freed for all of us to sit around holding Alva's hand and coloring with him when he felt like it, giving him clues for crosswords, then filling in the squares for him, moaning like crazy when we thought he had the right answer and the next word across or down proved he'd missed it. Watching his eyes grow bigger, the shadows around them darker, as his skull grew smaller. The long days siphoning his voice, shrinking his curiosity. The smell of this shrinking filled first the room, then the house, the way butchering a deer does. I asked him one day if the world looked bigger from inside those bigger eyes, if he was afraid of what was happening.

"Hell," he said, and we giggled at the cuss word, which we were temporarily allowed to use since that was number one on Alva's list of "Final Wishes." "Remember *The Velveteen Rabbit*, Jerry? I'm just becoming, that's all."

I don't know why I made the promise to Alva that, once he died, I would never eat meat, especially bone marrow, and I don't really know why he asked. Was it ugly for him, the thought of animal bones dying and people breaking them open, sucking out the spongy middle? I don't know. Right now, I'm too busy looking for this woman's right-sized alternator to think about it. European car owners. Finicky but spunky. But always, always, beautiful, mindful women. The whole package mostly worth it, and they never argue about the fee. As for Uncle Jessup, he won't look at a European car. Says a woman who drives a European car almost always has missed her calling, settled for money and fine things. But I like the foreign-ness of the leather and the dashboard design and those little sachet packs they hide someplace inside the car that smell so good, like gardenias or lilies or apple blossoms. Like the parlor of our home filled with funeral flowers in the days after Alva died. Or my mother after a rodeo, having dolled herself up to cheer my father, hoping to make the air sweet enough for him to stop and take a deep breath.

SOMEBODY SHOULD HAVE SCOLDED THE GIRL

IT'S A FARMHOUSE, and it's February, and it's cold. Donnie is gone to work at the A&P in town and Philip and Ginny, named for Donnie's mother's sister Virginia, are off to school. The mom, the wife, Marlette, is home cleaning, cooking. The inside windows today, the kitchen and bathroom throw rugs. The pumpkins that have been sitting in the cold cellar since November frost are finally packed into jars, still hot, waiting for the lids to seal. She fools with the radio dial, finds WQNW, the Evansville hippy station. She can't help it. She likes this young generation, such a loud afterthought to her own, so colorful. They're regularly on the news, dunking themselves into the Pacific Ocean out in California, hands raised to Jesus, smoking marijuana and taking window-jumping acid trips. Staging events called "Be-ins." Women at the beauty parlor where she sweeps and mops afternoons gripe over the heated wind of hair dryers and the smell of permanent wave solution about how they'd like those spoiled-brat college kids to try Being-in over a hump of dirty baby diapers and mill-dusty husbands who demand dinner on time and the sheets hung in the sun and the checkbook balanced. She disapproves along with them, of course, but a tiny deepness way inside her admires the hippies' bravery, their ability to insist on remaking the world according to their young vision. A religion itself, the way they drip hair and love beads and flowers on their blue jeans, write songs devoted more to words than music. She watched a young man on *The Huntley-Brinkley Report* waving an American flag and a placard with what David Brinkley called "a peace sign," which the pastor that weekend pointed out was truly a broken, upside-down cross. The sign of the anti-Christ, he said, after which the drugstore and the Shop 'n' Save pulled their little souvenir versions off the front-counter display stands.

Her day starts at 4:30. Cows to milk, eggs to fry, sack lunches to make. Donnie hauls out of bed at 4:45 to help with the milking, after his coffee cup is full and his stack of toast buttered, which he stuffs in his mouth as the two of them pick their way to the barn. The job isn't as hard to get up for in summer as it is in the frost, the dead grass matted and frozen at kooky angles and noisy as they walk through the before-daylight. The sky overhead feels hinged shut, the new day knocking to be let in.

After the milking, after her and Donnie's boots are rinsed of manure and stuck hay with dippers of water from the rain barrel, she goes upstairs to the new shower next to their bedroom to wash off the cold, put on a fresh nightgown, and crawl back into bed with Donnie, who has done the same, for twenty minutes of cuddling or sex, whichever one or the other of them feels like. They oblige each other and always agree it makes the muck of the barn worth it. Once in a while in summer they pass those moments on the porch with coffee, talking about the field corn and the planting, new pups to be spayed, the hog lot fence they wish would just go ahead and rot so they can turn that land into a storage shed for the tractor, soon as the hogs make enough money to pay for it. The decision about how to spend this time is never mentioned. They simply move toward the activity and go through it, right for who they are and no question to it.

Then breakfast and Philip and Ginny's chatter. They're growing up strong and hopeful, rosy-cheeked, full of ideas. She and Donnie tolerate it. Watching the late news, however, Donnie prays aloud they don't grow up to be hippies, but Marlette decided a long time ago she wouldn't mind if they did.

She lets the breakfast dishes soak while she mixes vinegar water in a pail to wash the windows and runs the kitchen throw rugs through the washer with a shave of lye soap, a cup of borax, and a hand of baking soda, then pulls them through the wringer, hangs them across the dinette chairs to dry. She figures to save water and soap by waiting for the last of the pumpkin to cook, washing those pans and utensils in the leftover water from this earlier mess. She'll add a little boiling water if she has to.

The house still smells of vinegar and wet newspaper from washing the windows by the time she turns up the radio and sinks her hands into the whitish dishwater. A woman has committed suicide, the announcer reports, a famous writer in England. Marlette stops at the words *children* and *gas oven*, dries her hands, stares first at the radio, then walks over to look at her cookstove. "Cookright" it says in nickel letters across the front. The brand Donnie's mother owns and so, good enough for them. She opens the oven door, speckled granite and clean as new, from last week's scrubbing with steel wool and baking soda and its own dose of vinegar. Every night before he goes to bed, Donnie checks to make sure the pilot lights are lit, the little blue flames that prove his house is safe for sleeping. Used to be no fans allowed in the kitchen. In summertime he fussed if the kitchen windows were open, even knowing how much Marlette liked to see her dotted Swiss curtains blow. "Huff 'em out and put us all in the ground," he would say. Donnie tried to make a cover for the stove, first of plywood scraps, then of soldered sheet metal, but Marlette wouldn't have either of the ugly things in her kitchen. She finally found a hinged, enamel stovetop cover that clipped to the back of the grill surface in a mail order catalog and spent part of her saved money to order it.

"Well, I'll be. Good enough," Donnie had said, and when it got hot, surprised them all with a box fan for the kitchen window. Marlette kept it set to low, liked nothing better than once in a while to sit at the kitchen table, feet propped on the chair opposite, hands around a tumbler of ice water and leaf of mint and teaspoon of honey, letting that spun air whisper across her forehead, dabbing her cheeks and chin with the chilled glass.

The news announcer goes on to comment about this Sylvia woman's life, about the way she grew up in America and who her parents were and her schooling. Shocking to Marlette to hear the newscaster talk about such things as the woman writing about hiding in a basement and cutting herself for psychological reasons. Marlette wondered what had to have transpired to make a person do that. One of her books was called *The Bell Jar* and another *The Colossus*, which made Marlette think of Greyhound buses and long-distance travel. She'll ask him later, but Marlette doesn't think she or Donnie has ever heard of the woman, much less had to read books by that name for school, and they both graduated from the same high school in Terre Haute. She isn't even sure what a "colossus" is or "a bell jar," but she knows what sound a jar makes when a lid seals, and hers are doing just that. It's a good sound, one that verifies a job done right. Lots can go wrong when you put a seed in the ground, and the sound of a jar sealing is the reassurance it hasn't. There'll be pumpkin soup through the rest of the cold months, plus pie and pudding for Valentine's and Easter and more in between and after if she's rationed the year's sugar right, and the flour. Out of season for some, but Donnie and the kids don't care. Of course, raising hogs allows for plenty of lard for crusts, but they have to depend on Donnie's A&P town job and the cash discount he gets for sugar and flour.

Marlette guesses somebody should have scolded the girl early on for expecting too much of herself and of life. She looks around at the butter yellow of her kitchen walls and the white of the cupboards, the glass doorknobs, at the slow plans she and Donnie made when they bought the place at the beginning of their marriage finally evolved into existence—new sink and washboard, the lowered ceiling and modern lamp globe, the gas cookstove, purchased to replace the wood-burning one the previous owners left behind, which is now kept wrapped in newspaper and stored in the mud porch in case the gas one ever gives out or Donnie gets laid off and they can't afford fuel. It's a mystery to Marlette, how other people live. But then, what's to know—as Donnie puts it, the rich sit around thinking about themselves; that's the only way to get richer.

Three more jars of pumpkin make their metallic sound, an overlapping series of *enk!s*. The dishes are done, but the bedsheets still need washed and changed. It's the fourth of the month. She has to get bills paid and the woodwork dusted before she sets the bacon to thaw for the corn muffins, which will round out the chili for supper. "Most bone-warming meal there is," Donnie always says. Then to the beauty parlor for the afternoon job that allows her to surprise him and the kids with birthday presents and store-bought candy from time to time. "Oh Lordy," Marlette says when the announcer on the radio interrupts the music again with the story of Sylvia Plath being dead. She wonders if the library keeps books by people nobody's heard of. The last of the pumpkin goes *enk! enk!* Softer this time, muffled by her distance from the kitchen and the tenor of her old Keds on waxed wood as she heads upstairs to the bedroom for the sheets.

*　*　*

Donnie asks when he gets home from work that night if they have money for feed. "Feed?" she says, "What kind of feed?"

"For this little fellow," he says, and pulls a squash-sized puppy from under his wool jacket, navy plaid, the lamb's wool collar she's had to re-felt time and again, from his habit of sitting at church and grange meetings with it across his lap, pulling at the hand-whipped stitches. He never admits to his part in it, just leaves it on her sewing table to be mended. "Well, maybe fellow's the wrong word. She's a she-dog. A bitch."

"Donnie K. Peel," Marlette says, ruffs the fuzz on the dog's head, tight as boiled wool, brown and black with little white tufts of four or five hairs each. A mutt. "I don't remember talk about another dog."

"Aw, Marlette. Some kids had a mess of 'em in a box in front of the store. For a quarter. All but one sold. They walked off and left her. You see what I was up against, can'tcha?"

"Her? Well, it'll be another spaying bill, too. Guess you're planning on doing the milking by yourself while I build a bed?"

Donnie lifts the pup to Marlette's nose. When the animal doesn't cooperate, he leans and kisses Marlette himself, then the pup. "See that?" he says to the dog. "That's how it's done."

Around midnight, Marlette hears whining, gets up to check on their little lodger, which is squalling by the time she gets there, scratching and clawing her way up the deep sides of the cardboard box, the one Baldwin's store sent last winter's coat order in. Philip and Ginny both still required a new coat every year. They grew as fast as they ate. "Don't feed 'em so much," Donnie once had argued, as if the plan had possibility.

"Sylvia Plath," Marlette says, and picks up the pup. The dog nuzzles Marlette's neck like it's trying to bury itself. "Miss your family, don't you, pup?" She walks barefoot across a chilled floor to the utility room, looking for one of the feeder bottles they used to nurse orphaned kittens and pups. The puppy climbs up Marlette's shoulder and across, lands on a shelf, knocks off a box of jar rings. "Shhhst!" she says, "You'll wake the house." The pup looks at her, head sideways a bit, the way pups on calendar pictures do. Marlette shakes her head. "You've done it now," she says, "guess I'm fool enough to fall, too. Same way as with every orphaned thing in this world." *As if Donnie doesn't know it.* The box with the feeder bottles smells like bleach and old milk, cardboard dust. She doubts if anybody's been in there in two years, not since Tweak and Billy, parents of this current litter of heelers, died of something the vet couldn't name, within a day of each other, and the pups but weeks old.

"Blasted, Marlette," Donnie had said, "I told you to get those dogs vaccinated."

"Donnie Peel," Marlette replied, "You're telling me to cut back feeding the kids to save the clothes budget and you want me to get shots for a dog?"

Donnie had thrown the shovel. "You bury them, then," he said. "I'm late for work."

Was that what this pup was? A way of saying two years later, *Boy was I a nut or what*?

*   *   *

Marlette is awake half the night, feeding and playing the pup, which refuses to be left alone else it whines like a kitten. When Donnie and the kids get up, she is still in her nightgown, dozing in Donnie's recliner with the pup on her lap. "Shoot, Marlette. You could have woke me. I would have done a shift," he says.

"What you can't come up with," she says. "I'll get the coffee on. Meet you in the barn."

"No lovin' this morning, looks like," he says. "Already five."

Marlette lowers the pup, still sleeping, onto the old quilt inside the cardboard box. Seems she and Donnie are to trade one habit for another for a while. The mutt can't even be bred for income as the heelers were. Sylvia Plath, or whatever they decide to name it, will be outgo with no income. Marlette expects some dog-realm guardian angel is to blame. A pup must be special if a human is making sacrifices to save it. She hopes that guardian angel will bring the price of feed and whisper to the pup that it ought to appreciate its turn of luck, wondering what they'll have to give up until it's old enough for the cheap farm supply brand the older dogs get by on.

Around noon, Pink calls from the beauty salon. Pink is, as her name declares, a pink-skinned woman with red hair, her body plumped out the least bit, enough so the polyester pantsuits she favors look tugged at the seams and makes Marlette wish things came in half-sizes just so she and Pink both didn't have to feel so confined. "Please don't hold it against me, Marlette," she says, "but I ain't got business enough to go around. Things are slow. My Durenda's going to sweep the floor for a dollar a week. She's near twelve, and I just can't be spending my money lightly. Even for a friend. Surely you can see my side of it."

Marlette looks at Sylvia Plath lapping milk and cornbread crumbs out of a cast-iron skillet. "What gets me, Pink," she says, "is that you'd call me on the phone instead of telling me to my face." Marlette can hear Pink's protest in the background as she drops the receiver. "Never count on nothing, Sylvie," she says. "Never count on a single thing in this God-blamed world."

Well, losing her job doesn't mean there isn't still dinner to cook, so Marlette goes about it. She totes the numbers—mortgage, feed, vet bills, fuel—as she cuts apart a whole fryer and drops the parts in saltwater, dices a pan of potatoes, grates a few shreds of cheese, beats a pair of eggs, and pours the mess together in an old casserole she bought at a rummage sale. She feels like she doesn't care what it turns into. She has never in her life put a pan of anything in the oven and walked out of the house, but she is going to today. She covers the casserole with a piece of used tinfoil, turns the oven temperature to two-seventy-five, just enough below the usual three-fifty to buy time, gets her coat and purse, and heads out the door to start the Mercury. Some years down the road she'll think back on that car and others she and Donnie owned, when twenty-three-cent gas made everybody freebirds, and chastise herself for the wastefulness, but right now she figures she'd ordinarily burn gas going to town for work, so she didn't see it as frivolous.

*   *   *

The library in Dunes Park, Indiana, is a timid affair, one of the smallest buildings Marlette has ever seen. In fact, the library isn't its own separate building at all, but a long, slender room of shelves tucked between the Chamber of Commerce and City Hall on Main Street. From what the sandwich board sign out front says, it is open afternoons, eleven to four, and Saturdays, ten to two. It has Children's Reading Hour on Saturday morning, Women's Book Circle Wednesdays at noon. Marlette ponders the goal of a book circle and then it becomes apparent: the poster says they'll be "continuing their series on Ernest Hemingway with *The Old Man and the Sea*." Marlette has heard of him. She believes he might have been mentioned in her Literary Studies class in high school. Obviously, the women read their books together.

Marlette always gets a little bright wind in her stomach whenever she comes against something new. She counts it as gained strength if she can extinguish the sensation by facing whatever is causing it. She feels it now, walking through the door of the library, drawn halfway against her will to whatever is beyond the shellacked mahogany and riffled glass. The address and hours of service are painted on the pane in archaic lettering. She wonders whether some people paint letters and numbers at a whim, or whether they have to cut a template, draw an outline on the glass with a grease pencil, then fill the inside space with paint. Maybe it is a little of both. Maybe there are some people who can do it one way, others who can do it another.

The woman behind the library counter is Avis Eads. Marlette knows her from Pink's. Avis is older than Marlette by fourteen years. She knows this because they share a June twelfth birthday and remembers their discussion and discovery of this fact one day last summer, after which Pink baked a red velvet cake decorated with the phrase, "Happy

40 and 26 to Avis and Marlette," in alphabetical order, which seemed logical to everybody but which apparently nipped Avis's feelings as it meant she did not get her usual personal birthday cake. Consequently, Avis has held a public grudge against Marlette for most of the last year.

On this day, Avis wears dark-framed cat-eye glasses and has her sweater sleeves pushed above the elbows. Pale blue mohair, in loose-knit button-front style Marlette has seen at Fashion Fair. Underneath, a gray dress with a princess waist, similar to the pattern Marlette made herself in butter-yellow gingham last Easter.

"Well, Marlette," Avis says. "Honey, I'm sorry. I heard about it from Pink herself. I'm with you. She should have looked you in the eye."

Marlette feels the bright wind in her stomach turn a little brighter. "I won't talk about it, Avis. I'm looking for a book by that dead poet. Sylvia Plath."

Avis walks over to the card catalog. Marlette hasn't seen one since high school. The small oak drawers have brass handles shaped like wide hooks. On the front of each, a little brass frame holding a tiny white card: A-Ba; Be-Cl; Clo-De, and so on. "Plath," Avis says. "You say she's dead? Is she local? We don't have much on current writers. Walt Whitman. He was a poet. We have lots of Walt Whitman. I think the last director had a fixation. We have a new book in on the guy who carved Mt. Rushmore. You've heard of that. Presidents carved into rock? Wyoming or some place." Avis opens the drawer marked "St-Ta." Marlette smells the age of the catalog cards, the oak and shellac of the wood holding them, focuses hard to keep from screaming that Plath might be listed under P. After a few moments of pulling and replacing cards, Avis says, "No. I guess not. You might drive to Evansville. They have a bigger library. Two, in fact, but one belongs to the college, and I think you have to belong there to get a card. Heck, but then you'll just have to turn around and take them back. Too, Evansville's got Harney's. They sell books. But I guess without a job it's not a good time to buy." Avis looks down at the narrow file drawer, still open. "Aw, honey. There goes my foot. Let me strap it to my teeth. Does Donnie know? You told him yet? I hear Woolworth's is looking. Ruedale Hawkins has been put to bed until the baby comes. Who ever heard of working P-G anyway. I don't know about that woman. Sour, if you ask me. Lazy, Pink says. Tries to make people feel sorry for her."

Marlette wishes for a gas oven to hush Avis Eads and Pink for good. "Don't worry it, Avis," she says. "Tell the rest the same. Unless somebody blabbed it at the A&P, Donnie doesn't know. I'd just as soon be allowed to tell him, but I know that to be an impossible wish."

* * *

Evansville, Indiana, is far and away the biggest city a hundred miles in any direction from Dunes Park. Dunes Park got its name same as Evansville, from somebody who came through and tacked the title on a door. It is Wednesday, and Marlette should be home doing chores. No point adding to the misery with a messy house. As it is, Donnie will be slamming cabinets, then sitting over supper solemn as a funeral when he finds out about her trip, same as he was when he heard about her losing her job. "I know it isn't much, Marlette," Donnie said last night, "but why do you think I brought home the pup? I figured what little she'd need could come out of the pocket money you make at Pink's. Is that so much? For a family to have one little thing the sole purpose of which is to produce joy? It ain't like we're gambling pennies for marbles. It's a pup. A tiny pup. I couldn't leave her to freeze in the sleet and rain."

"I guess I just don't see why you're fussing at me," Marlette said at one point, which hit off a debate that lasted long into the night, dredging old grieves and sealed hurts until both turned cold shoulders to the other and awaited the clock's ring. Two weeks now since Pink's phone call and Donnie still can't see what Marlette does: that one thing has very little to do with the other. That losing her job the day after he brought home an un-agreed upon pup with begging eyes and an empty stomach was pure coincidence. Donnie seems to think of it as just another example of the way the world continuously plots against him. The way life is bound and determined to drag him low. In the disquiet they still haven't named the pup, although Donnie says over and over he can't see why Marlette would want to name a dog after a dead foreign woman. Marlette keeps telling him, "It's Sylvie, Donnie Peel. Sylvia Plath was American. I want to call the dog Sylvie. Hadn't nothing to do with the human girl other than to give me the idea, that's all."

Ginny, sitting at the dinner table Saturday night with new dental braces and one of Donnie's bandanas tied hippy-style over blonde curls that otherwise refused to be captured, thought they should name the dog Pink, since Pink was the cause of the trouble. Donnie slapped her for that and tore the bandana from her head. "No kid of mine is going about like a gall-danged hippy," he said, and poor Ginny left the table crying. Cried herself to sleep that night and refused church and her beloved Sunday School the morning after.

The Evansville City Library is, as Avis promised, much larger than the one in Dunes Park and is a free-standing structure. According to the raised-letter brass sign on the lawn, it is an historic landmark, the stones quarried from local limestone, the tall, white-washed columns hewn from giant yellow poplars once common to the area. Marlette parks the old sedan, self-conscious of its age next to a new little hump-shaped foreign car and a white car in a newish style called a fastback. The sedan's a behemoth next to them, a black and grey and chrome torpedo beside tiny arrowheads. The bright wind in her stomach is too quick; she can't catch her breath from it. She has spent a dollar in gasoline to get here, and it will take a dollar to return. She tries to calm herself, but the sun shining through the car window heats the sedan's dusty upholstery, making her feel nauseated. Now wouldn't that be something. After all this time to find herself pregnant. A policeman taps his billy stick against the passenger side glass, points to the meter head. "Takes pennies, Miss," she sees him mouth, wonders if he spoke it aloud or only fashioned his lips around the words. The sedan's motor running makes it too loud to hear. She nods her head and watches the officer walk on, but rather than switching off the ignition and setting the emergency brake, Marlette pulls back into the traffic lane instead.

*   *   *

Harney's Stationery doesn't have Sylvia Plath's books, but they have plenty of others under a printed tag tacked to the top bookshelf which reads "Literature." Oh, there are other sections: cookbooks and reference books and paperbacks, but Marlette feels drawn to these. People by the name of Sexton and Eliot and Du Maurier and Bradbury and Woolf and Stein and Vonnegut. A large display of a book written by a woman named Rachel Carson called, *Silent Spring*. She sits in the dark red velvet armchair in the browsing section thumbing through her stack, intending to sit there skimming and reading until she's had her fill, and Donnie can go to hell.

When she looks up again, the sun has set and the streetlamps have blinked on. It feels very late, even though it is only the gray of the waning afternoon. She sees the Greyhound is pulling loose from the curb, the five o'clock departure, she guesses, likely full of hippies heading West. She wonders what it must feel like to be one of them, to feel that free, to go wandering about in search of whatever people who travelled to the American West were searching for, had been searching for since the days of Lewis and Clark and what she had learned in high school was called "Manifest Destiny." She can only catch a dream glimpse of a shadow just now of what those words truly mean. The clerk, a college-age young man with a ponytail, psychedelic T-shirt pulled over the top of a long-john shirt, walks over, perches himself on the arm of the chair opposite and says, "Sorry we can't help with Plath's books. Backlog, you dig? Everybody in a heartbeat wants to read her. Poor Sylvia. Just didn't take to mothering, I guess. It's ten to close. Did you want any of the books?" Marlette looks up, dumbstruck. She blinks, concerned this foreigner has broken into her living room. Donnie will have a fit. In the same second, the veil splits, and she recalls the day. She is in Evansville, and this is a bookstore, and she has to get home. "No. No," she says, "I'm sorry. I just got so drawn in."

"It happens. Anytime. Absolutely anytime. It's all yours," he says, lifting his hands toward the sky, then clapping them together, turning in a quick puff, his soles squeaking as he marches toward the front of the store. "Five minutes, my fair ladies and gentlemen. Five minutes to close." Marlette hears the sound of cash register bells, the doors opening, closing. She stands, lifts the tweed coat off the back of the chair and holds it to her nose, smells the fragrance of herself, Donnie, her home, pulls it on one arm at a time, feels the slick of the lining as it passes over her dress. She looks at the books again, the books and their hard backs and protective paper covers, titles dancing along the spine as if letter-painted.

If nothing else has come of it, she knows how to get to Harney's Stationery in Evansville. She will drive the miles back to Dunes Park and Donnie and Ginny and Philip and tell the story. Donnie will rant. He might throw a plate. He will tell her not to drive the car except once a month for groceries, until she finds a way to bring in income.

Marlette will do this. No way around it. She will. She'll do what he says.

One thing she'll insist on, however, and she'll make him see the right in it. She'll give in to keep that pup, but on the condition that they name her Sylvia, Sylvie for short, and they'll find a way to pay for getting her spayed, and on the day Sylvie dies, they'll pay somebody from town to paint a grave marker. Or maybe Philip will grow up to have that talent. He's the quiet one, the one who watches and takes things in and never questions. The one with sideways crooked teeth he's embarrassed of and that will require dental work far beyond what Ginny has had to endure. They're already anticipating the expense of that.

CURLIE'S ALIBI

Question 1: Do peaches wear pillbox hats?
Question 2: Do Martian dogs chew sapphires?
Question 3: Does bacon sing Italian opera?
Question 4: Do podiatrists walk on tulip beds?

THIS IS JUANITA. Sometimes we call her J. A beautiful girl with hearing aids, scribbling on a napkin, in response to a bet that she can't think of six questions no human has ever asked another human. She's on number five, punctuating the air with her hands as she imagines aloud. Curlie interrupts her, says he's willing to bet she can't tell a story while stifling her fingers. Hito and I throw tens on the bar. Curlie follows suit. J says, "I'll raise you ten," and we all throw down again.

She tries, telling an old yarn about two French women who came to New Albany, Indiana, in the early 1800s, dreaming to open a restaurant for steamboat passengers, only to discover they'd each lied to the other about talent and funds, that is to say, they'd overstated themselves. What other choice did two enterprising women of that era have but to open a brothel and saloon, so that's what they did, in an abandoned bank, in the exact place known today as Curlie's Bar. Of course, as civilized as the new world was by then, the brothel part was a secret.

J loses the bet. She runs her fingers through her hair, which we count as foul, as she is wrapping up her story with, "New Albany was full of wealth, but you'd never know it today." Her penalty is to buy a round of tequila shots for the bar, all of four people, including herself, Curlie, Hito, who is tending bar, and me.

J we have known forever. We went to school with her, and then she was a 'Nam nurse early in the war, went to college a second time on her G.I. bill at the university over in Louisville and eventually became a divorce attorney. According to her, as of 1972, she was still the first and only woman divorce lawyer in Floyd County. She has been known to write stories about us and our town, which she sends out in the mail to high-brow brainiac magazines, hoping to get published, and when she does, Curlie sets her up at the microphone and she reads for everybody. It's a comforting and intellectually stimulating endeavor, and one we all look forward to. When Curlie's feeling flush, he puts an ad in the paper, but people come whether he does or doesn't. Folks love her stories and keep on top of her goings on. To us, she's funny, especially the more she drinks, and J, just like the rest of us, will string them together if a happy audience is buying.

"Don't you see?" she says, a few sips of a whiskey on the rocks to her credit, "Two people talking and one asking questions that don't make sense. Or, how about this? Take these four questions and make them into a game. What if each question on this napkin is a spy code? How would you answer if you were a spy agent duty-bound to confirm your identity? What does the question then even mean? Does it have two meanings? More? Is each individual word a separate code or is it only a code if the words are strung together in that particular sentence? Do you see what I mean? Maybe all the questions in the world don't make any more sense than these do. Maybe if we line ourselves up right, we can see we've gotten used to what we think a question is. Maybe tonight is the only true question: what will happen tonight? In this place or some other place? Will we have fun? Will someone? Will anyone laugh? Maybe we four are the only story, and this napkin and this writing don't even exist."

Juanita shouldn't drink. Curlie, the bar owner, tells her just that while he fills the napkin and silverware baskets, just like he is always telling her that, because, as he's told me, he thinks he has some kind of right, since he used to be married to her. Not for long, and he's still in love with her, which is why he devotes time to talking about her wellbeing behind her back. Juanita acts affectionate toward him, but respectfully so, as if Curlie is just a great bartender or waiter.

Neither of them ever said what happened. When J drinks too much, she talks too much, doesn't make room for anybody else, but that's no reason for divorce. True, nobody can keep up with her ideas and often, somebody has to take her beautiful body home because she refuses to drive if she's had more than two drinks, and that's a good thing. It's hard on the men, being around somebody that smart, that pretty, that special, and not think about the one thing that never in hell is going to come to them. Let alone lay her. Hell, half of Curlie's patrons probably dream about *marrying* her, not that she'd stoop to washing out teacups for one of them. Nobody's smart enough for J around here except Curlie, and he's blown his chance already.

Me? Well, I listen to her, but sex is not an option. Not that she asks, other than to flirt, which is a sort of kindness I get on occasion from women, and not just those I know and love. Excuse the narcissism, but I'm not completely terrifying. I love my Becky, and I aim to keep it so. She, too, has got a brain like a locomotive, is practical and good-looking, and she makes me want to be the best human I can, and because a wedding ring is protection and a home and safety for both of us, not that she isn't every bit capable of making it on her own, and in style. Lucky me, she doesn't see me as a circumstance, but as her Man. Never has she called me her husband, rather, her *man*. Me, I need her same as I love her, if I am to keep from becoming a youthful casualty of the VA old farts home. Becky needs a smart, good-looking, muscular man. She told me that once. You push a wheel chair, you get muscular, all right.

Juanita's wild, barely conceivable theories are something I enjoy pondering. I go home and worry her diatribes with Becky. We discuss matters such as "questions no human has ever asked." Becky jokes that these conversations have replaced sex. Not true, but, where before we'd have gone at it a bit first, now we at times start jaw-jacking and forget about the sex part. We kid about it, calling it intellectual sex. I think it's more the case that you can be with someone long enough and wholly enough that sex becomes a redundancy. I think it is possible to love someone so much that you transcend sex or at least the need for sex. Becky worries about whether that is true in our relationship, but the bottom line for me, and I know she gets this absolutely, is that I don't hanker for any other woman. Becky is my one hundred percent desire. Period.

Discussions with J have led me to believe in this sort of loftier possibility. I confessed to her and Hito one night that I can see where, as a male, I've been fed a diet of sexuality from the moment I became conscious in the world, sometime in my very early teens. I saw in movies that I was supposed to want to look at girlie magazines. TV and magazine ads seemed to me to have the potential to train me to be obsessed with being attractive to women, to see a woman's body as an object of my sexual need, and, again, obsessively. None of which is close to how I've ever felt. I've felt respectful of girls, of women. I never understood why every photo of a woman has to insinuate that I should see her as a slut. So, it's an easy leap of logic to me. This is me as a human being arriving back around to my original instinct about the way of things.

All of this is to say that J.'s public transmittal of knowledge and weirdness have left me with new viewpoints, and Becky, too. We're in a sense addicted now to imagining a myriad of answers to the questions of the world. Becky and J got to know each other over the years from talking outside Curlie's while Hito and I enjoy a last smoke for the evening. Honestly, if I did sleep with J., Becky would probably understand. She's wired a little differently that way. For her, life is all about the long haul, not the day-to-day mistakes and annoyances that tend to trip people up emotionally. But she'd be disappointed, and I'm not going to purposefully cause her pain. Besides, those two women love each other as friends now, and Juanita would never lift a finger to hurt Becky's heart. Privately, it has flicked through my brain, of course. No man my age could prevent it one hundred percent.

Becky and I refer to these talks as The J-File. We keep track of our discussions in a notebook. Subjects such as, "What the world would be like if women were in charge." That's one of J.'s and Becky's favorites. The plan is to type it up into a book and have it bound and give it to J someday as a gift. Maybe she'll get it published and make us all a fortune.

Talking to Juanita and people who come to this place is a great alibi for having a drink or two. I like having a drink or two. People can be religious to the point of staying one hundred percent away from alcohol, even beer. Just the opposite, the humid climate around here makes non-teetotalers swill cases and think nothing of it. Likewise, I know folks who steer clear of dancing and swimming and common things like that. A number of my fellow VFW members belong to the Nazarenes, and they don't partake in much public fun. It's a side effect of being an injured Vet for some, religion is, so I'm around those types at Vet rehab, too. They might look down on me, think I'm weak for preferring booze to the Bible, but never say as much. It's more an attitude. Becky and me, we like to pour a cocktail at home on occasion. Other times, I prefer to go sit on a bar stool—for the social aspect, I guess. Becky doesn't mind me coming to Curlie's for karaoke and especially not for open mic. She doesn't appreciate the vibe around drinking establishments, so she stays home. Old wounds having to do with her mother. But she'll drop me off and pick me up with a smile and a kiss. I roll myself in and folks help me onto one of the two hydraulic barstools they keep for vets. Tonight, it is Hito and Ruthie, who joke that my workouts aren't doing them a lot of good, and who then leave to go dress for their performances.

It's Tuesday, and Tuesday is open mic night set aside for disabled singers, which means a crowd is starting to accumulate. We've all been doing this long enough that a progression has developed that has nothing to do with talent and everything to do with habit. That is to say, the usual suspects start filing in, first one, then the other, over the course of the next fifteen minutes. The place becomes full of people hello-ing and catching up on the week's news.

Curlie organizes the singers the same way he wears his jeans: tight and high up the ass. Tonight, he's lobbying for a rearrangement of the usual order, and people are objecting. He has no good reason. He just wants to mix it up. Usually first on the billing is Meredith, a Raphaelite beauty who has worn polio braces since we were all kids and walks with handheld crutches that make her move like a spider and who has a good voice but needs lessons to get control of her vibrato. Meredith is always first because she is proud, well-groomed, and gets to the stage on her own, kindly refusing help, even though it takes her a long time and she knows we are all waiting. In other words, she sets a good example of a person who is being herself, doing her own thing. Tonight, we sing while she's working her way to the front, the entire audience—"Let It Be"—which makes Meredith at first laugh so hard she can't move. She sets a good tone to the night, and you could say she one hundred percent never walks up there alone.

Next usually comes the man with the hook, Caiaphas Caiaphas II, he calls himself, which is a name he legally adopted as his given name was Charles Evan Manson, which brought him a measure of grief after the big murder rampage carried out on those Hollywood folks back in 1969. Calling himself Caiaphas Caiaphas II is kind of funny, if you think of it, because Caiaphas was the one in the Bible who plotted Jesus's execution. One night I made note of the fact that his chosen name might offend as many people as being called Charles Manson did, and that he had traded one bad name for another. He came back at me with a story about Caiaphas Caiaphas being the name of the fishing boat he owned and captained most of his life up out of Ilwaco, Washington. Mainly, his goal was to rile people, but from his point of view, one Caiaphas cancels the other out, so the name is a moot point. With his white beard, he looks like an old sea captain and sings songs he writes himself about old voyages, lost loves, and the search for love. He sometimes sings old Irish sea songs, too. The hook is a phony thing he holds onto with a good hand, but nobody cares. We know it's his form of showing unity and respect.

Another singer who is not sideways-abled, as we like to call it, is a beautiful brown-haired girl named Lizzie, who ties her curls in a bun with a piece of yellow ribbon. Nobody knows the significance of that. She doesn't drink, but she sings Dolly Parton songs to beat Jesus and is always accompanied by her husband, Chet, who has black braids and a North Carolina accent, wears a wool Indian-patterned vest and a beaded rodeo buckle, and told us one night he is an enrolled member of the Eastern Band of the Cherokee from North Carolina. He says he's named after Chet Atkins, and I believe it, because he plays guitar good enough to go into competition with the man. He took a bunch of shrapnel in 'Nam, also, and usually occupies the other "silver suppository," as we call Curlie's two special-made barstools. Chet rolls a chair, too. It's not redundant to say Lizzie and Chet make a seriously perfect duet in more than one way, the same as my Becky and I do.

Everybody's favorite person is an older man named Bob, who sings Bobby Darin and Johnny Mathis hits. He talks every week before he sings about how he has hardening of the arteries and quit both booze and his three-packs-a-day of cigarettes all at once and that young people would do well to never get started with those two demons. Once in a while he'll talk a bit about his dead wife. Bob has a brain for dates, and it always seems to be the anniversary of something he and she did together. He's already told us tonight that it's the ten-year anniversary of their last trip to Florida together.

Among the lesser known regulars are the two cute-in-a-Goldie-Hawn-kind-of-way sisters with the twin skinny husbands who sing harmonies to make you weep. Curlie couldn't tell you their names, and neither could I. They don't drink either. They order colas, sing one song, usually a Johnny Cash or a Willie Nelson, sometimes two, and leave without visiting.

As Curlie likes to say, Tuesday nights don't make him any money, but "the talent is worth the price of omission."

The early-shift bartender Hito, whose parents had to go to the internment camps during World War Two, every week goes home to clean up and comes back and turns out a great Elvis, swivel hips and all. Rhinestone costume, too. He's not sideways-abled either, but nobody cares. We just like it that he graces us with his gifts. Hito blows my mind. He actually has won a number of Elvis impersonator contests. Third place at the big Vegas show last year. A true phenomenon. Transports us all. Juanita once said impersonators are people who haven't "exacted identity from their assigned natures." I don't think that's the case with Hito. He's just as good with a set of vise grips or a carburetor as he is at mixing drinks and taking people's breaths away with his true-as-true Elvis bit. He works hard at being good at all the things he enjoys. I once told J I thought it was fun, the artistry involved in an average person pretending to be Elvis. It's just a type of performance, a stage act, same as it is for female impersonators. Maybe Elvis has to work just as hard at being himself. Nothing wrong with any of it. She rolled her eyes and said I didn't understand the meta of it. No idea what that means, and I keep forgetting to look it up.

Then comes the young, tough waitress Ruthie with long, wavy strawberry blonde hair who told Curlie and me one night when Becky was late picking me up and the rest of the crowd had already shoved off that at the age of twenty-eight she had already seen five years of hard time in the prison at La Grange for killing her abusive boyfriend, but Curlie said later he didn't know that to be true. He said he didn't doubt she had it in her, because she was known to fight and fight mean. He had seen her bloody a grabby drunk's nose once: smashed him in the face with a stone crock lid, but she also was fond of telling stories that fell into the realm of far-fetched. I knew what he was talking about. For example, she once told me she had spent a summer in Greece during high school, but then didn't have a clue I was pulling her leg when I questioned her about the Great Pyramid and Michelangelo's statue David. She claimed to have seen them both when she was in Athens, which is, of course, not where they exist. I guess you could say, when it comes to Ruthie's tales, we suspect them as a sort of performance, too. No matter, I always tip her good. Ruthie loves to sing Janis Joplin hits, and we love to hear her. She can wail. Just like Hito, she dresses herself to look the part, feathers, beads, and fringe. It's Woodstock all over again, minus drugs, although who knows what Ruthie does in between work and open mic.

The closing act every Tuesday night is Curlie, who always tells about how he grew up next door to Marty Robbins, who taught him and his sister to two-step, which he presumes to prove by dancing with Juanita to end the show.

Tonight's show eventually gets going pretty well, except Lizzie and Chet are not here. Curlie offers to help me into my chair so I can get closer to the stage, but I tell him I won't sing tonight. "Too pooped," I tell him. "Therapy at the VA today." Curlie nods, walks up to start the show. He gives out the door prize of a free pint of beer, introduces Meredith, who has an entire program planned of Barbra Streisand hits. Becky loves "Evergreen," which is what Meredith closes with.

Ruthie jumps in next, for some reason, and she's not wailing Janis but Grace Slick, ahead of Caiaphas and Hito. People have been singing in the same order for so long that it makes me agitated, gives the night a jittery feel. Then Caiaphas comes on, minus his hook, apologizes to anyone he offended with it. What the heck? As far as I know, no one has ever mentioned a word about it, good or bad. Caiaphas is in rare form, singing a string of old Gaelic tunes, surprising us all with a Celtic drum to punctuate the wordless parts. I didn't know Curlie's eight-track archives included old Gaelic tunes, but there you go. I'm guessing nobody in the crowd knew Caiaphas had it in him. The beat washes through my body, the parts that I can feel, surges like courage, to where I imagine I can stand and walk, even levitate. If J.'s way of thinking is right, maybe I am levitating. Maybe we all are. The magic transfers to the string-bean couples who sing several 50s hits, including the Everly Brothers' "Dream" and Frank Sinatra's "I Did It My Way." Then, just to throw us off further, even though the show is not finished, Curlie and Juanita go on stage and do their Marty Robbins tribute, dancing and twirling to "El Paso." Those two might as well be Ginger Rogers and Fred Astaire, one hundred percent. Watching them chokes me up, but nobody's close enough to notice. Becky and I used to cut a rug. More than once, we cleared a dance floor back at senior dances and two years of proms. Not sure why so many of our graduating class turned out to be good dancers, but it was a thing back then, going out and honing your moves. Curlie almost drops Juanita on her bum when he misses a beat on his last lift. He takes it as his cue to give it up for the night, and starts calling at Hito, who lets himself be edged toward to the front of the crowd under protest. Hito is trying to be courteous, insisting Bob go next. "Beauty before age," Bob says, and bows deep in Hito's direction.

Hito nails "Love Me Tender," then "Ain't Nothing but a Hound Dog," and then, as if the night isn't oddball enough, he picks up his guitar and does a medley from Elvis's first Christmas album—and here we are in the heat of July. It works to the point that several holler out, claiming to be cooled off enough, just as he gets to "I'm Dreaming of a White Christmas," such that Hito urges the crowd to warm back up by singing with him.

By the time Bob picks his way to the front and is halfway through "Puff the Magic Dragon," I'm starting to think we've all gone off our gourds, since Bob usually sings Lester Flat and Earl Scruggs and once in a while a Patsy Cline song or two. About that time, it sinks to a few of us that Bob is dripping sweat from his forehead, darkening the blue of his cotton shirt, has dropped the microphone, and is clutching his left collarbone region. Curlie silences the eight-track, goes running to the stage. People knock over chairs trying to get to Bob. Since Lizzie and Chet didn't show tonight, his silver suppository is vacant. Best I can do is watch. Bob's microphone is still on, so we hear every word. "You can change your mind, Bob. You certain? You're sure?" Curlie says.

Bob nods his head, best he can, the force of his pain evident even from my distant vantage point. I don't hear his response, but later Curlie tells me he said, "No flowers." He also whispers that Bob left what little money he had to Meredith, but I'm not supposed to tell. J passes by me, moving like a mad bull and says, "Like hell. Point me to the damned phone. I'm calling the ambulance." When I do, she dives over the bar for the phone.

Ruthie, who has been chasing J from all the way across the building, grabs her by her Levi's 501 belt loops and pulls her back over the bar. "Curlie made a pact with Bob, Juanita," she says. "We all did. You weren't here. We pricked fingers and marked it in blood. Bob's made his choice."

"I am not going to sit here and watch him die," J says, crying, her tears a torrent, which Ruthie dabs at with a tissue.

"Let me call you a cab, then," Ruthie says. "I'll walk you out, and we'll have a smoke."

I saw death aplenty in 'Nam, so watching life leave a body is not one-hundred-percent new, but I don't like watching Bob die. It's not the spirit-leaving-flesh part that bothers me, it's the afterward I hate, that feeling that the roof has been ripped from its trusses and time is pouring in, compressing and reshaping, the humanity of our tiny community now crystal clear and solid but heavy, like a glass weight. Curlie tries to make us feel better by sharing the story of the pact they made, and Bob's hope that his death be an act of protest, a statement about people as late as the 1970s in the U.S. having to choose between death and paying a bill. "I expect our founding fathers would be astonished and ashamed about the undemocratic nature of the condition of our money system," Curlie claims Bob said, and Ruthie nods in agreement with the account.

After it's done, after Bob hasn't taken a breath for a good ten minutes, after he has upchucked from the pain, and we can smell the shit he's leaked, and people have left the building bawling like newborns, Curlie calls cabs to transport everybody to their various homes, a few of whom are sniffling into bar towels, paying the tab for the whole night himself, including tips for the cabbies. Then he calls the cops. It must be a busy night for New Albany's blue squad, either that or nobody's in a hurry to check on an old man having a heart attack in a bar. Happens every day, right? Maybe it's just the nature of time that it seems like they took forever to arrive. Slow motion. I back up Curlie's story that it has been an easy night, not too many folks in, and that Bob was singing his guts out when he collapsed on stage. We don't realize Meredith is sitting in the back with her crutches, watching it all, until one of the cops walks back and chats with her. She must have corroborated our story, because the officer closes his notebook and we hear him radioing in that he is all clear.

Hardest thing I've ever had to do is lie about the progression of events to Becky when she picks me up, telling her he went peacefully, and that we'll be going to a funeral in a few days.

CHEMO, THEN GAINESVILLE

THE NAUSEA WAS no worse than a hangover, but losing her hair was sad, even though she wore a wig almost every night anyway. She had a few costumes that required batteries, for example, the one where her breasts went off like sparklers. But mostly it was just tasteful outfits and wigs. For some reason, audiences loved having her rip from her head an artificial hairpiece. As soon as her hair started falling out in clumps, however, she shaved her head, and asked Nardo to tattoo a big peace sign on her scalp. The crowd stood and applauded that night as she carefully lifted her wig, the peach-colored one, revealing reddened, inked flesh under a film of plastic wrap affixed with white adhesive tape. Of course, word was around that she had cancer, but they all could see she intended to fight it, and they more or less tipped her out every night from then on. People admire bravery, even in nightclubs.

Plus, most of them knew about her daughters, little Melanie and Angela. Minute by minute, day by day, she'd gotten them through their diaper years and now to third grade and kindergarten. Both cute as buttons and little flirts with Nardo and the bartenders when she brought them with her during lunch hour when the club was just a place for a burger and a cup of coffee. Before the lights went down and the dancers came to work. Yes, they lived part of that time in what was essentially a motel, but it had had a kitchenette, and she could pay by the day if necessary, which circumstances at times forced her to do. But both girls always had clothes on their backs, even if they were from thrift shops; they had a roof and a warm place to sleep and food enough. Sometimes she fantasized about the nightmare of them getting to high school and boys swarming about. That part was going to be hard, if she lived to see it. She remembered what it was like to be crazy over a boy. Melanie had been born when Tracy was just fifteen.

She was only eighteen when she came up pregnant a second time, at which point her mother threw her out. What could she say? She was a sucker for the closeness she felt with boys she went steady with in high school who, after five or six dates, wanted her in the backseat of their souped-up muscle cars. Lots of jobs for keypunch operators in Louisville, Kentucky, in 1976, jobs that paid well enough to afford a small walk-up apartment and childcare, so she tried that, working all day surrounded by rows and rows of young women just like her, and whirring machines, stamping holes in computer data cards, her girls dropped at a nearby daycare center that smelled of sour milk and baby piss and cigarette smoke. After about six months, when a credit card application came in the mail, referencing the offer as a "perk" of the computer company, she applied for it, thinking it would be a nice fallback in case of emergencies. The payment was taken directly from her check. It wouldn't even cost her a stamp.

Pretty soon she was twelve hundred dollars in debt, mostly for the sake of trying to keep up with the company's dress code, which required her to look "modish and put-together," in the words of the memo she was handed her first day on the job, after she showed up in a plaid wool skirt and sweater left over from high school. Her lack of stylish clothing during those first months meant her probation was extended to nine months instead of six. With interest, her weekly paychecks were twelve dollars lighter than they originally had been, the card was nearly maxed out, and she was wearing underarm shields to absorb perspiration and spot-cleaning her nice, new clothes by hand to postpone dry cleaning bills. Every night she went over whatever she had worn that day with a damp sponge and baby soap, steaming out wrinkles with a wet hanky and a hot iron.

The stress of the debt was more than she could handle. She began stopping off with a group of co-workers at the end of her shift for a scotch and a beer. One night, a year in, after her mother had finally fallen in love with Melanie and Angela enough that she was willing to watch them from time to time, Tracy went out with a friend named Joanie, who just days before had been let go because she had passed the tardy limit: keypunch operators were required to clock in no later than five minutes *before* the eight o-clock bell. Arrive at eight o'clock, and you were already late. You got three lates a year, and that was it. Joanie was excited because she had answered an ad for a waitress and dancer job at a club a few blocks away and was hired on the spot. The first night she made two hundred dollars, which was roughly what she made in two weeks as a keypunch operator. She insisted Tracy give it a try, even just one night a week, pay off her company credit card in no time flat. Days, really. She could think of it as an art form, as all the other girls did, making up their own routines and costumes.

The only catch was that Tracy would have to work up to the privilege of creating her costumes. To begin, she'd have to dance in a bikini, and, if the customers called for it, topless. Topless was where the big money was.

It only took a few seconds to realize that at two hundred per night, she could pay off her entire debt in exactly six days.

*   *   *

Joanie was right. Tracy was hired during her interview and committing to work only a few nights a month was completely allowable. As her mother already had established a routine of keeping the girls overnight on occasion, it didn't take much talking to convince her to make it a regular thing, so that Tracy "could have a social life," which is what Tracy's argument had been. What could she do but pick up a couple of cute bikinis with the credit card, pay the bartenders under the table—as drinking on the job was against the rules—for shots of vodka to loosen herself, take off her clothes, and dance?

The freedom she felt when she was on stage was like nothing she had ever known. It was fresh air. It was fire in her blood. It was swimming a mile under water then plunging skyward for deep, gulping breaths. It was walking in moonlight along a golden beach then rocketing among the stars and the planets. It was, Tracy often mused, a drug. Removing her bikini top was no big deal at all. Freedom multiplied. She read a magazine about women bodybuilders and discovered that by lifting weights she could change the proportions of her upper body and her strength. She quickly became toned and athletic, and at the same time a favorite among customers, and just as quickly, her debt was paid off, but she used that card again and again once she was allowed to advance to creating her own costumes, which was code for stripping.

"Butterfly Girl" was her first costume dance. She put on a long fairy dress and blue glittery wings nearly as tall as she was, pointe shoes, and imagined she was a ballerina dancer. All those lessons her mother bought her as a girl didn't amount to nothing. She'd *plié* and curtsy and leap and stay on pointe until people applauded. The girl version of her loved that she could dance for that long and in that outfit.

Then, of course, the snare drum started and men on the front row helped her one-by-one slip off her wings. Pieces of her skirt, button-looped to her waistband, also fell to the floor, section by section. By the time she was down to her G-string and bra, she was feeling the pull from home, the girls wanting her. Butterfly Girl became her end-of-the-night scene, and she never stripped all the way on her first or last dance.

*   *   *

Cancer set her back. After she moved to Florida with the girls in 1978, where the money was said to be so much better, and certainly the air and the weather, she and her daughters reached the point where they were not only surviving, but she was able to buy herself a used station wagon and move into a little rental house with a year-to-year lease. They had lived in that blue adobe cottage for four years when she got the diagnosis. Blood in her urine. Bladder cancer, probably from smoking cigarettes. Everybody said the same thing: "You are too young for cancer." Unfortunately, nobody thought to inform the cancer. It turned out to be fortunate that she had moved to Tampa Bay, which was only three hours from Jacksonville, where she was able to get the best and newest and most advanced treatment. If she had gotten sick a few years sooner, she'd have been toast. As it was, they took a piece of her bowel to make a bladder. It wasn't cheap, but she volunteered to be a guinea pig, the first person in Florida to undergo her particular regimen of treatments, so she got a big discount. Now, with the burden of medical bills—and who could possibly keep up with those, discount or no— she'd never be able to save a down payment or qualify to purchase a house of her own, at least not anytime soon. She had known there was such a thing as health insurance, she just thought she was too healthy to need it. It seemed like every time she was close to pulling ahead, something would happen to toss a rod in the works. Always had plenty but never extra. "Enough is as good as a feast," Nardo always said. The girls needed work on their teeth and after-school daycare and never-ending upgrades in the size of their clothes. She didn't dare hope to send them to private schools and only daydreamed of the possibility that she could one day send them to college.

First chemo, then Gainesville, and a new life for her and her girls. That was the new plan. Money in Tampa Bay had been enormous compared to Louisville. She could make up to twelve hundred a week during tourist season, even only working four nights a week, but she was finally learning that money only smelled green for so long, then it started to stink. Cancer had her re-thinking things. Maybe she could get one of those government grants and go to school herself. But no sooner did she have the thought than the brakes and the alternator went out on her car, pretty much all at once, which Nardo, her boss of now more than four years, had towed at his expense to a mechanic friend of his. New alternator, brakes, and a new rear axle seal for $200. *A bargain.* Nardo would front her cash. Ten percent per week out of her tips until it was paid, interest-free. Which meant, once she recovered from bladder surgery, working through the many weeks of chemo, no matter what. All she had to promise was that she'd do the deed with the mechanic. He was maybe twenty-five, laughed instead of saying hello while shaking her hand. "Best mechanic you ever seen," Nardo said. "You ought to marry the poor guy, Tracy. You could do worse than young Matìas here."

She never felt embarrassed anymore when she ran into men who came to the club. *It's a job, guys.* She was sure she recognized Matìas from an occasional Friday night, but not enough to know what kind of tipper he was. Everybody local came in at one time or another. Travelers, too, of course. The police at first were repeatedly trying to bust the place, even though all the girls were permitted. Now sometimes a cluster of them came in off-duty, but understandably didn't tip, even if they were friendly and fun to spend time with.

Matìas told a story that seemed to go with the red grease-rag smell of the garage. One of those macho stories where he got two girls pregnant at once. There was nothing to stop her from running, from leaving the car there on the lift two feet into the air with Matìas's voice and legs extended from under it, Nardo's cash roll in her pocket, but she didn't. Nardo's trust in her made her not want to cheat him. Not that she ever did or would. But it crossed her mind.

She gave Matìas his quick little blow after Nardo left, the young man's body folded onto the toilet seat and surrounded by the grunge of a bare-wood stall ages old and which had never seen a coat of paint or a dusting, his oil-stained trousers around his ankles, between his legs smelling amazingly clean, like Irish Spring. Being that close, she got the impression of a man who took pains with himself. She imagined he caught plenty of eyes on Friday nights. He came almost as quick as she got her mouth on him. They almost always did, which is why she did not qualify these acts as sex—the time spent was just too short—and she was not sharing any more of herself than she'd share with the average chili dog. Much less, in fact. Not even with the extra money he gave her just before she drove out. Especially not with the way he slipped his leather wallet from his back pocket like he was hesitant to do so, and the way it stuck there where the fabric met itself in the corner to make a welt, the way fat wallets do. Not even when she pulled out into traffic in her loaner car, only briefly aware of the cold pad of his folded dollar bills and the moment or two it took to conform within her bra to the curve of her breast.

THE COWBOY BAR

PEOPLE TOLD STORIES about a tavern at the west end of New Albany. The West End, meaning the so-called wrong side of the tracks, was where just-getting-by folks with a casual lawn care esthetic and the more exotic religious advocates had scattered themselves. Their houses flanked at random intervals Highway 150, a swerve-y state road cut through limestone knolls that drained west out of New Albany toward the cornfields and tobacco farms pondering the Ohio River. When the Ohio flooded, which it did every few decades or so, residents of 150 had to haul out their angling skiffs and crank up the outboard to get to town.

The tavern was called The Cowboy Bar, for reasons nobody could remember. A name that hardly suited southern Indiana, with its Italianate mansions, steel fabrication plants, and farming villages. It was a box built of concrete block with two high windows out front, both sporting neon beer signs. The door, situated between the windows, or *winderlites*, as some of the older regulars called them, was turquoise blue. The building itself had once been painted white, but so much of that effort had chipped and worn away that the facade looked dotted, like a Dalmatian dog. The original builder and purpose of the structure was a source of argument for bar regulars. Some thought it had been built to be a tavern, others thought, with its rough-plank wood floors, that it had been intended to house animals. At least one person thought it had been meant as a tornado shelter, since the walls were a foot thick and the building was set into a berm, appearing to be a story and a half from the river side, although there was no entrance from the back. Etched into the front door facing was the crude inscription Culpepper 1911, but patrons argued that concrete blocks did not exist until after the second big war, so that could not possibly be the year of construction. This was incorrect, of course, as was proven when the owner, Diane, went to the New Albany Public Library and checked out a book on the history of masonry and learned the manufacture of concrete blocks dated back nearly a hundred years.

Anyone could have gone to the Floyd County courthouse and looked up the detailed history of the building and the land it was built on, but no one did. In fact, after Diane spilled the secrets of the development of concrete blocks, it took two weeks for someone to come up with a subject to argue about. Diane herself put a topic on the table. She asked what her patrons thought of abortion, a question she wrote out on the chalkboard, which hung next to the cash register and where she usually announced drink specials. The chalkboard was a handmade gift from an old codger named Custer whose nickname was Yellow Hair, for obvious reasons, and who had since passed on. Custer had carved naked, lounging female figures around the chalkboard's frame and finished it with old-fashioned beetle-shell shellac, now yellowed with age. The black writing surface itself was from the old Lanesville one-room schoolhouse, which was torn down once the newer four-room Edwardsville school was built. That was back in the forties. Since many of Diane's regulars had gone to school at Lanesville, they were downright proud of that chalkboard, but they were used to words like "Cans 25¢" or "Out of Pull Tabs only this week," as usually happened around Derby time or during the summer when college types home for the season were stopping by to pick up packaged beer. On the day regulars started strolling in at four o'clock as usual and saw the question, "What is your opinion of abortion?" they all, to a one, all men, started grumbling about looking for a new bar. The problem was that driving farther into town meant burning more gasoline and risking running amok of the cops on the way home.

Abortion was a subject of the times, just like civil rights. After people got used to the question, they began the discussion in earnest, and from all angles.

After a while, the conditional circumstances far outweighed the yeses and nos. Rape was easy. So was disease, or a case where the mother's life was threatened. Medical equipment was becoming pretty sophisticated in 1975. Tests could be done. Sometimes it was possible to know ahead of time if a baby was deformed. If it was, if doctors could tell, should you get rid of it? This was a point on which the regular patrons were divided. At least one person pointed out that all of them might fail a doctor's test, but weren't they all, Diane included, happy nobody routed them out for failure to be perfect?

The Cowboy Bar's turquoise door was also the portal through which any number of rural residents passed if they needed to use the head after the winding drive from their farms and treed acreages. Except for kids, of course. Kids had to wait for the service stations on State Street. Diane never would have written such a question if kids might be exposed. She couldn't help but notice that restroomers glanced around and went straight to the back once that question was on the board. It made her laugh. She loved making people uncomfortable. Her strategy for letting people use the head was that often they stayed for a beer or to grab packaged to go. No one, not one restroomer stayed once she posited the abortion question. Not one. Which almost made her giggle. The glee she felt was nearly worth the lost revenue.

Through that portal was also said to be available moonshine and, if you had enough cash, you supposedly could adopt yourself a baby.

Or so it was said.

The acquisition of Kentucky moonshine was a potential that most interested college boys home for the holidays, high school seniors, summer boaters, football fans, and hill boys who had recreated their Appalachian homesteads along the loopy backroads and buffalo traces of Southern Indiana, down which you were just as apt to be met by snarling dogs and shotguns as not. Supposedly, as part of the trading Diane did to get that moonshine, she helped a family of girls get across the river to Louisville for abortions, although nobody ever had enough courage to ask her to verify that. Some kind of liberal-hippie group over there thought getting rid of an unwanted pregnancy ought to be just fine and that women themselves should have a right to choose the fate of a baby. They shouldn't need the consent of their man. That's what abortion clinic pamphlets tucked in tiny corners of health departments and counseling offices all over the Falls City area declared. Something about a legal case in the news called Roe v. Wade.

Occasionally, toward the end of an evening, when the regulars were starting to grumble about heading out into the cold, or, in the summer, it still being light enough out that their wives might expect some chore to be done, a slight knock could be heard. A specific kind of knock, just a tap, tap, not the kind of hard banging you could get with a knuckled fist, but a *ting! ting!* with a slight metal ring to it. No one ever asked about the sound, but as soon as she heard it, Diane would say, "All right fellows, mop up," and the men would begin tallying their tabs and arguing over tips and line up to pay their bills. Diane was very careful about the number of beers a man could drink in her establishment. You got one every thirty minutes, and after four, you had to wait an hour while you chugged coffee and ate a bag of popcorn. Peanuts could be had all night long, and the floor was littered with shells that got swept up once a week or so, usually by one of the men. Popcorn was for the seventh-inning stretch, as it was fondly called. At the end of a normal night, nights when the *ting! ting!* was not heard, Diane cut everyone off a full thirty minutes before they headed out to their cars. In fact, before you sat down on Diane's barstools, no matter how long you planned to imbibe, she stood in front of you with a fishbowl to collect your keys. No car keys, no beer.

Life went along just fine for Diane and her operation for a number of decades, or so it was said. She took possession of the place on the first of January, 1950, and by 1975, as she estimated aloud to the boys, she had sold close to a million cans or bottles of beer. No one knew exactly how old she was, but she had served their grandpas, some of whom were now gone, like old Custer, and she was serving them, and one or two had started bringing in their older boys. Three generations. She could have sold other beverages, colas or mixed drinks, even hard liquor—she was licensed as a cocktail bar—but she preferred the common and ordinary, as did her customers, and that came down to commonly advertised pilsners, and, in the summer when the college boys happened around, maybe a brown beer. You couldn't buy a draft from her or a keg, or a burger, or any other fancy thing. Not even a bag of potato chips.

But you could, supposedly, if you came to her under just the right set of circumstances, even if none of her patrons truly knew this, even if none of them had proof or ever had dared pose the question, get yourself a baby or an abortion.

The reason none of her regulars knew the history of The Cowboy Bar's building, is that Diane made good and sure to keep it from them, or so it was said. Beneath it was rumored to be situated a World War I bunker, an oddball thing that almost nobody who knew anything about that period of time would expect to find in New Albany, Indiana. But just like anxious folks built fallout shelters in the 1960s, so people built underground bunkers and put camouflage buildings on top of them at the turn of the century. This one was said to have been constructed by the feds to house female spies intercepting telegrams sent between foreign operatives who had managed to ferret themselves into the country. Indeed, perhaps the upstairs was designed to serve as a tavern, but only to cover for what work went on below. Diane had likely found all manner of paperwork left behind at the end of World War I when she started clearing out the lower level, a cavernous room accessible only through a hatch door not visible to the average beer drinker.

Yes, Diane sold bootleg moonshine under the counter. It was why she stayed away from cocktails otherwise, but like everything else, she had a catch. You could only purchase a tiny bottle at a time, and you had to bring the container yourself. It had to be a flask of no more than eight ounces. That was it. You couldn't bring in more than one flask. The second catch was that she had to know you. If you came in wink-winking asking for "the good stuff" or "still liquor" or "something stronger," you'd be met with Diane's raised eyebrows and uninterested glance and rote answer, "Bottles and cans. Packaged or here. The sign tells you what I got. What will it be?" and she'd hold the fishbowl and point to her beer pacing rules which were painted on the wall above where it met the thick slab of cedar plank that served as the resting place for elbows, forearms, bottles, cans, and bowls of peanuts.

The code was a question, of course. "Have you seen Dr. Chang lately?" If Diane did not know you, and you did not know that question, you drank beer or left. No exceptions.

In the summer of 1976, Diane somehow managed to get her hands on a couple of cases of bootleg beer all the way from Colorado. Everyone had been hearing about this new beer supposedly brewed with mountain spring water. It had her customers' imagination, for sure, most of the regulars referring to it as "hippie beer." She gave each of the men a free one, and most everybody liked it, all but the oldest ones who were pretty much stuck in their ways. "It's coming," she said. "One of these days you'll be able to get it in Indiana. College types will like it." You could see by the gleam in her eye that she'd already started counting the dollars she'd bring in. "I wouldn't mind having a few women be part of my regular crowd," she said. "Women will drink it. What would you boys think if I started carrying it when it's available in Indiana? Wouldn't you rather be playing pool with something prettier than this bunch of mutts?" she said.

This started another round of grumbling. "We don't want no women in here, Diane. You're plenty. We love our wives, but this place is what keeps our marriages going. This is our second living room. We come in here to get away from all that. This place is too man-ified for women. Women would just spoil everything."

It wasn't much later that some of the college boys got wind of what the code was and came in asking for Dr.

Chang. But they didn't say it quite right. They said, "I hear you know Dr. Chang?"

"Never heard of him," Diane said, then casually reached for a fastener of some kind, lifted her mass of blonde hair, and pinned it to the top of her head. Nobody had ever seen her do that. Nobody had ever seen her except the way she always was, hair down, no make-up, blue jeans, and a top or sweater, usually black or yellow or coral. Or turquoise, same color as the door. Once it was all over, looking back, the regulars, who quickly found another hangout a half-mile east of The Cowboy Bar, a place called Curlie's Alibi, realized that the color of Diane's upper garments were code themselves. They realized that the *ting! ting!* never sounded unless she was wearing turquoise. They couldn't prove it, but they were sure of it. Regardless, that was the end of Dr. Chang. Diane wasn't stupid. She had a mole. If she ever found out who he was, he'd be booted from the bar forever. She never had to speak the words. It was evident. From that day forward, her hair was always up, and no one ever asked the Dr. Chang question again.

In 1977, the FBI raided some government office downtown because of some bookkeeping problems and, supposedly, during the process, got wind of what The Cowboy Bar was known for. That was the rumor. Supposedly, a half-dozen big men showed up in dark gray overcoats with badges and shoulder holsters and canon-sized firearms, looking like revenuers in the old days of prohibition. Supposedly, Diane showed them around, let them go in the walk-in cooler where they dumped out a big barrel of peanuts—"looking for contraband"—then demanded to be let into the lower level. "Are you boys blind? Ain't but one door into this place," Diane supposedly said, and, "As far as I know, and I've owned this building going on thirty years, the only way to do that is to rent yourself a concrete saw. I aim to tell you, you're going to have one hell of a headache if you start cutting down my tavern."

"Is that a threat, Miss?" one of those bruisers was reported to have said.

"Sorry," Diane supposedly said. "I'm hard of hearing. You'll have to speak louder."

One of the agents came in from looking around the perimeter of the building, carrying something that looked like a tabletop Chinese gong, a brass thing on a little black stand with an ebony striker hanging from the top by a pink ribbon. He said he found it in the back wall, on the river side of the building, inside a little wooden door about five feet off the ground. He said inside the door was made of zinc and looked to be connected to the upper level by a tube of some sort, said there looked to be a sound system or speaker wired in.

Then it was all over for Diane, or so it was said. They came back with a warrant, gave her notice the bar was going to close. She was not cooperating. She could be charged with all kinds of things, including bootlegging, if they found what they expected to find. The lower level would have to be accessed. The regulars showed up for their usual rounds to find a typed piece of paper taped to the turquoise door, the place locked up tight.

Supposedly, those agents did rent a concrete saw and what they found was a dormitory set up just right for a woman to deliver a baby. A nursery, sterile equipment, like a hospital on a one-woman scale. Nobody ever saw any of this actually. They just heard rumors. The *New Albany Herald* only reported that Diane had shut herself up tight that last night, loaded herself high on weed, that Colorado beer, and LSD, and had to be carted out strapped to a gurney. Supposedly, she got shipped to the state hospital in Madison, but nobody could say for sure.

THE UNREAD DIARY OF
CHARLOTTE DODGE

Oct. 4, 1977

I DIDN'T BELIEVE it when Cash told me, and at times I still
don't, but the court had its say, and that's what we have to
live with. By the time Cash gets out, I'll be thirty-four. You,
baby, will be six years and six months, if you are born on
time. Seven years without parole. It seems a bit much. Callie
Anne may have been only fourteen, but Cash was only
nineteen and it was nearly eight years ago! He's almost
twenty-seven years old himself! No leniency because his
wife was having a baby, either. None. Not one drop. Cash
might as well have been fifty and Callie Anne ten and it was
yesterday, because that's the way the judge treated it. Seven
years. Seven years inside a minimum-security prison.

I am almost to my first trimester with you, my first baby.
My husband, Cash Dodge, your daddy, is on his way to the
Eagle Mountain Correctional Facility near Baker City, and I
have a cherry orchard to tend, hogs to raise big enough to

slaughter, a pair of horses, and now I've got to find myself some kind of paying job. This is not remotely close to what I signed up for. Writing letters to you is the only way I can think of to keep myself from going crazy and to give you in some future day a way of understanding what you were born into.

Oct. 6

Well, they do let them make phone calls, and today was the first, and Cash was pretty sullen. Still, his voice on the other end of the phone is one of the things I love about him. His voice in general, really. He only has to mumble and a little fireworks show takes place in my gut. That's a good thing, although keeping a love fire going over the phone is one of the least sure things I know of. I tried it once when I was a teenager. A boy named Rick Belden who came to speak at our church. He was awfully handsome. Dark haired, blue-eyed, and a talker. They had him in all the way from Indiana to tell about how he got himself out of drug abuse. Giving testimony, we were taught to call it. The Cove Assembly of God at that time was big into bringing in addicts and alcoholics who has been saved by Jesus. Now that was always something that intrigued me, how people got themselves messed up on drugs and then suddenly overcame it they minute they give their lives to Jesus. Not that I don't doubt the possibility, I just doubt the probability. I tried drugs. M.J. Marijuana. You'll learn when you are older it's sometimes called different things. Cash said he tried to grow some once when he was just out of high school, probably about the time he took up with Callie Anne, but he said it didn't amount to much. He had heard you could put foil and an incubator light in a closet. He didn't have a full closet to devote to it, so he lined a big packing box and stuck it behind his shoes and under his shirts and jeans. Once every day or so he raised the lid to water it. Him putting that level of effort into something he's curious about or cares about is typical. Same way he delivered our shoats and blew breath into them. Same way he herded our pigs into the cherry groves because he believed hoof beats and scat benefited the ground and trees. "Salmon feed the bears, bears feed the trees," he always says. Didn't surprise me to find out he poured his fish tank water into the soil of that little plant, too.

The thing about Rick Belden was the exciting life he'd led. He came up to me after church that morning and said he couldn't get his eyes off of me during his entire speech. I had noticed him sitting more or less sideways in the pew trying to get a look at me. I wore my green and white dotted Swiss that day. A dress I sewed myself. He asked me what that material was, and I told him. Cap sleeves and a Juliet waist. A u-neckline my mother said was too low. I let him, *LET HIM* run his finger around the edge of it. He slipped a piece of paper with his address in my hand before he left. Odd enough, he lived in New Albany, Indiana, where I've been many times because my father had cousins there. One of them works as a doctor for the Kentuckiana County Fair Rodeo Association, and several times as kids we went to watch her work. We used to take summer road trips to visit his family when I was little. I still remember every bit of those hot, dusty summer drives. I would get so carsick. It took five days. We had a little pull trailer. Some of it was interesting, seeing the sights and all, but some of it was misery, until we arrived, and then it was always lots of fun. All of my cousins and their parents and grandparents have southern accents, and by the time we left, we did, too. I've been back a dozen times by bus and train since Mom and Dad died. Dad's Uncle Jessup in Nebraska won't hear of anything else. He mails me a ticket for some mode of transportation every few years as his offspring regularly hold a family reunion at a nature preserve, about an hour's drive from New Albany. One cousin who is about my age comes from Kentucky. Mercy Grace. I particularly enjoy her, and we have much in common as we both enjoy farming. She is smart and a very innovative person who works with women who served in the war in Vietnam.

Because of this coincidence, I think, I began to view myself as married to Rick. Strong enough that after four or five letters, when he managed to get himself another invite to our church, I let him take me down a long road up above Elgin and sat with him in his car. You could say we went to new territory together. I thought I had peed and apologized to him. "No," he whispered to me, "you're all right. You've done everything just right." I was willing to breach my virginity with him, and I told him so. I knew about condoms. I'd seen packages of them in a box hidden under underwear and socks in my father's bureau drawer. I'd heard about the secret things men and women do to each other. We could easily go back to my house and get one.

To his credit, he wouldn't have it. "No," he said, "We'll be glad if we save it." We went on courting through the mail until one day the preacher who was in charge of Rick's drug rehabilitation program wrote a letter to my mother and told her that he had just intercepted one of our letters and that he thought my parents should know that Rick was not who he made himself out to be. That he'd been in trouble with the law, was on probation for robbery and selling drugs. I was to abstain from all contact.

Of course, I ranted and screamed and hollered and lay in my bed at night with my fingers, remembering. No point writing letters since my parents made no bones about the fact that they would see to it I hadn't two nickels together to buy a stamp and would take away my bicycle so there was no getting to town—and at fifteen miles nothing would make you want to ride that far in the summer heat for a stamp and a mailbox if not love.

If you are reading this, I am dead, and you are a woman, so you might as well know that your mother was human, too, once young with the same urges you have.

So, came the end to my first try at long-distance romance. I relished the experience when it came to Cash having to go to prison, phone calls being all we're going to get for a month or so until he "acclimates" as the Family Transition Counselor called it. Your father. Immediately started calling the woman the FTC, like the flower delivery people. Well. There you go—fine example of his goofy sense of humor.

Anyway, time to bear up.

Oct. 9

I thought I'd keep track of the news. Is it big-headed of me to think my own child might want to know my thoughts for seven straight years? You might also one day be interested in the current events of this time. Here it is, nearing 1978, and nobody knows what the '80s are going to bring. We all imagine nuclear war and humanity evaporating. Preachers are saying how close it is to Jesus's return, and I don't doubt it a bit. Perhaps this diary can serve two purposes: keep a promise to you and a record of end times.

Which has me writing this morning with the paper open. In today's paper is an article about bones found in Montana. The bones were in the mountains about twenty miles cross-country from the hot springs at Lolo. In a rockslide. They think they could belong to an Indian woman whose husband was a fur trapper. Some speculate he might have killed her. He wrote a book about her, but that's not the way he told the story. Nobody could ever find where she was buried all these years, even though people had looked for her, which of course fueled the notion that he tried to hide evidence. She was the only woman to be shot and survive the Big Hole Battle. You can look that up for yourself. It's a sad story about the Nez Perce Indians who lived in Wallowa County, Oregon. I know archaeology, at least a bit. I started to study it at Eastern Oregon State College, but then I learned I couldn't make any money at it.

Oct. 10

Today, unborn baby—Jayne or Jarrod or Lucy or Luke or Cassandra or Cash, Jr.—grief reached out its black claws. I turn to God in times of despair. I guess most people do. Faith is pretty powerful. I once heard a preacher say what is important is possessing faith, no matter what you have faith in. You could have faith that the ground you stand on will support you. Maybe I brought this period of time on myself as I didn't have faith in Cash's ability to manifest what he wanted to do—grow the cherry trees and raise the hogs and remodel this house and build a barn and keep fifty acres from returning to the wild. I thought we were too young to take so much on. His father, Burrell, said the same thing. Right at our kitchen table. I didn't know Burrell knew about Cash and Callie Anne at the time, but he did. One of the things the judge brought up is just how many people around Cove knew about those two and didn't make an issue of it. Cash insisted at the trial that even Callie Anne's parents knew, but they turned around and swore under oath that they didn't. Poor Callie Anne. She's a classic example of what jealousy will do. Maybe if Cash and I hadn't married, she wouldn't have turned him in.

I bawl and I bawl. Your daddy just learned he won't get to live in the same house with you in seven years when he is released. Burrell and Suzette are already making plans to set him up in a trailer on their land. Because Callie Anne was a minor, he will have to stay a certain distance away from all children, even his own. He will be able to have visitations, supervised visitations. But until they are sure he won't "reoffend," he will not be able to live in a house with children and won't be able to come within five hundred feet of a school. He won't be able to come to school plays or concerts unsupervised, not for parent-teacher conferences—none of it. Cash Dodge, your father, will be a ghost in your life until the judge decides he is not a threat to you. Even if it turns out that you are a boy.

I've been poring over my mother's diaries. Why isn't she here to help me? Her entries say the same thing again and again, that there is no predicting what life will put on us. Marilyn Jeffreys at the post office whispered to me the other day that I ought to get a divorce. Maybe she's right. I could just get a divorce. But what would it solve? Cash would still be your father. He'd still have a right to you in limited ways, not that anybody else thinks he'd ever hurt you or any child or even a flea as far as that's concerned. Cash Dodge won't even kill a spider! He jars them up and takes them outside, turns them loose. I've seen him bawl like a newborn calf when he had to drown a pup that was so badly deformed it would never walk.

Truth is, I'm not so certain that what he did was altogether wrong. I hate it, sure. Was Callie Anne under-aged? Sure she was. Obviously. But they were kids. He was still a kid. Maybe over eighteen, but kid enough. It sure as hell wasn't molestation. As everyone has been saying, Suzette and Burrell included, you can't rape the willing. People know her to have thrown herself at every boy in town. What we called in high school your basic slut. I hate using that word, but it's true. She was a few years behind me in school, and I've known her all my life, and she's forever and a day been after the boys. Boy-crazy, is what we all used to say about her, and emphasis on crazy. What we know now is that her daddy beat her all the time and her uncle did all kinds of wrong things to her, got too close when she was little and those things affect a person's psychology. But is the uncle in prison? Nope. Is her father in prison? Nope. So, tell me how these things are your father's fault? How is it Cash Dodge's fault? You can't find one person in this entire valley who can give a good answer to that question. He said he pushed her off as long as he could, and I believe it. This is a small farming community, most of us have known each other since birth, and we all saw her coming up, saw life had made her into something different from the rest of us, and was Cash weak? Was your father weak? Yes, you could argue he was. That doesn't make him criminal. That doesn't mean you and I should have to suffer for it, that your life, in particular, should be marred and impacted the way children are marred and impacted when their fathers aren't present, that you should suffer the scrutiny of school children the way you will, the way children treat other children when something about them is off. You'll be taunted because your father went to prison. The story will get turned around every which way and far from truth, and you will suffer for it. You will suffer and every time you come home crying and bloody, we will all die a little more. I can see it now, and it's why I'm running through boxes of tissue like water and why I'm taking time to write this down because if I don't, I think I will fall to the ground and give up the ghost right here on the spot. Because I think that someday you will want to know. That you will want to know that I loved you enough to stand by your father. I don't believe in divorce. I believe it's wrong. I pledged *in sickness and in health* and this time right now is just a kind of sickness. If I trudge through these years, you will learn more about what it takes to survive in this life than if I don't. So, yes, I'm staying for you, and we will, as a family, survive and no regrets.

Oct. 16

The sun shines bright this morning, like it can't help but be a happy day. I woke up early, 4 a.m., headed to the sow pen to feed, and got there just in time to see the new one, Elsinore—which your daddy named after a famous theatre in Portland for some reason, again, an example of his goofy sense of humor—drop a farrow of piglets. Can't really call them shoats officially until they're weaned. Which is about all I know about them, and I got that part from the dictionary and Cash's high school collection of encyclopedias. No idea they were coming. I guess in all the commotion your daddy hadn't noticed or wasn't told when he bought the sow. Or just didn't tell me? When I see him, I'm going to double his ear over. I don't know how to go about caring for newborn pigs. Best I could think of was to wash them and lay them beside her, but she wasn't having none of it. You do not want a three-hundred-pound sow chasing you off her babies so I let her be. Waiting for it to be late enough to call Burrell, your grandfather, and catch him before he goes to church. Hopefully he can tell me how I at least keep Elsinore from rolling over on her own offspring, which is my fear. The happy part is that those babies mean money. If I can get them through the winter, they'll bring nice green dollars a year from now.

Oct. 19

Rain. Days and days and acres of rain. Caught myself a cold. Trip this morning to La Grande to see the obstetrician. He advises not to take cold tablets, just to let it wear itself out. I suppose I caught it looking after the piglets. It gave me the excuse in any case to go to the library to look up a few things. Burrell and Suzette ended up being out of town over the weekend. I hadn't known that. So, no help that first couple of days. Somehow all survived.

I love a trip to the library. Found a row of helpful-looking books on hog farming. A couple of novels plus Emerson. Had a thought to read him again. He makes me feel hopeful. Also picked up the book written by that Indian woman's husband. The Nez Perce woman whose skeleton was found on the day your daddy left for Powder River. *PRCF*. The book is called *Hell of a Paradise*. I'm curious to read it. Something went through me when I saw the article about that woman's bones.

Oct. 31

Thought I'd never get over that cold. Ended up in the doctor's office again and again. Finally sent me to the hospital for an x-ray—they are very skittish about giving a pregnant woman an x-ray. They lay a big, heavy drape with a layer of lead inside over your vital parts. The weight made it hard to breathe. Came back pneumonia. Dr. Gillespie quizzed me on me becoming pregnant when your daddy was headed for prison. "How could you be so stupid" was the meaning behind what he was asking, but of course he was just doing his job. Health isn't just about your body, he said. It's about making healthy choices.

You might as well know it, if you don't already by the time you're reading this. Living in a small town means everybody knows everything. Of course, the papers published a play-by-play about your daddy's trial and the sentencing, even down to mentioning that Judge Sinclair wouldn't allow anybody in his chambers except Cash and me. That was kind of a big deal, too. Some questioned whether it was legal. It was quite the controversy and even made mention on the editorial pages of Portland papers and who knows where else. Had to do with the law that governed his sentencing being newly ramped up and his "crime" being so old. Some law-makers thought Cash ought to be grandfathered in, so to speak, like he shouldn't be affected by a new law, rather he should be held to the laws that were in place during the years of his dalliance with Callie Anne. She was fourteen years old, plain and simple, and he was eighteen in the beginning. Old enough to know right from wrong, both of them.

Honestly, I think the problem was much deeper, and I tried to tell Cash's attorney, and he brought it up to the judge in front of the jury and found himself in contempt of court with a big fine. The Portland editorials said Cash should have gotten a change of venue. You reading this now are old enough to know what that means, but I had to ask.

It was eons ago, but the Judge, Gerald Sinclair, is actually the son of a man who was once and for a very brief time married to Cash's mother, Suzette. Like I said—long ago. Suzette was a teenager, then not even sixteen. Well, what Suzette told me was that the man, Gerald "Stormy" Lassiter, had raped her. Did she or her parents go whining to the law? Nope. Did Stormy have to stand before a judge? Nope. Instead, he and Suzette were forced to marry, part of it being based on the fact that they were both Catholic, and although she lost the baby almost right away, they chose not to have the marriage annulled. That was the way they handled things in those days. So, what happened to Cash is a bad thing for us, but a good thing for women, because it's a sign the law is coming around to favor women.

Stormy Lassiter came with a son, barely a year old, named Gerald, Jr., the mother of whom had signed over custody and run off. Suzette said she suspected the boy could actually be Stormy's brother or the child of one of his sisters. She never found out. Stormy got killed within the first few months of being drafted for Korea. He drowned during boot camp, and she was left with a baby boy to raise who was not her own. Fighting in wars. So many of our boys lost during Vietnam. The entire Cove High School football team got called up at once. Sequential draft numbers, all got their notices on the same day. The rumor is they got drunk and went skinny dipping here at our local hot springs—but first they painted their draft numbers all over themselves with markers. Supposedly their mothers scrubbed them with bleach but still couldn't get the ink off. I've heard the story many times about that group of boys standing naked in a row for their physicals in Portland two days later, the rest of the recruits and commanding officers and physicians laughing their asses off. Who knows how much is true, but this much is fact: only about half came back alive.

Suzette's family living in Cove, Oregon, goes way back. They were among the original settlers and helped to forge relationships with the Umatilla tribe, who used the Grande Ronde Valley as their summer land. I guess you could say the Umatilla were the original summer people for this region. Anyway, Suzette didn't want Gerald, Jr., to associate with Stormy's people, who were somewhat down on their luck, their extended family living in a string of trailer houses above town, so she went before the judge and easy enough got guardianship, changed her name along with Gerald, Jr.'s. They both took on her maiden name Sinclair. Gerald, Jr., became Gerald Sinclair period. She got a veteran's widow's benefits and sent him off to military boarding school. She didn't feel like the money belonged to her, given the nature of her marriage to Stormy. About the time young Gerald graduated and went off to West Point, she met Burrell.

But before that, way before that, at least the way the story Suzette tells goes, Stormy had been born with an abnormality. Horrible hernias that stuck so far out of his abdominal wall he couldn't bear to be on his feet very long, else they start throbbing and risk strangulation. A strangulated hernia, as I learned in my anatomy and physiology class in college, is a death sentence if it's not treated immediately. I saw photos in a textbook of what one of those looks like internally, so I know firsthand what a frightening thing it must have been. I guess the neighboring farm kids made a game of carting Stormy around in a wheel barrow to "save" him from the monster trying to break through the wall of his gut. Old Mr. Lassiter, Stormy's father, did not believe in modern medicine, and gave Stormy's mother strict orders that she was not to take the boy to a doctor. If God wanted him healed, God would heal him. Old Man Lassiter finally did give in and allowed Stormy to have a surgery to correct the worst of it. Stormy came back cured, but then he did some kid's thing he wasn't supposed to—who knows what—and Old Man Lassiter beat the devil out of him and busted open his surgical site. The hard part—and the part I can't believe coming out of any parent—is that Old Man L. refused to get the kid help. Stormy lay there for weeks with fever and his intestines falling out with his poor, tired mother trying to nurse him, feeling sorry for the situation, and the Old Man would not allow her get him to the hospital. When I heard that story, I thought right away that raping Suzette was Stormy's anger from his childhood coming out in that obscene way, just like his guts has tried to fall out.

Anybody with a brain could argue that there isn't much connection between Gerald Sinclair as he exists now and who he was at birth as Gerald Lassiter, Jr., By the time he was a grown man, he barely even knew Suzette existed. Suzette told me that once he went to West Point, she sent checks to the school's accounting office and had the receipts to prove it, but that was about it. With Gerald, Jr., being so ungrateful, Suzette didn't put out any effort either. But still, anybody with an imagination could conjure how it might be possible for some of his old unconscious feelings to leak into current situations. He may not have any true relation to Cash, in fact was no place near him in any way until the time of the trial, other than in the way that all people in a small community are near each other, and Gerald Sinclair had been living in the Grande Ronde Valley at that time for a span of years. Even if he did only travel in judgely circles and Cash only travelled in teenagerly circles, it certainly seems to me that Judge Sinclair never should have been allowed to oversee the trial, and Cash's attorney is even right now working on having it declared a mistrial and also an appeal to a higher court. Suzette has been mute on the subject. She carries on like nothing's happened, but the truth is that a boy she had guardianship over put her biological son in prison.

Antibiotics took care of my pneumonia. I'm weak but getting over it. Elsinore chewed the head off one of the not-yet-shoats. Burrell said pigs'll do that sometimes. It's a sign the sow won't be able to raise the young one. Either means a bad winter, or the sow for some reason senses she otherwise won't be up to the task of feeding and rearing that particular piglet or the offspring is deformed or in some other way ill-fated. Usually the weaker of the two, and this was definitely the case. Cute little bugger. I started calling it Little Pop and another Big Kernel. Couldn't help myself. Pigs eat corn, you see. That's your daddy's sense of humor having an effect on me. I wrote him a letter about it. The sight of that little piglet's head lying loose on the ground brought up a new round of morning sickness. Here I thought I was about done with that. Don't know what Elsinore did with the body. Burrell said she likely either ate or buried it.

Nov. 1

Baby Child, it's like you felt my suffering yesterday, and responded by making your presence known. I've been wondering what it would feel like, those first little kicks, and it's just like the books say. Like butterfly wings. I'm not quite as flat-bellied—I was a beanpole of a kid—and if I lie face down on the floor, it feels like an apple or an orange in there. Kind of off to one side a bit, but definitely a *something*. You are real! Not just a mark on a lab report. You are the actual beginnings of a live human. I was so happy I called Burrell and Suzette and got them out of bed. I wish I could have called your daddy, but I have to wait until the regularly scheduled time. So, another letter to him, which is why this entry to you is short. I had Suzette take a Polaroid of me sideways. I've got enough strength back after the pneumonia to herd leaves into the orchard. That's a job that involves not only a rake but the tractor and Cash's pull-trailer he built.

Nov. 2

Who knows if you'll live in this house long enough to remember it. I'm worried about my ability to make the payments for seven years by myself. Hopefully it isn't romantic to think you'd want to see the house you were born into through the eyes of your mother at the time of your gestation.

Well, it is just an old farmhouse, really, built in 1894, but I have a love for it. Drafty in the wintertime, steam radiators hiss, as does the plumbing, both of which were added after the fact, but it has a summer kitchen with an old-time wood cookstove still hooked to the flue where I do my canning, and a parlor with wood floors and bay windows, and the bathroom has a claw-foot tub, and the garden soil is so rich from the generations of women forking under their kitchen scraps that every seed puts forth a bounty. In fact, one of the ways I plan to add dollars to the in-column on my budget ledger is to expand the garden and open it up to u-pickers.

Other than that, it's painted white, like most old farmhouses—whitewashed, as Suzette still calls it. Two story, although to save on fuel oil for the boiler, I'll either close off the upstairs or take on boarders, like they did in the old days. That last one I'm not so fond of, but if I could find myself a job and take in people to help me work the place, well, I suppose I would. I started out on the road to nursing school, but when Cash came along, I let the idea go. I did work as a nurse's aide when I was going to college, which is a job I could easily get certified to do again.

The inside of the house is covered with layers and acres of wallpaper and coats of paint. I've started the long job of scraping it off to get down to the lathe and plaster, a look I like much better, and the kitchen is done, since that's the room where I spend most of my time. The original color is that old milk paint, kind of a hazy pale green that was common to the era, as I've come to know from reading remodeling books at the library. They bought a powder, and it bound itself to the fat in cow's milk—real cow's milk, of course, not that supermarket crud. How I hate the taste of that stuff. Put that next to what's in the pail from Jessamine every morning and night and you've got the difference between ants and trees.

We talk about it, all of us who are trying to keep doing things the old way, about why the government thinks you have to pasteurize milk. None of us ever got sick from it the way they say we could. The day I give up Jessamine's milk is the day I'll take up marching in Washington, D.C., with a sign, and it's a day the old-timers insist is coming. Politicians deciding the best way to sell milk. To quote Burrell, "It's the stupidest thing I've ever heard of."

Luckily Oregon is a long way from D.C., and I doubt anybody's going to come haul me off over the jars of milk I sell, or the ones in my fridge, or the blocks of butter I trade to Suzette for her home-milled flour.

Cash is the one who wanted this place. It's the way he proposed to me. I was living in La Grande going to school at Eastern Oregon State, but I had a weekend job as a nurse's aide here in Cove at the Sisters of Grace Retirement Home. I was the relief for the three duty nurses who shared the job during week. It was easy—taking blood pressures and handing out pills to folks who were basically independent but still needed a bit of oversight. They shut its doors after the big Sunday storm in '76 brought a pair of ponderosas down on top of the church side of the building. It was an old building with lots of what they call "deferred maintenance." No services during part of the winter because the boiler was old and coal-fired and didn't generate enough heat to keep the frost off the insides of the stained glass. Still, it was a pretty church that held many memories, and we all hated to see it go. Plus, everybody loved Father Cobb, even if he was a bit cranky at times and complained loudly about skinny dippers at the hot springs. I think we loved his crazy hair more than anything. He looked like Einstein, something he and Judge Sinclair have in common. They both as they aged ended up with wild, crazy, heads of white hair.

Father Cobb was also just plain good to everybody and would organize potlucks to bring the farming community together with the townspeople, as well as clothes and food drives and book drives for school kids. He didn't give a hang if you were Catholic or not, he just wanted you to come and join whatever he was putting together. He believed an active social community to be a community of hope and support. When the Church said Sisters of Grace Retirement Home had to shut because it had been running at a deficit and the repairs were too costly, Father Cobb one by one helped a dozen residents find similar living situations in La Grande and Elgin.

The only human casualty the night of the big storm was old Mrs. Rebbin, a former school teacher who had a heart attack and died before anybody thought to check on her. We all worried about that for a long time, how scary the sound of those trees falling must have been.

Nov. 10

Everyone fears it's going to be a long, cold winter this year. I'm almost afraid to stop at six cords, but I have to. I told Burrell to quit cutting, because I can't pay for any more. He just laughed at me, since, probably obviously I'm not paying him for the cutting, only the fuel for his truck and the Forest Service permits, which isn't that much. He doesn't even want me to do that, but I pay my way. Meantime, I'm bringing in a woman, Doris Blessing, because I know once you're born, we're all going to need the help. I know, it sounds like too much of a coincidence, the name, but it's true. I asked for a blessing, and he gave me many, but most currently, he gave me Mrs. Blessing and you. She doesn't know what she's doing in her life, really. She left her husband, who was a good man but a drinker (why do you hear that so regularly? *He was a good man but a drinker?*), then he died in his sleep one night—heart attack or stroke, she didn't say which—before she filed papers. So, she got some money from his insurance and was able to sell their house for a profit—she didn't want to keep it after he died in it. But then, she had to have some place to stay, so while trying to figure everything out after becoming a widow at sixty-four, she decided to save what was left after funeral expenses and rent for a few months. She hadn't had any means of seeing to herself other than Blue, her man, she says, but she likes to think of herself as self-sufficient, too, and she says if she knows anything, she knows to go slow when making big decisions. These are all things she said to me sitting at the kitchen table.

Putting in a private entrance into the upstairs may be trouble, in terms of time and mess, but I hope it will be worth the money and the insult to daily existence. Your Grandpa Burrell is going to help put it in, and we still have a handful of hired men from cherry season who haven't moved on. These are people who come back to the Grande Ronde Valley year after year, which means I know them, so having them in the proximity of my living space doesn't bother me. In fact, we have a feast at the start and finish of every harvest with these folks. Some bring their families, live in old RVs—we take only men in the pickers' quarters—and there isn't a year passes that we don't have the health department out for a picnic to talk about health care services for migrants. You get to know people and you grow to love them, no matter the differences in your ways of approaching life. I call myself a Christian, but sometimes I believe in the reincarnation way of thinking about things. I learned about it in my world religions class at Eastern Oregon State. Some religions believe that our souls come back around and keep running through life like it was a rock tumbler. Cash has one of those things out in the shop. He's been that way as long as I've known him: picks up pretty rocks and brings them home to polish. One year for Christmas when he was a kid, Burrell bought him a used rock tumbler for polishing stones. We have old flower vases and Mason jars full of them around the house. They're like good luck things for your daddy. I imagine when you get big enough, you'll be fascinated with them. I love to hold one to the sun and pick out the various shades and sparkles and colors. You can't see the detail of a rock unless it's polished. Reincarnation is supposed to work like that. You keep getting born again until your soul is spit-shined. Our preacher at Mt. Emily Assembly talks about being born again, but I don't think he means it in the same way. In fact, I know he doesn't. To the Christian faith, being born again means buying the history of Jesus as told in the Bible as truth. I confess to believing it, but I have questions. One lifetime is too short. The heaven and hell business has me baffled. It seems they might have their meanings confused. If you've got a heaven and you've got a hell, you've got several dimensions of existing, right? Well, that right there implies something counter to what they're saying, because, what happens *after* heaven? What happens *after* hell? They say eternal lake of fire, but how long is eternity?

I have this idea that time doesn't exist. The calendar is invented. Anybody who farms or breeds animals knows the cycles of the moon have more of an effect on God's creatures than any calendar pages. I can tell you when Julie, our old sheep dog, is going to come into heat. Happens every sixth full moon. Cash says I'm imagining it, so I started keeping track. I suppose after I've been around the horses long enough, and the sheep, I'll see the same thing. The milk cows, well, I don't know. We keep them artificially stimulated, so it's hard to say.

Anyway, we take good care of our seasonal employees, and we pay them well enough, so when it comes end of harvest, and we need help, no question one or more of them is going to be willing stay about and help.

Nov. 15

Finished painting the upstairs. The doctor wasn't sure about me doing it and exposing you to paint fumes, but we've had unseasonably warm days, so I threw open the sashes and went to work. Mrs. Blessing was going to help, but she had meetings about her husband's estate. It didn't matter. I love putting up paint. The way the upstairs is configured, with two bedrooms and a bath off a single hall, makes it an easy switch to boarding rooms. Mrs. Blessing is going cook for us, too, so in exchange I'm giving her the bigger bedroom on the south end with the corner bank of windows and the sitting area. She seems well thrilled by it and thought it worth the exchange, so she'll cook during the week, and I'll take weekends.

Well, the first visit with your daddy. Let's see. He looked pretty good. Better than his voice has sounded over the phone these last weeks. He was happy about the boarder idea, and happy to know I'd found Mrs. Blessing. He laughed, too, at the name coincidence. Cash is a much more faithful person than I am, and he keeps saying he believes nothing but good will come out of all this. He says he's been reading his Bible and praying, that there's a scripture study group and a prayer group and another therapy art class of some kind. He says prison is not as people imagine. He says it's not like TV, not where he is. He says everybody has jobs and hobbies. Some men make the best of it and try to get along, and some struggle with loneliness and depression. Some are manipulators and try to get your goad and some are scared and some take classes and plan new and better lives for once they get out. Those who create trouble are moved. It's minimum-security, so the men serve on work crews outside the prison ground. If the powers think you can't be trusted or are an escape risk or if any tiny thing is off-color, you find yourself getting shipped to Pendleton, where more of the ugly stuff does take place.

That's what he's telling me, but I see the dark circles under his eyes, and I see the way he's holding his shoulders less square than normal. I felt his back when I hugged him and the tightness in his neck and shoulder muscles. He's used to being in charge, making decisions. He's a good man, your daddy is, and you have to always know that. I do not believe he deserves to be where he is, and your grandpa Burrell and I have several attorneys working on it. Goodness knows how we are going to pay for it, but the point stands that people around here know it was no more statutory *rape* than this desk I'm sitting at is. There wasn't no rape to it. But law is law is law is law. I wish he could feel your butterfly wings flapping around in there. He tried but he just couldn't, but he did tear up when I tried to tell him how it felt, how it's gotten stronger over the past week to where it feels more akin to a little egg beater whirring around in there. He grinned over how big my breasts have gotten, which made us want each other. At one point the guard cleared his throat, so I know it was a little too obvious. I shouldn't be writing this down, but who knows—maybe you'll end up never reading this thing at all because maybe such things just won't matter. Maybe it will only be me, at the end of my life, and I'll be glad as a crinkly old lady that I can look back and remember a time when I had those kinds of sensations in my body.

As for the painting, well, it looks pretty good upstairs. New white on the mopboards and trim, dusky peach in Mrs. Blessing's room, pale gold in the unrented one, and a faint yellowy cream in the bath and hallway. I didn't repaint the floors. Too much work and they aren't that bad anyway. Hasn't been that much traffic up there since we bought the place, and they're a nice dove gray color that matches the rest of the new paint anyway. In fact, the whole upstairs has a feel to it that I'm kind of glad to have reason to bring about. If I were a tenant, I'd be proud to live here. I took snapshots to show Cash, and he approved. Burrell has to take a chainsaw and carve the new door out, so the upstairs is draped with plastic sheeting. It's like walking into a bread bag.

Nov. 18

Did we ever get tripped up with a surprise snow dump! Got the doorway opened up yesterday, and that was the end of it. Burrell had to close it with insulation and wrap the water pipes. Started about mid-afternoon. Was a clear, blue morning, then the sky clotted and started sleeting, and then big, quarter-sized flakes began. It was warm enough during the day to where you wouldn't expect anything to stick, but cold, night-time temperatures can seal the deal. The goats and pigs were loose in the north pasture, and the horses and Jessamine were loose on the south end. Burrell and Raul were up on the scaffolding putting the new doorframe in. They planned to drill staircase braces before dark. Jaime was in the shop creating risers and runners plus landing underlayment. Burrell posted a flood lamp, hoping to continue working after dark and finishing the job before bedtime, but they were so drenched and cold by the time the doorframe was in that he just had Jaime cut a door-sized piece of insulation and roofing tin and sealed it up that way for the night. It worked pretty well, because I had not a bit of breeze through the downstairs ceiling vents, which I expected to, and the downstairs stayed plenty warm.

It's the kind of weather we tend to get here in the Grande Ronde Valley in November sometimes. Unpredictable. I've read about it quite a bit, the history of the Grande Ronde Valley. I've become more interested in this Nez Perce woman, Lah-tis-i-yet, who was married to this Albert Garza back in the 1800s. He was a fur trapper. They found her bones right around the time Cash went to prison. A hundred years her bones were lost. I was thinking about her last night, sitting here watching the snow through the big picture window on the east side of the living room where the company dining table sits. I kept thinking about the snow falling on her bones that first winter. The Nez Perce were Indians that lived during the summer not far from here, over to the east in Wallowa County. The Grande Ronde Valley is the place where the Nez Perce, the Umatilla, the Warm Springs, and the Paiutes came together in the summer to trade and pow-wow. They called it The Peaceful Valley. I've always had an interest in the original people of the world. What happened at the hands of the whites was wrong. All the colonizing. As if whites were a virus. A relative of my family belonged to one of the tribes back east. A multiple great-grandfather on my father's side. Daddy came out of the mountains of Kentucky. His brother is the father of my favorite cousin, Mercy Grace. The more I think about Lah-tis-i-yet, and the more curious I am. Who was she? What was it like being in the middle of the Indian wars, running from the U.S. Army, leaving your dead people behind? Here you have a good glimpse of your mama. That was me, last night, watching the first snow fall of 1977, your daddy in prison, and me by myself in this big old house.

At least the hole is cut open. It won't take much tomorrow for them to get the door hung and the rest of it done. Snow won't stop Burrell. Sleet, yes, but not snow.

January 14, 1978

Well, happy new year! As you can see I'm faithful as a hen from time to time, and then, all of a sudden, gaps. I've read enough diaries of settler women moving from back East to the West to know that's how many of them did it, too. Work has to get done, and it's hard to justify the time it takes to sit to make a record or to make sense of things on paper. The short story is that the snow has been here for most of the last two months. I have shoveled and shoveled, spread salt and spread salt. The path to the barn and pig shelter has been flanked by thigh-height drifts since Thanksgiving, and we are now in the middle of our usual January cold streak, so the temperature has been near zero or below since New Year's. Beautiful, of course, and magical, but you are getting so big and my torso is magnified to the point that it is no longer suitable for my usual clothing. I don't know which extends further, my breasts or my belly. I laugh at the pregnancy book that says, "You may notice swelling in your breasts." I have gained two cup sizes. Two! That talk they give you about how you have to be careful about how much weight you gain? Forget it. I'm only six months in and already I've gained thirty pounds. Mostly in my boobs.

Still, I manage. Mrs. Blessing has moved in upstairs, and she's a big help. The rent she pays brings in extra feed and cord wood, so although finances are tight, I can glimpse a hint of possibility that we'll arrive at spring with our savings intact.

Cash is well as can be expected. It's dangerous for me to travel over to Baker to see him, but Burrell drives, and we take the four-wheel, and so far, so good. We had a long visit with Cash and his attorney. They're still talking about an appeal bond, but I don't see it. Another article came out in the paper this week about how steep the legal problems are now for people who commit crimes against children, and Cash's is classified as a "crime against children." I mean, I'm a pretty capable woman, even young as I am, and I just turned twenty-seven on January 4, but this is flat tough, this staying on here in this house, trying to keep the animals going and thinking about hay and feed and realizing I completely forgot to finish carting leaves off the lawn and over to the orchard beds. Well, I didn't forget, exactly, but the snow came and never left before I got to it. I know what this means—fungus in the lawn—and cherry trees with cold feet. Burrell thought I shouldn't be so alarmed over it. He said the snow would protect them, but I became obsessed one night when I was over at his and Suzanne's and bust out crying like the bereaved for the dead. Seriously. Suzette said she had never seen anyone keep at it even after falling asleep. I guess Burrell went and explained things to Mrs. Blessing and shut down the house for the night, and Suzette put me to bed on the couch. I don't remember a bit of it, other than I woke up the next morning feeling like I'd been beat to shit. I find myself wondering what it feels like to be drunk. To drink alcohol. I don't know if I am to survive this or not.

January 22

You were early. And you are not normal.

March 30

Before I go on, let me say one thing. I love you. So does your daddy. Nothing in the sky above or the earth below can change that. But when I first saw you, when they could not get you to cry, and I saw your strange hand, I did wonder what I had done to deserve all that has been put on me. I'm not even twenty-eight, and in one year I've seen my husband behind bars and given birth to a child with a *syndrome*. A *disorder*. You aren't home from the neonatal nursery yet. I'm writing this from Portland, from Northwest Children's Hospital. I'm living in a place called Hill Street Cottages. It's housing for the parents of ill children. You aren't ill so much as you are just small. You were born at thirty weeks, as if my body, when it figured out something was wrong, tried to spit you out. Nature works like that. Right after we were married, Esther calved a two-legged thing at fifteen weeks. You were breach. My nurse was rushing to get ready for a caesarean section because your heart rate bottomed out, then, with no warning—chaos. My nurse told me later that your butt cheeks were showing between my legs. It felt like a bowling ball trying to get out of there, and I could feel and smell the blood strong as butchering. One of the nurses yelled, "She's hemorrhaging!" and that's the last I knew. They said I "coded," which means I lost so much blood my heart stopped. If it weren't for the advancements in treating cardiac arrest in the last ten years, I wouldn't be here. Later I learned you had the cord around your neck. At some point neither of us was breathing. Your grandparents, Burrell and Suzette Dodge, were in the waiting room. They heard people yelling and running with carts and they both started praying. Suzette said she felt a hand on her shoulder but there was nobody there. Burrell said he felt something similar. They both thought it was the hand of God telling them we'd be okay. It wasn't another minute before the ward clerk came to say your daddy was on the phone. He'd been given privileges because of the situation. We were still in La Grande, at the hospital. The nurses set up a private spot in a conference room for Burrell and Suzette to explain to Cash what was going on. Brought in cots so they could stay the night.

We named you Bethany Grace, after my cousin Mercy Grace, but also after my great-great-grandmother Bethany Grace Hardsaw Murrell, who, along with my great-great-grandfather Benjamin Murrell, came over on the Oregon Trail from Kentucky. I think it fits you, and it fits our situation since even getting through a day right now feels like it takes the pure grace of whatever God is out there. Plus, it's a pretty name, and you, even as tiny and undeveloped as you are, are a very pretty little girl.

April 12

Now you have a feeding tube. It turned out you have a cleft palate and can't nurse, can't take a nipple. You are too young for surgery, so they stuck a feeding tube down your nose. I hook to an electric pump every two hours and squeeze out the breast milk, then they have me push it slow into your feeding tube with a large syringe, similar to the kind we use to artificially inseminate livestock. Jessamine has to give birth once in a while to keep giving milk, although, since Cash has been in prison, we've been giving her hormone injections. Burrell has been helping oversee our operations, and with me being pregnant, I've just let him do things the way he sees best. He doesn't like to artificially inseminate, and I don't want some big bull mulling around my pastures, scaring the geese and the goats. I hate the way bulls act when the females are in heat. Makes me think of a bunch of drunk teenagers, and when I think of drunk teenagers I think of Callie Anne, and I don't need her memory in my mind any more often than it has to be.

She came up here. Can you believe that? Of all the gall. Came all the way to Portland and the Hill Street Trust Cottages to look me up and tell me how sorry she was. Burrell and Suzette happened to be here in my little apartment at the Cottages. Burrell yelled and grabbed her by her long, yellow hair, and carted her to the parking lot, screaming the whole way. By the time he got her shoved into her car, the cops came. According to Burrell, she was bawling and sniveling and one cop was talking to her while the other was talking to him, and by the time Burrell had finished his story, the other cop went over to her and said, "Young lady, you did these people a grave wrong showing up here, now pull yourself together and move on." Burrell said he about fell in love with that cop in that moment. Said he shook the officer's hand and promised to make a donation to the Hill Street Trust Cottages in his name. I imagine by now Burrell has, too, because he's just that kind of person. I hate feeling so bad toward Callie Anne. I mean, she's a woman, and her problems are all connected to a man, and I know how it is between men and women and how women get mistreated. She told on Cash out of pure meanness, out of spite. I believe what she did inspired the devil. Whether that influenced the way you turned out, I don't know. I worry about painting the upstairs while I was pregnant. Turpentine and oil paint. I asked the pediatrician here whether that caused it. Dr. Cadena. She heads your care team. She said nobody knows what causes the "constellation" of conditions you have. She said we live in a complicated world. Dr. Gillespie in La Grande told me to stay away from chemicals, and I didn't. I mowed, planted, sprayed, and did the things we always do. And I painted that danged upstairs.

Plus, as winter grew on, I became fond of sitting by the fire with my night-time brandy.

April 14

Dr. Cadena had asked me to see her this morning at ten, and so I did. I've lost count of the number of visits and consultations, the forms and the questionnaires. I've talked with surgeons and pediatric gynecologists and hearing specialists and urologists and physical therapists. Dr. Cadena said this morning that they've finally decided on a name for what you have. She says it's likely not my fault. Just a thing that happens. She said it's connected to genetics or simply an accident. It's a long name, but the short of it is EEC Syndrome. One of the nurses photocopied pages of a book so I could read about it. Your hand is called a lobster claw in laymen's terms, but officially it's *ectrodactyly*. You are lucky because you have your thumb free. Sometimes people don't. Your three middle fingers just look like tiny balls. When you are older, the surgeons will remove them. They say there is no reason you can't live a normal life. The cleft palate can be repaired, and they say you are lucky because you don't have a cleft lip. So that's one of the E's and the C. The other E is for *ectodermal dysplasia*. It means you may have stringy hair or undeveloped fingernails or teeth or sensitive skin or scaly patches. Your fingernails look fine and so does your hair. Burrell and Suzette have the prayer chain going at church, and they've called the 700 Club hotline, so hopefully we won't have to worry about the rest.

To me, to us, to your daddy, who now has pictures of you, and your Grandpa Burrell and Grandma Suzette, you are beautiful and perfect. Your eyes are big and blue and wide awake. Dr. Cadena expects no problem with your intelligence or your mental ability.

April 16

Portland this morning was bright, sunny, cheerful and buzzing, Bethie. Nobody would know the rooms in these high-rise buildings house the worst human misery and the saddest of human stories. Life on Hospital Hill, which is where the big medical university and Northwest Children's Hospital sit, was busy as what I imagine New York City must be like: full of workers getting to their jobs, beginning and ending shifts, carting fresh lunches or empty pails. Full of anticipation or anxiety, depending on their relationship with their work. I see them from my room here in the Hill Street Trust Cottages, white uniforms and blue scrubs, hefty-soled shoes designed for the wear on the body a life of being on your feet all day brings. My own shoes are my dressy ones, black slip-ons, somewhat clunky, I guess, looking like they belong to a woman who lives on a farm, like someone who keeps them in a closet in their original box.

April 17

I don't know if time is my friend or my enemy right now, Bethie. I look in the mirror, and I don't know who I'm seeing. I'm a mother. I get that part. Similar to most new mothers, I am deprived of sleep. But I am also deprived of my husband, deprived of my home, and in a way deprived of you. I've come to hate that electric pump. It hurts much worse than likely you would. I want to put you to my breast, but the nurses say it might confuse you. I don't want you to be confused. I'm confused enough for the both of us. My body doesn't belong to me anymore. It belongs to a machine. It has a sound and a rhythm, like Burrell's electric milker. I shouldn't hate it. It delivers a part of me to you. But still. I have to wake up every three hours. This is an improvement over every two hours. I'm tired. I beg the nurse to come and plug me into it herself. To carry either me or it via the elevator and plug us in. But, no, I have to set my alarm, get up, go downstairs, cross the street, take another elevator, and plug myself in. I fall asleep every time. The charge nurse offered to let me sleep through the night and to give you formula if I wanted. I can't let myself. It feels like a failure. So, all day long I keep to this schedule. Everything else— holding you, eating myself, bathing—comes in between. Your nurse tonight said it is not in my best interest to keep up the routine. That I will be no good to you if I collapse. I asked her how on earth I am to take care of you at home if I can't do it here with all this help. With all these machines, all this technology. So, I keep it up. It feels like years, and it's not even been two months.

Every day seems to bring more bad news. Bethie, at this moment I don't know if you'll ever read these words. Today it was your heart. You have a false vaginal opening and you have a hole in your heart. A *patent ductus arteriosus*. More surgery. The hole in your heart won't cause any problems yet, but if it doesn't close on its own—which they sometimes do—it will keep you from growing. The false vaginal opening is the rarest, and it will come first, otherwise your own secretions will cause infection. You have labia and a clitoris and what looks like a large hymen but which is actually a benign tumor. The toss up is whether after the removal of that they'll do your heart next or your cleft palate.

Meanwhile, Burrell and Suzette are working to keep my place going. Mrs. Blessing is taking care of the house, but she refuses to interview boarders. If she hears of someone, she'll tell me, but she's too worried about the other chores she's taken on to concern herself with an ad and with fielding phone calls. I don't blame her. She's milking and keeping up with my butter, cream, and egg orders. She's also feeding the horses and keeping the water thawed. It was wickedly cold, but now spring is coming up. I told her don't bother with the garden, but she said she'd take it on, cook for the hired help who'll come in with the cherries, and generally oversee the place—in exchange for free rent. Who am I to argue? Burrell and Suzette are doing their part, and other folks: the farrier is shoeing the horses at no cost to me; that saves a bundle. Mrs. Blessing said somebody dropped off two cords of wood. I had laid plenty in, but it will keep.

I think about spraying the cherries, about hatching chicks, about whether the roof will hold another year, about weeding the flower plots and getting the ads out for folks to come pick blossoms. That was my idea, and Cash didn't seem to mind. I figured if you could advertise u-pick for strawberries and peaches, why not flowers? We put an entire acre into tulips and irises, and another one in zinnias and hyacinths. It's amazing how many people drive in from La Grande, Union, and Elgin to cut their own bouquet. Even Baker and Pendleton. I get two dollars for all a person can hold in their fist. Three for a gallon bucketful. Sell bulbs in the fall. I've had people come from Enterprise and Walla Walla. It's a nice Saturday or Sunday outing, I guess. On a lark, I put in a row of Shasta daisies. Nothing prettier than a stand of daisies. I almost hate to sell them; always keep a handful in a mason jar of water for myself.

Bethie, honey, I think I'd be okay if I could get you out of here and take you home. Dr. Cadena said she's going to send another type of social worker to see me, one that helps with adjustment. I don't feel adjustment is possible as long as you are not in your natural environment.

April 23

Well, Bethie, finally some good news today. The nurse is pretty sure you tracked her finger when she moved it from your nose to your ear. You are a bit late with that skill, but she said it's not unusual in preemies. She's going to report it to Dr. Cadena. It's a point in your favor.

Got word your daddy is going to be shipped over here. His attorney took it before a judge and determined the state would allow it. He'll hitch a ride when they transport some mentally ill prisoners to the state hospital at Salem. He'll be here the 28th. I'm so excited I can hardly breathe.

April 29

I guess I'm starting to figure out that life is a series of both sad and happy changes. No matter how much you might want life to stay the same, might want to sit in front of the fire of an evening in your chair with your cup of tea or curl on the sofa with a good book, bad times are coming. You will be stretched and pulled far beyond what you imagined your limits to be. If you're lucky, you find out what you thought was solid about yourself was in truth elastic. If you're not lucky, well, then, you learn exactly how brittle you are, and exactly what it takes to break you. Burrell once told me he thought it took three years to heal once a person broke. He never defined how he came to know that, but I thought it might have had something to do with his younger years. We do stuff in our younger years.

Things an older version of ourselves might think twice about. In church it falls under the category of sinning, and we're supposed to abstain from it. Did I sin when I married Cash Dodge? Can loving be a sin? I'll bet a thousand million humans have asked that question. Was it you, Bethie, I felt pulling me to want him?

Cash and I grew up in the same one stop-sign town. Not a town, really, because we're both farming kids. But we went to the same school, sat in the same church pews, pulled in with a carload of friends to the same drive-in theatre in La Grande, ate twirled vanilla ice-cream out of the same silver sweet-milk machine at Creamtop Burger Shack, where all of us teenagers loved to show off our freshly-waxed cars and trucks on Saturday nights, even if for most of us, they did belong to our parents.

I have known Cash Dodge for so long, I don't remember when I first saw him. We had to have been infants, but we didn't know each other until later in school. I do remember him coming up to me to tell me how sorry he was, after the accident, after my father and mother decided to take that back-road Sunday drive without me, a date, a little afternoon break for them, before Dad swerved to avoid hitting the deer or the bear or the elk or the cougar or whatever it was that sent him and Mom barreling off into the hereafter. I was a teenager, still desperately wanted and needed them both, and Cash was always passing me funny notes, trying to make me feel better. They said my mother bit off her tongue; Daddy was folded over onto her, his hand smeared with her lipstick, her cheek awash with blood. Burrell said the coroner told him Mom died first. Dad's hand was clutched to an opening in her side where he tried to hold her life into her. He was known about the area for his generosity. "He'd give up his shirt and button it for you, too," people still tell me. I have often thought about those last moments, Dad watching the blood of my mother flowing, seeping onto the floorboard of that funky old Studebaker he loved so much. For a long time, Burrell kept a photograph of that car taped over his tool bench in the tack shed, where he repairs buckles and replaces brass studs and grommets. I don't know why he held onto it, although I know my father was a good friend to him, and that Burrell's family had come out of the same part of Kentucky as Dad's earlier generations had, before Dad's parents moved to Indiana.

It's awful to have to watch your husband walk into a white-walled hospital room in prison denims and handcuffs with a uniformed prison guard eyeing every move. The guard acted like Cash wanting to see his newborn baby daughter and wife was a wrong against society. But then, he probably had a gut full of watching those bad others in the van on the drive over, keeping them from acting out their various criminal craziness on each other, and from what Cash told me on the phone this morning—since they did let him make one last phone call to me from a phone booth while they gassed up here in Portland on the route back to Baker, since it was a local call—was that there had been trouble on the ride over. One of the mentals smuggled on what Cash called a "shiv," which is a piece of sharpened metal or altered hand tool meant to serve as a weapon. Cash said people in prisons become very inventive with these kinds of things. They make a kind of liquor they call "pruno" out of anything that will rot. Some find ways to have sex with each other. Yes, Delicate Ears, some men let themselves be used like women. I didn't see anything in the morning paper, so it either was not newsworthy or it was not reported.

He looked like, well, like he did after he had meningitis in high school. It was a big thing, because we all had to take antibiotics. His team had travelled to Pilot Rock to play football, and two of them came down with spinal meningitis, as did one of the Pilot Rock players. It was caught early but is extremely contagious, and worrisome enough that it made the papers. People die from meningitis. Anybody who'd been around the football team had to get doped up with pills to prevent it from spreading. I remember Cash came back to school looking shriveled, and Burrell or Suzette drove him to school and picked him up in the afternoon for the rest of the school year, rather than letting him wait out in the weather for the bus.

Of course, being Cash, he downplayed his looks, said it was called "prison pallor" from too much time indoors. "Cash Ezekiel Dodge," I told him, "I've known you long enough to know better." But he wouldn't tell me anything more, just if I had a chance when you got out of the hospital to bring him over a basket of fruit. A basket of fruit! Now isn't that funny? I thought it was a joke or a pun or a secret message, but I laid awake last night turning it over in my head, and I still can't make hide nor hoof of it.

What else came of his visit? Well, he got to lay eyes on you. He fairly well burst into crying. The guard surprised us all by tearing up, too. At that point, he left us alone in the NICU and stood outside the door, and even though he wasn't supposed to uncuff Cash, he did. "I'm a daddy, too, Dodge, so don't go making nothing of it," he said. Told Cash there'd be hell to pay if he breathed a word, and Cash swore he wouldn't. We got to embrace, and Cash got to hold you. Bethie, he bawled and bawled. I hadn't told him half of it, but I had to then. He said surely it was enough to pursue a new motion from the judge. I told him I didn't know, but I'd be behind him if he did. Anybody who knew rough, tough Cash Dodge from the past would not believe seeing him sitting there in his prison denims with that number on his chest and the brackets around his ankles and a nearly handless baby three months old and not even ten pounds lying there across his arms and him bawling and bawling, heaving from deep in his ribcage, like a kid with a jawbreaker some bully had just stomped to bits. The guard did tell me on the way out that the ankle chains were only necessary because they had to transport Cash with mental criminals. Funny the way he told me that, as if an explanation made any of it better.

June 10

Sometimes I swear I hear someone crying. Not you, Bethie. But a woman.

Aug. 1

Yes, the summer is full on us and just about gone. Bethie, Bethie. Lord. What has happened since I last wrote. So, first off, you decided to come back to us. On the hottest day we've had all summer. I feel it, but I don't feel it, the heat and Portland humidity. I took some time off after your daddy visited. Bethie, I love you more than my soul, but I got so tired. Went back home. Mrs. Blessing and Burrell and Suzette had done just fine getting the garden in and tending the flower crop, but the place had been overrun with flower pickers. People came this year from as far away as Spokane, they said! Just on account of you! On account of wanting to help us out and lend support! Amazing! But that was the least of it. I felt like after nearly six months for my own good-keeping I should take a spell and sleep in my own bed. The day after your daddy came to see us you had a heart attack. A heart attack! In a tiny baby! They said it was that hole in your heart letting blood pool in your ventricle. They said it had never been done before, heart surgery on one so young or so small, but if we were willing to sign for it, for an experimental procedure, it would be free, as would all your follow-up care from now on. I didn't want you experimented on, Bethie. Never in a million centuries. But we were out of insurance, siphoning off what was left of the money from Mom and Dad—which, to Cash's credit, he always insisted I not use, that we keep it untouched so our children might have a college fund, but I saw no other recourse.

So, Bethie, we signed you over. They put you in a drug-induced coma, put you on a ventilator to keep you breathing, put you on an ice blanket to lower your body temperature to where your metabolism was near nothing, bypassed your heart and ran your blood through a machine to keep your brain and kidneys alive, and fixed the hole in your heart and the one in the roof of your mouth. We let you be a medical experiment. You were too young for all of it, but it was your only chance.

Fourteen hours. For fourteen solid hours, Burrell and Suzette and I sat there. They had Cash sitting on the phone at the Powder River Correctional Facility. We had that feeling again, all of us, each of us, of that presence, the one Burrell and Suzette had when I was delivering you, of a solid hand on each of our shoulders. It sent what I would describe as a chill through my mid-section, like I'd been flushed by a shivery wall of 7UP. Like a spirit passing through or what I'd imagine a spirit passing through a human might feel like. Burrell thought it was my mother or father or maybe both. Suzette thought it was an angel. Or God himself.

Then you didn't wake up. You didn't wake up and you didn't wake up and you didn't wake up. This went on for days. Every time the doctors tried to take you off the ventilator, you went into cardiac arrest. They resuscitated you with drugs and electro-shocks four times before they finally decided you were on the ventilator for good. None of us left the hospital to even so much as shower. The surgeons came and stood around us in their scrubs and surgical caps time and again and shook their heads. They didn't know. They couldn't understand. Dr. Stark was the leading cardiac surgeon in the country. Dr. Hammond was the leading pediatric cardiac surgeon in the country. They had studied and studied. A very similar surgery had worked on several babies who were only barely older than you, Bethie, but no heavier and no further along developmentally. They said time was on our side. They wondered if we could suspend judgment. "Who knows what that little gal has going on in there," Dr. Hammond said. "If I've learned anything in my work as a surgeon, is that miracles can and do take time, especially in the case of preemies."

So, we waited. I waited. Burrell and Suzette went back home and ran things on both places. The summer workers came and—can you believe this, Bethie? They banded together and came to Burrell one night and tried to give him several thousand dollars to pass on to me. Twenty-five percent of what they had collectively earned for the months of June and July! We don't pay those poor people but minimum wage, plus a small commission on our crops. They tried to give us the cut they usually send home to their families. They come up here to do harvest labor so they can send money back home. Most of them spend very little on themselves, other than what it takes in gas to get from one place to another. We cook for them while they're working for us, so most of their wages are profit. What they send back home is meant to feed their families all year! They were going to take money out of the mouths of their own children and wives and mothers. Of course, I told Burrell under no circumstances was I going to take it, but he said they got very upset. Said all they were giving back was their commissions. I finally told Burrell to take the cash and put it in a special account, and we'll buy new bunk mattresses and give them a small raise next year. They don't have to know I didn't use the money myself.

The hard part was that Powder River wouldn't let Cash come back to see you, but they let the Hill Street Trust Foundation send by courier an audio tape explaining the surgery and its potential aftermath. Hill Street Trust has kept me alive. The other mothers. The grandparents. The ministers who come and go. The children who've been through cancer hell and survived and who come around to hug and read us stories. I guess I'll never get the smell of hospital sanitizing solutions out of my nose, that red stuff they call Betadine that they swipe around your various scalp IVs, thin as spaghetti, as everyone who comes in here smells like it. *No reason*, they'd been telling us for months, *no reason* she does not wake up. Except you didn't. Until yesterday, pretty much right about the time I arrived back here at the house. What else could I do but grab a bit of sleep, repack the suitcases, and return back along I-84 and the Columbia River corridor and Portland again. I thought it would kill me. Honestly, Bethie, I was so tired I sobbed like a baby myself when I found out I had to turn around and drive back. I'm sorry. I truly am. It's nothing against you. It's just that there is only so much a person can take. That lasted five minutes. You bear up, you know? Suzette and Burrell tried to get me to wait a week. Cash over the phone begged me to come see him first. I've got one thing on my mind, and one thing only, and that is to look into those peepers of yours again and finally, for the first time in your little life, put your chirping mouth to my breast.

January 8, 1979

Well, Happy New Year, Merry Christmas, and all that. Now here it is winter again, and you are back in Hill Street's.

Which is the roundabout way of saying, that you did come home for a spell. A few months. But your inter-cranial shunt got blocked for the fifth time. It gets backed up with gunk and your head circumference can balloon in a matter of days. They finally replaced it. Your doctors have been holding off because they hoped you'd outgrow the need for it. The surgeon told me today that she hopes by this time next year she'll see you in surgery to remove it. Meantime, I had to go see a doctor again myself. I haven't had my period, and no way I'm pregnant. Can't get pregnant in a prison visiting room. Well. I suppose you *could*, but that definitely is not the case. Stress, he said, and I just laughed at him. "Well," I told him, "if that's the diagnosis, then what's the remedy?"

He just smiled and said, "Charlotte, you are too thin. You need to go eat a pizza or two." Well, I didn't eat a pizza, but one way I know to put on weight is to eat more bread, so I asked Mrs. Blessing to make a pan of cinnamon rolls from my mother's recipe and to double the vanilla icing, which she did. I ate three of them in the car on the way here, then gave the rest to the nurses. It didn't make my period start up, not so far, but it did make me feel better. Sugar high.

Now I know you likely will never read this, Bethie, since they're telling us you are showing signs of what the pediatrician called "significant developmental delay," but I've started the habit, so I'll keep going. The hospital in La Grande where I've been trying to hold down a job has been good about letting me have time off. Doctors in La Grande have been able to deal with your blocked shunt up until this time, so I've continued to work shifts as much as possible, even with you in our very hospital as a patient. Mrs. Blessing has been wonderful. We all tease her about her name. She kept the whole damn show running this past year. Neat as a pin. I love her. She's gentle and warm but so damned capable. I'm sure she's the way Mom would have been had she lived, I'm just sure of it. Bethie, I promise you I will not leave your side. We'll get through all we have to get through. They've already told us we may not have you long. You don't exactly have cerebral palsy, but something akin to it. Some kind of brain damage from lowering your metabolism and running your blood through that machine. They told us ahead of time that fifty percent of infants who have open-heart surgery end up with CP. So, we knew the risk. Your situation is a bit different. Not exactly full-blown CP, but not exactly not, either. Time will tell, they said, how severe your problems are. So far there's no sign of the palsy part, just the developmental delay part.

Cash is so broke up they had to put him in the infirmary. I guess he blacked out when he got the news. Then he got into some kind of fight with the orderlies and had to be restrained and then went into some kind of spell—a catatonic fugue, they call it. His caseworker said it was a temporary response to stress. He ended up in the state mental hospital at Pendleton for thirty days. Now he's back at Powder River and on some type of depression drug. I wish we could get him out. The appeals, well, that drags on. Takes time. His attorney remains optimistic, but I don't know anymore. Burrell called yesterday to tell me a citizens' group had formed to fight his sentence. No way I'm getting my hopes up, but Burrell and Suzette felt pretty touched by the gesture, and I guess I do, too. Still.

Snow's two feet deep, Burrell said. Started falling almost the moment I drove off. And with it the annual cold snap. Dropped below zero. Wind chill into the minus thirties. Said he could skate to the barn if he wanted to. Crust got that deep that quick. Makes me glad for the Hill Street Trust Cottages. Never would have thought I'd get to know a place like this.

Should be all of it for a while, Bethie. We'll get you back home in your own little room. With the new shunt we shouldn't have to worry about blockages, and the level of fluid collecting on your brain has dropped significantly over the months. I may have aged twenty years in the last two, but you will perk up, they told me. You will grow, but you will not be like other children. You might or might not ever know your colors or count to ten or say your ABCs, but one day, you will be over all this initial stuff. So, the cleft palate, the hole in your heart, and the vaginal opening. All done. Eventually they'll do the plastic surgery on your lobster hand.

January 9, 1979

I don't know that I believe doctors all the time. This morning, Bethie, I left Hill Street Cottages and took a long walk in the freezing Portland fog. Below zero in Cove on the east side of the state translates to freezing fog here, I guess. It's like a crystal palace. The entire world is covered in what looks like thin glass. The trees, the shrubs, the streetlamps. I saw on the news this morning that homeless shelters are overflowing, and two homeless people were found dead from sleeping on the ground last night. In a park not that far from such a huge medical complex. Right here on Hospital Hill. It made the walk a little more unsettling than it otherwise might have been. To think of those poor wandering spirits.

After your surgery to replace the shunt, the doctors are now telling me to expect the worst, to expect that you might not even live to see your second birthday, that I shouldn't count the twinkle in your eye as recognition and the sounds you make as potential words, but I believe they are not looking at you right. I see changes in you every day, and they say I shouldn't mistake "anomaly for increments." I swear to you, that is what one resident said to me. Well, posh. I'm not going to trust the opinion of somebody who's still being trained, anyway. They are talking like city folks. I may still be young, but I've been around long enough to have seen a miracle or two. If a sow bites off the head of an offspring it instinctively knows it can't raise or won't survive, then why might a human not have an opposite instinct? Know her baby is going to survive and thrive despite odds?

None of that is what I thought about as I picked my way around the trails on Hospital Hill this morning, through the small parks that dot the area, places where, I'm sure, on good days, hospital workers bring lunches and share their crumbs with the pigeons and squirrels. Where they found the bodies of those two frozen homeless men. All these big, warm buildings, and they couldn't think to duck inside one of them—or one of the many-storied garages?

What I thought of was your daddy and Callie Anne.

You can't pick and choose the things in life that befall you, but you can choose what you let bother you. Then there are other things, the ones the effects of which you can't control, the ones that, unbeknownst to you, form a tiny leak in you, like a little one-hole sieve. Invisible, but they can turn you into your own shadow. You can sense the leak, but you can't actually feel it, can't describe it, so you invent language for it, imagine it. Some days you feel like you are alone on a high cliff, nothing left in the world but you and the sea. Other days you imagine yourself a black forest, so dense you can't see between your own trees. Once in a while you feel you might be beginning to glimpse that leak, the teensy portal through which the substance of you dribbles out, knowing if you can see it, you can plug it closed, but almost as soon as the vision presents, a kind of gauze descends, and in a flash becomes a machete, hacking off the vision, and with it, the entire population of possibilities for your life. You are left empty as a rusted barrel.

What did they think, once their tongues touched, those two, Cash, at eighteen, my future husband and your future father, Bethie, and Callie Anne, voluptuous and boy-crazy at fourteen? How ironic that the one thing Callie Anne gave so easily, that part of herself that she had so little respect for, was the very thing you were born without, that surgeons had to unblock for you? What does it say that you were born with a hole in the heart but not between your legs? I ought to be able to understand. Like there's a connection, but if it's water it's full of salt, you know? Because I can't see my way through at all. Not well enough to craft meaning.

What was the essence of that initial touch? Was it a morning glory, ripening in early stillness? Was it honesty's most pure form, like a housecoat and old slippers—trusted, reliable? Familiar but not forlorn? Why did Cash not see and want and choose me first? He certainly knew me. What was it about me then that failed me? Why did he not recognize me and us and by the mere fact of my existence *choose me then*? What is it about men when they are around women like Callie Anne? Why could he not, at eighteen and nineteen years old, perceive of what would happen were he to actually *sleep* with, have sex with, put his erect penis—his baby-making, life-wrecking, erect penis—inside a young woman fourteen-years old? Again and again and again? Two years! Two years they went at it! Back of the barn! Burrell's hayloft. Maybe even the same road my mother and father died on. Who knows? Part of that time, Bethie, and this is what bottom-of-the-bucket actually slays me, Cash Dodge was also putting his erect penis into me. Telling me he loved me. Begging me to marry him. *Verboten* didn't translate to English for him. Burrell says a stallion might as well be a gelding until he rides a mare the first time. Maybe the same thing holds for people. There's an invisible gravity beam that keeps hauling you back. Like getting hooked on dope or cigarettes.

These are the same thoughts I had in Judge Sinclair's chambers, too. Now and again it washes over me. Judge Sinclair had me come to the sentencing because he said Cash's crime was against an entire family—me and you included, Bethie. We were all sentenced to serve the next seven years in a prison. Cash isn't the only one behind bars. Why I planned to stand beside him, Judge Sinclair said he didn't know, but I must have been daft to have opened myself up to him, to Cash, to accomplish "this, this *thing*, this *other thing*" as he put it, eyes to my belly, which at that point wasn't yet obvious, so that I wasn't in the moment exactly sure what he was referring to, since he was looking at me from over the top of half-lensed glasses which magnified print for him without apparently interfering with his concept of the rest of the world, and that appeared to be the most stable thing about him, the way his jowls moved and wavered as he talked on and on. The lecture he gave about Cash's responsibility to me and to you and the way Cash ought to be ashamed, forcing himself *yet again* on an unassuming woman (really? did he actually think Callie Anne was *unassuming*? Did he think *I* was unassuming? Suzette and I talked it over and over, believe you me) and then Judge Sinclair had the gall to drop on us then and there the fact that Cash would not be allowed visitation rights to his own child! A thing which obviously had to be side-stepped when they brought him in to see you at Hill Street, but he laid it out: your daddy was not to be allowed to live in the same house as his own child—son or daughter—until that child reached the age of accountability, which in Oregon is twelve years old. He sat there, his eyes glaring at us over the top of those half-moon glasses, his wild, crazy Einstein hair so light and white and airy it filtered the sunlight beaming through the window behind him, creating the effect of an aura, or a halo. Like Jesus or the Madonna. Cash, seemed to take it with the designed resignation he told me he'd decided to adopt about the whole situation. "This is not a witch hunt," Judge Sinclair then said. "This is the fate you created for yourself." I wanted to wallop him one, but I didn't. Down at the root bottom is the fact that what Cash did was to hurt my ego, which is what I finally decided this morning on my walk. Simply put, I wish Cash had wanted only me.

January 10, 1979

Bethie, it's still the weather holding us back, keeping us from going home, and you are sleeping. Since I no longer pump myself for breast milk, I now can sleep when you sleep. The nurses at night feed you formula. They wanted me to try you on a bit of rice cereal once you'd recovered from anesthesia, to see how you'd do, and you took to it right away. It's the one thing about having a child like you, Bethie—they want all your firsts done under supervision. If you tolerate the rice cereal without problem for a week, then we can add bananas and so on. I can't believe in just a few short days I will get to take you back home, almost for good! A nurse will resume coming out to see you a couple of times a week to weigh and measure you, make sure your head circumference stays down and to make sure you are growing but not too fast. They don't want to you to gain too quickly, which they say could happen with the addition of solid food. A quick bump in weight could also mean congestive heart failure, which, so far, you've shown no signs of, but apparently sometimes it's hard to tell, thanks to the atrial fibrillation which you will now always live with— a result of the heart attack, which was actually caused by the atrial fibrillation, which sometimes goes with a hole in the heart. Poor little snookies. What a lotto card you drew.

But what made today a banner day was that you smiled. The nurse was holding you in her lap, and I was feeding you the rice cereal, and you lifted your little face at me, at your mama, and you smiled. "No way that was gas," the nurse—Patrice was her name, she's been with you from the start, and her little girl is seven and has Down's—said, and that just made you smile bigger. "It's a milestone," Patrice said, "may be a few months late, but that was a bonafide smile. And lookit that. She's got teeth coming through!"

Sure enough, there at the crest of your lower gums, right in front, were two shiny, whitish rims trying like anything to push their way through. Two little March crocuses. The resident didn't want me to make too much of it, the smile or the teeth, but Patrice said, "Don't you dare pay him mind. He doesn't know diddly. Next thing you know she'll be trying to sit up." Then you lifted your chin and smiled at us again. At *me*. You smiled at *me*, Bethie, you smiled at *me*.

January 14

All this time, and I have not been to see your father, Bethie, so when we get home, that is just about the first thing we are going to do. Burrell and Suzette did not want me to drive back with you alone, even though Shriners outfitted us with a special car seat and a contraption of a hat to make sure your head stays warm but that your shunt is not disturbed. It looks like a beanie with a little chimney, basically.

They took the passenger train from La Grande to Portland, just so they could ride back with us. With you and me and the yards of diapers and blankets and extra beanies and balloons and teddy bears and flowers and the gracious mountain of gifts from all the other Hill Street Trust Cottage parents we've become acquainted with over the months.

Even though you came home for what was going to be a while, I had not closed down our little studio unit until now. Suzette, bless her, couldn't help stripping the beds and scrubbing the shower, even though the resident social worker insisted it wasn't necessary. Pearl. What a warm, caring, gentle woman. She was originally from Atlanta, very southern. Said her parents had immigrated to this country from Tangier, in Morocco, when she was a little girl. They were medical researchers. Her mother was French; her father originally from a village in Zaire. Both ended up working at the Centers for Disease Control in the U.S. Pearl trained as an RN, then got her degree in social work so she could work as a counselor. Her laugh could be heard a block away. I loved to get a laugh from that woman. So infectious. So beautiful! I wanted to give her a gift, to thank her for all she did for us. "Honey, you were the gift to me. You and your baby girl. What you don't know is that I think your little Bethany is special. She's going to talk to you one day, I know it. I sneak over to hold her every chance I get. I sneak over and hold all the babies. Which is why I know so much about the ones who have a chance and the ones who don't. That little Bethany? She does have a chance.

There are angels on this earth, and Pearl is one, Bethie, but she's only one of legions of angels who abide on Hospital Hill in Portland, Oregon. I hope some of them follow me home.

February 3

We made an agreement, Bethie, no Christmas presents this last holiday season, except for Cash and you. We pooled the money we had each budgeted, and Burrell, Suzette, and Mrs. Blessing drove to Boise to buy books, chocolates, and toiletries for Cash, and a crib mattress and nursery fixings for you. I had my colors decided on. I wanted sort of a raspberry with pale lemon. You can't find raspberry and pale lemon in La Grande. Not enough shops and not the traditional girl colors they carry at the department store downtown. We could have ordered from the catalog, but we wanted unique and handpicked just for you, Bethie. You've had your head shaved since you were born because of IVs and the shunt so that none of us realized how much of a redhead you are. Yep. Bright as a copper penny. You still can't have hair around the shunt, but you no longer need an IV, so the nurses stopped shaving all but that immediate area. If you do grow up to read this, you might wonder about that shunt. The science and medicine of it isn't quite clear to me, but part of your *syndrome* includes what's known as *hydrocephaly* or water on the brain. The shunt drains the water from your brain into a large vein, so that it can be carried out of the body by the kidneys. I've looked at so many anatomy charts and plastic figures that I can't even count, but this is the way your doctor explained it. She likened it to hooking a garden hose to a portable sump pump to drain a flooded basement directly into the septic tank. Which made Burrell laugh because he'd drain that water into a field, but oh well.

Of course, your crib is handmade by Burrell. Every rail and spoke hand-turned, hand-rubbed, and hand-stained and varnished. I had no heart for telling him I wanted it painted white. Around here, it's all about wood grain. Not one soul knows I do not care for the dark cherry finish he put on your crib, and not one soul ever will know. That's the way I mean to keep it.

I'm feeling a little tired, Bethie, but let me see if I can capture your homecoming.

First, as I've already told you, they made that trip to Boise to outfit your room. They got my raspberry paint I asked for and unbeknownst to me and without asking, really, painted the walls above your wainscoting with it and then the wainscoting and trim and doors white. It was pretty and so perfect I nearly cried. Well, the truth is, I did cry. Then Mrs. Blessing had taken lemon yellow chiffon and made not only breezy curtains for the windows but somehow managed to cover roller shades with the same fabric. She says there's a technique she'll show me one day, but I can't get over the suspicion that she had them custom made. I know she can sew very well, but I just don't see where she'd have the time to do it all. Then she found every little bit of lemon yellow that exists on the face of the earth, and I'm telling you pillows and rocker seat cushions and teddy bears and receiving blankets and sheets and bumper pads and throw rugs and curtain tie-backs and little dresses and sweaters and bonnets and socks and booties, and she rolled up what could be rolled up and tied them with lemon-yellow satin ribbons and piled every bit of it into this monster of a raspberry pink wicker basket. She took photos of each of us and put them into tiny frames and made them into a mobile and hung it over your crib—and the mobile arms she hand-painted raspberry as she did the frames. On the walls are a lemon-yellow moon and stars dotted with little raspberry polka dots. Burrell said he felt like he was in a sherbet factory, but Bethie, the whole thing turned out so cute. Cash had bought an oak rocking chair before he got locked up when he first found out I was pregnant and so that was there, along with a beautiful white afghan Mrs. Elmer from down the road made for me. I asked Mrs. Blessing how on earth she got it all done and in such short order, and do you know what she said? She said she had a feeling all along that you were eventually coming home, and so she banked on it. She'd been working on that mess of gifts from before you were even born!

Then I got another surprise when I opened your closet door, because stacked from ceiling to floor were packages—

gifts from people all over, apparently, who heard about you or read about us or were in some other way privy to the circumstances surrounding your birth. What I didn't know until this morning is that Suzette has another closetful at her house. She was worried about overwhelming me with it, so she waited until I'd had a chance to settle in before she told me. She and Mrs. Blessing have been keeping strict track of what came from where, and they've been steadily sending out cards telling people their gifts have been received and that they will hear from me as soon as I've had a chance to open them. Oh, and get this—Mrs. Blessing has already addressed the thank you cards for me. All I have to do is open gifts and write a tiny note of thanks. I've never seen so many presents in one place in all my life. I have no idea what we will do with all this stuff, or even where to store it, and in the case of clothing, some of the newborn things you've already outgrown.

February 8

Oh, my goodness, Bethie. Today I walked into your room and you were sitting up! Your visiting nurse was here. We were chatting in the living room while you finished a nap. We heard you cooing! You were cooing! And what do we find when we hurry down the hall to investigate? You, sitting up in your crib. She was so startled she called Dr. Cadena, who said something she'd never mentioned before, and that is that once you get out from under the "artificiality of the hospital environment" you could very well begin rapidly catching up on your development. She cautioned us that we should not be overly optimistic, that sitting up is a milestone to be expected at six months, not nearly thirteen, which, she added, and rather coarsely, I thought, on a standardized test would put your IQ at roughly 50.

Well, you know what we all had to say about that: *BS.*

February 10

Finally. Home is solid and secure. You are here. Mrs. Blessing is here. Suzette and Burrell are in their place and continuing to do all they do. I have an ad in the paper for a boarder. Haven't got the room decked out, but that will come. Right now, I'm trying to figure out the best way to get to Baker, to the Powder River Correctional Facility to see your dad. Trying to decide whether to take you or whether to bring photographs, of which I have scads, of course. Trying, trying, to figure out how to reach out to this man I no longer know. A year and a half! It's a year and a half, and I have been to see him only six times. Too much for one life, you know, Bethie? There is only so much a person can do.

February 14

Oh, Bethie. Now I know things will never be the same. Your father, he is—changed. I guess it's the lack of sun, but even his hair looks different. Darker. He told me they have him on two pills for depression but that they make him— they have some kind of effect on his man parts. It's called *priapism*. Not to be crude, but it's an eternal erection. Long story short, Bethie, I went to see your father, and I am just heartbroken. His attorney, Pete Frame, came over yesterday, and what he said was just astonishing. The Oregon supreme court denied the appeal. I can't stop the rush of feelings. He said he wanted to kill himself, and if he keeps that up, he could find himself transferred to the state mental hospital in Salem, which is not a place anyone would want to be.

Anyway, the pills shut him down. He's just this side of a zombie. Oh! He was so bright and young and handsome! Hair always sun-bleached, always muscled and browned from the sun. I miss that man, Bethie! I don't know who this new person is! I wasn't married long enough to get to know and appreciate his quirks and talents. Mrs. Blessing talks about how she misses the man her husband once was. She was trying to commiserate. But nobody knows what this feels like. Nobody! I look at that little lobster claw hand of yours, those little knobs where fingers are supposed to be, and I think, what fate, what monstrous fate would bestow such a thing on such a precious little soul as yours. Then I stop and think, what kind of monster fate would cast such a thing on such a capable and loving man as Cash Dodge. A man with so much love he couldn't contain it to just one woman? I think of Suzette and Burrell and how painful it's been for them to stand up in the community, to go to town, to church, to be known as the parents of a criminal? One who has let his tragedies overcome him? Do I dare think of me? Of myself? I'm not even thirty! Some people I went to high school with aren't even married yet! I have a farm and livestock and a disabled child and a husband in prison and I hold a job, too, and now I'm having to take in a second boarder. When does it end? When is somebody besides a ghost going to lay a hand on *my* shoulder? I'm almost glad you won't live to a grown-up life because at least in the condition you are in, you can be happy and smile. What if you have an IQ of only 50? You are smiling and at peace.

June 14

Well, let's see. We butchered Elsinore, I guess that's the big thing. Let me tell you about raising hogs, Bethie. Don't ever try it. They are intelligent, dear animals most of the time, but once in a while you can get one that turns frightening and mean, and that was Elsinore. She just wouldn't stop eating her own babies! Three years in a row! When I walked out to the pen one morning last week and saw the torn head of three more piglets, I decided that was enough. No more hogs. It's hard on Burrell who is such a premiere pig farmer. He got his sows over the eat-your-children habit by hand-rearing them. He literally removes the piglets as soon as they are born and returns them day and night to their mother for suckling and stands guard until they are done. He weans at the earliest possible moment and bottle feeds. Bottle feeds! He says there's no way to get a sow over it. Once she's destroyed one, she'll destroy them all. He offered to haul Elsinore over to his place, offered to even pay me for her, but I said no. I said I'd rather turn the feedlot into another iris field and I might grow half of it in cooking sage. He laughed, but I'm going to show him. I believe I can make more money selling irises and cooking sage than hogs I have to slop and bottle feed. I'd rather turn kitchen scraps into compost over pig slop. Burrell said pigs are nothing if not composting machines. I said to him, "Bullshit." Ha! You should have seen the size of his eyes. "Never thought I'd see the day when Charlotte Dodge would grow a dirty mouth," he said. "I thought your Christian faith run deeper than that."

"My faith does run deeper than that, Burrell," I told him, "but I can't find a word in the Bible to express it, else I'd use it."

A rare thing: Burrell Dodge gave me a hug. We've been trudging through a day, an hour, a minute at a time, and I suspect today was the first time he recognized how enormous this experience is for every one of us. It's mind-blowing. We've been under siege here.

Standing there in his manure-stained overalls and thermal shirt with that bit-lip grin of his—the same grin your daddy has: full of the devil. The thing I noticed in that moment was the white that has come into Burrell's beard and mustache. His hair is blonde as it's always been, but that beard is starting to tell on him. I like my father-in-law. He made it possible to keep Cash's and my dreams alive, else you and I'd be living in welfare housing, likely in Baker City, more jobs and cheaper housing there. That's what you get for being a freeway town and opening yourself to hosting a state correctional institution. That way we'd get to see your daddy more often.

September 10

Well, Bethie, we got the harvest about behind us, all except the sunflowers, and their seeds won't be ready for a bit. Already got a wholesaler who has put down a deposit on every bushel they yield. Plus, the sage. I told Burrell my cooking sage crop was a good idea. He bet me twenty dollars against it, and now he has to pay up. Herbs you sell by the ounce, and I sold every leaf. Same goes for the extra bed of irises. Sold flowers and bulbs. You can't believe how easy it was to sell that sage. I dried some of mine and took it around to restaurants alongside a sample I bought at the store. Sold itself. Don't come close to comparing. You should have seen me the day I got my first order. I was dancing around this kitchen. You were in your little swing laughing. Laughing! Yes, Bethie, you have taken to laughing. You still can't pull yourself up, but they fit you with a little set of braces and a tiny walker kind of gadget with wheels that you push along, and you motor your tiny self all over this house. The physical therapist came two times a day at first, morning and late afternoon. I was on day shift at the hospital, so Mrs. Blessing had to serve as your assistant— God love her heart, she went and got her certified nursing assistant training and license so she would feel better prepared to help with you. Initially, she only took a first aid course and CPR, but then we found out the state would pay for an assistant for you, so *voila!* Almost overnight, it seems, she had extra income, which improved her self-image a substantial amount, and I had the trained help I needed for you, which made all the difference when the call came from Dr. Cadena about the possibility of putting you in these baby-sized braces as soon as you were big enough. More or less to get Shriners to pay for them, you had to have oversight by somebody trained for a period of time, and it couldn't be a parent. A relative would do, except Suzette is already too danged busy. You hadn't quite grown as much as the doctors would like. You still have trouble putting on weight. But then Suzette and Mrs. Blessing came up with the idea almost at once to take you off formula and put you on full-cream milk. We tried cow's milk, but that did nothing but cause ear infections, to the point of possibly putting you through surgery to place drainage tubes in your ear, at which case I drew the line, as you hopefully might expect. Several women at church—Mrs. Elmer, Mrs. Timberlake, and Suzette—told me their children had runny noses and ear infections until they took them off cow's milk. Mrs. Elmer gave her kids powdered soy formula, but I don't like the idea of giving a baby something that isn't natural.

So, I went to the library in La Grande. Actually, I took you with me, Bethie. You are a little celebrity. Everyone wants to hold and play with you, but we have to be careful of exposing you. You have to wear a little surgeon's mask. For this reason, I rarely take you off the farm. But when I do, behind that mask you are 100% smiling. People are amazed that you don't tear it off. You just act like it's regular as rain.

I read all I could find on goat's milk and discovered it is easier on humans than cow's milk, and so got myself a pair of nannies, Polly and Molly, to breed with Horace and Jackson, the billies we've employed for ages to keep down weeds. To make certain, we also bred them with a 4-H prize-winning stud from over in Union, and soon we will have our own little flock. Burrell calls me Bo-Peep. I kept telling him Bo-Peep had sheep, but that doesn't stop him. Kid goats are the cutest blasted things you ever saw. Of course, I will sell the kids (oh my aching heart, I can already hear those mothers bleating and crying for days and days) after they are weaned. Right away, Polly and Molly kicked down the wire pen door and chewed up an azalea plant that should have been high enough off the ground to be out of reach, but dummy me, I had planted a half-barrel with petunias and had it sitting under the hanging azalea, and both those dang nannies climbed up and helped themselves to what had been my oldest and biggest azalea. I guess trying to settle their stomachs, they went after every lettuce leaf I had—don't know why they chose those two things when there was so much else, but they did—and the azalea made them so sick, I had vomit and diarrhea all over the yard. Called the vet, and he filled them full of charcoal, gave me a slew of instructions for keeping them hydrated and following up with a probiotic. If you can imagine, I have to feed them yogurt for thirty days, too. Never have I seen such a mess. I guess azaleas can kill a goat, and the vet basically scolded me for not doing a bit more research. The billies have never gone after the azaleas, and I have them hanging all over the place, but, as I said, most of them are too high for a goat to reach. The ones hanging on the front of the house are so high I have to attach a three-foot wand to the hose to water them.

The goat bills keep stacking up. I had to have built their own little paddock and run an electric row around it top and bottom—no way will I have them tethered. Grady (that's my new boarder; I don't know if I mentioned him, more about that later, I guess) built the pen and will be in charge of milking the two nannies when the time comes, and Jessamine, whose milk I will continue to sell. We should have enough extra goat's milk to sell to the health food store in La Grande and some to Mrs. Elmer who makes us cheese, and still keep enough for you. We had to get certified, which was pure tediousness, but it will be worth it, not only for your sake, but for the income, even if the endeavor has started out in the red. You picked up the weight you needed pretty quickly on what we bought from the Elmers, after which you and I and Suzette and Mrs. Blessing travelled to Shriners along with several physical therapy aides from the Health Dept. and Grande Ronde Physical Therapy and everybody trained at once on how to help you.

September 11

Twenty-nine. I am twenty-nine years old today. It was mid-afternoon before I remembered. Suzette baked me a cake. I wish my mother were here. I wish Cash were here. I am surrounded by people, but sometimes I get so lonely I want to drive up Rimrock Road and jump off. A mother shouldn't admit that to her child. We're supposed to persevere. God tells us to. The Bible tells us to, but lately, I sit in my church pew, and I can't feel a thing of God.

September 13

Grady talked me in to taking boarders of another kind. He thinks I ought to board more horses. Says horses are less work than flowers and produce. Says their manure would be good for the cherry orchard. Says he recommends not plowing leaves into the orchard floor. Says it will cause a fungus if you have a late, wet fall. Says we could lose the entire orchard. I called the county extension agent and he said leaves couldn't make that much difference. That orchard covers four acres. That's a lot of cherry leaves to rake out and plowing them under is quick and easy and to me makes sense. But that orchard is also many decades old. I don't know. Our cherries come out fine. We spray them like everybody else. They are worm-free. I don't see any reason to change. Maybe if you've got horses turned loose and tromping the leaves into the ground you wouldn't have to plow them under. Eight hundred dollars a month, though. Grady says if I took in six more head I could rake in eight hundred a month. Certainly, we have pasture enough. He says also he wouldn't mind sowing a field of hay. He says he'd do that and oversee care of the boarder horses for a reduction in rent. I don't know. I have to think about it. Plus, three of our regular seasonal employees—Miguel, Jaime, and Jesus—just now told me they won't be back next year. No reason that was clear to me, although, I suspect they don't like having to answer to Grady. He makes his living as a farrier, has for some time—hence his interest in boarding horses, I suppose. He can do the shoeing right here and charge for it. He showed me how he could turn the barn into stalls and a smithy. He used to be a deputy sheriff, and I'm guessing that makes the men nervous. I don't see why, really, I mean, that was quite a while back, as I understand it from Grady. It's a thing I like about him, except I don't necessarily like him having guns in the house. I do make him keep them locked in a strong box in the cellar. Either way, I hate to lose those three good men. They know how I like things done. They are good pickers, and they always have stayed on to help me through the end of flower season and pumpkin harvest rather than following the fruit otherwise. Talked to Cash's lawyer, Pete Frame, on the phone this morning about it, but he didn't have much to offer, just to be careful who I listen to. He says he thinks Cash is doing better, and I agree, he sounds better over the phone to me, too. Cash asked me to drive over with you and stay a few days. He says there's a possibility of a conjugal visit. If you are old enough and smart enough to be reading this, you likely know what that is.

September 30

Shit. Yes, I said it. Shit, shit, shit, shit, shit. Oh my gosh, Bethie, I kissed Grady Bell. I didn't mean to. Shit, shit, shit, shit. Damn brandy. Damn, damn, damn. Now what? He has to move, that's what.

October 7

Okay, well, I had a long talk with a priest. Lord help me. I left you with Mrs. Blessing and drove to Walla Walla. Can you believe it? Walla Walla to find a priest who would not know who I am. I went to a priest over a minister because I wanted to go into one of those booths where no one could see me and get it out of my head and body. I threw every drop of brandy I had down the sink. I told Grady he had to move. He said it made him sad, but he is gone. I didn't like his guns in the house anyway. I swear he did not touch me otherwise. I immediately agreed to the conjugal visit with Cash. I never knew anything in life could move me to such cussing, but I came so close to screwing up that I no longer trust myself. The priest said I need to see a counselor, that I have too much, too much, too much on my plate for any one human. I hate the idea of that. It makes me feel weak. So, I decided to go ahead with the horses. It'll bring in some money, it'll give me one more thing to keep me out of trouble. Funny thing, no one questioned Grady taking off like that. Suzette said she wondered about him from the beginning. Said she thought it was a little strange, him trying to push his ideas over on me and creating so much confusion. He did basically move in and try to take over. Cinnamon gum. When he kissed me, he had a piece of cinnamon gum in his mouth. It's the smell that I can't put away.

October 8

We were sitting in the kitchen this morning, Bethie. You and me. I had coffee water on. It was, oh, I don't know, six o-clock. Not quite dawn. You were fed and warbling like a little chick. I swear you are trying to speak, but you haven't figured out how to maneuver your little lips to control the sound. Without warning, the door flew open. The inside door. I checked the storm door—still locked. No wind outside. That was it. The inside door burst open. Nothing else. You looked at me and started laughing. I was fairly raining goose bumps. Shivered to my bones. My first thought was to book a reservation in Baker. If I'm hallucinating, clearly, it's time for a break. We're going for three days, you and me, to see your daddy.

October 13

Grady came by this morning to apologize. Said he doesn't have to live here to help with the horse business. Said the rest of it can disappear into the air and never be thought of or spoke of again. Says he'll still grow a hay crop, and I can trust him to the farrier work, and he swore he'll never lay a hand on me. I want to let it go. I like the horse idea. It's a good bit of money, and I could drop a shift at the hospital. Pete Frame is working on the conjugal visit. Cash's caseworker called yesterday. We have to make provisions for you. Can't have you physically in the cottage "during the conjugating." Ha! Sex in prison parlance is conjugating. I thought that only had to do with verbs. I can't believe I have to involve so many people in my business, but I had to go to Suzette and Burrell and ask them to check on the house. We set the date for a week from today. Mrs. Blessing will go with me to care for you during "the act." Can't have sex in front of a child. Still so much to do here, and the pumpkin harvest coming up before long. I'm letting them go u-pick this year. I didn't organize the festival. I hate that because it's so much fun. We normally pull out the cider press and dress in old-fashioned garb. People bring potluck, and Burrell drags over his big tent his family used to use as a dining hall on cattle drives way back when, so people can file through and fill their plates out of the weather. It's quite a time. We normally have kids and families tromping all over, petting livestock, etc. We let the peacocks loose to strut. I make a big kettle of fudge from a recipe card my mother left in her diary. I made the fudge, but I'm taking it to your daddy. I made a flyer for Burrell and Suzette to hand out explaining that the festival will return next year.

October 20—a little before noon

We are here. You are sitting in your chair across from me, batting at a toy Mrs. Blessing is teasing you with. No problems with the drive. We are staying at a motel called The Maverick. It's not bad. I have almost never stayed in a hotel or a motel, unless you count the Hill Street Trust Cottages. The drive was fine. It's a simple trip down I-84 from La Grande to Baker City. Takes about an hour. Simple, that is, unless it's closed because of snow on the pass. The Grande Ronde Valley has a mountain pass at either end, and sometimes it gets snowed in and closed off from the world in winter. I love that time, really. I mean, I guess it's frightening on account of not being able to get a person in and out in a severe trauma case or medical emergency. Don't know if anybody has ever died because of it, but both passes at times have been closed for as much as three days. We haven't had snow to speak of yet this year. The foothills had a dusting, enough to fill in the Oregon Trail ruts on the south side of the freeway and make them much more visible. Maybe you'll learn about the Oregon Trail in school one day, but it's the route your ancestors came over when they emigrated from the mountains of Kentucky. Somewhere I have old papers and diaries belonging to my mother's side of the family. My great-great grandmother wrote about the hardships they had coming over in covered wagons. Babies and children dying of smallpox and cholera. Struggles with the Indians. One thing I brought with me was the book I started around the time you were born—*Hell in Paradise*. It's written by a man, but he had an Indian wife. I read a few pages and then have to put it down. I like to say her name—Lah-tis-i-yet. If I ever came up with a flower hybrid, I think I'd give it that name. Lah-tis-i-yet. It sounds like the name of a flower. I bring it up because I haven't read a book since you were born that didn't have to do with goats or irises or growing something—one even about nothing but sage—and I hate not finishing what I've started, so I'm hoping, when I'm not *conjugating*, to get a little reading in and to try to finish *Paradise*.

Otherwise, Baker City doesn't have a whole lot to keep a person busy. A few little shops downtown. I'll actually have to backtrack to get to the correctional facility—it's west of town, but not far. Mrs. Blessing and I will get ourselves a pizza tonight. I love Klondike pizza. Maybe we'll take in the Natatorium tomorrow, which is now an historical museum. Lots of things for you to look at. I imagine we'll head to Safeway and grab a few things. Oh, and disposable diapers. Being on the road, I didn't want to fool with cloth diapers.

1:30 p.m.

I get to see your daddy in a little more than an hour. I'm set to meet him in the visiting room at 2:45. The off time has to do with his caseworker's schedule. We have to go through a session about not bringing in drugs or weapons. I can give him the fudge, but it has to be x-rayed. Rather than lose my good Tupperware, I put it in a gift box lined with wax paper. I was only allowed to bring as much as we could eat while we are in the conjugal. I'm nervous! I was warned ahead of time not to wear a dress to the visiting area, not to show cleavage, etc. I feel more like I'm getting ready for surgery than having sex. Rules, rules. Oh. And no spiked heels. They can be used as weapons. No strings of beads or anything that could be used to choke somebody. You'd think I was the criminal! Oh! And no perfume! He can't go back to his dormitory smelling like a woman. In fact, we both have to shower before we can leave.

First, we will hear about birth control and be admonished to avoid getting pregnant, how conjugal visits are a privilege, and how, if we screw up, it will affect Cash's parole possibilities and eliminate our chances for further conjugals, and on, and on.

7:30 p.m.

Bethie. I'm your mother, and you are my child, and if you are reading this then you already know so many things about me that a child shouldn't know about her mother. But for my own self, I have to write these words on paper. Maybe I should write and burn them.

One of the hardest things I have ever done is sit across from your daddy this afternoon, knowing that I'd kissed Grady Bell. A kiss may seem like a small thing, but when you are a married person it is a betrayal. We didn't get to talk much privately today, so I didn't bring it up. I got the sense that life may be a little better for Cash than it was a few months ago. I've been hesitant to mention it here, because there's no real need for you to know, but if I'm writing to the white-haired version of myself, I might want to remember it. Plus, it's still a struggle, and he's still awash in the aftermath, which means I have to have somewhere to process it. I have never been raped. I can't say I know what it feels like to be physically forced into something like that, and especially for a man, it's got to be one of the most difficult things. Those men didn't quite rape him, but they roughed him up like they were going to. A guard walked in on it happening. Got them all tickets back to Pendleton, where they had come from. Powder River has a zero-tolerance policy. One screw up and you're back to what they call the Big House. I tried to ask about it over the phone in advance of my visit, but he's sullen around it and won't talk. I must say, to his credit, I believe he tried hard today to put on his best face and to make tomorrow seem as normal as possible, under the circumstances. He held my hand, told me how beautiful I looked, even though my blouse and slacks were prim and conservative with no accessories. He wore prison blues, of course, but I have to tell you, Cash Dodge in denim is not an undesirable thing. He passes the time now by lifting weights and running. I felt myself stir in my soul, in a way that I do not feel around Grady Bell, and I believe that is because of the history Cash and I have. I mean, we are a family, and prison or not, nothing changes that. I believe I have always loved him, even when we were children. It's the spark you can't explain that rises up between two people. Some couples are meant to be, and I believe that is the case with us. Could I have left him? Sure. Not one person in the entire of the Grande Ronde Valley would have held that against me. Somebody like Grady Bell come along and sweep me off my feet? Chances are nobody would bat an eyelash. But I feel proud of the fact that I've stood by him, that I, as a woman, and even young as I am, hormones giving me fits and all, could stand by my husband through the most difficult of times. I don't think I could have lived with myself otherwise, truth known.

October 21—8 p.m.

What a day, what a day! First, you and I went to the visitor's room to meet with your dad. He was overjoyed. I gave him instruction about your shunt. He was crazy over your pretty red hair. He thought Suzette had once mentioned somebody in the family with red hair, although as I told him, just about everybody has someone with red hair, and both of us have people in our lines from way back who came from Scotland. It's not that unusual. Meantime, you were a charmer. You cooed and blew raspberries and giggled and laughed. Cash was surprised that you were so interactive. He thought you'd just be more fragile. I felt badly that I hadn't given him a full understanding of how far you've come. We showed you off with the little walker and the braces, and you acted proud, trying even to get away from him when he acted like he was chasing you. I hadn't told him about your little glasses. That was a thing we learned when we went to Portland to get you fitted for the braces. They ran you through some eye exams and discovered that part of your developmental troubles could be related to the fact that you simply could not see! I didn't think it was a big deal, but you should have seen the change in you when we took you to the optometrist in La Grande. They fitted you with temporary little black frames and a little black gadget that holds the glasses on your head, and gosh did you squeal. Not a one of us thought about the fact that maybe you couldn't see. When I questioned Dr. Cadena about it in Portland, she said it's hard with preemies and a child with all your other conditions. You really have to wait until there is some way for the child to respond to testing. The thing with you is that you were doing some things. You could track an object with your eyes, but only if that object was close. She said what she noticed with you on this most recent visit was that you got upset when the object was moved away. She said it was something you hadn't done before. Anyway, short story is, they worked their magic in Portland, sent the prescription to the optometrist in La Grande, and we got you suited up. All things being equal, your vision can be followed just fine here at home. I can hardly wait to see how it changes your interactions with the world. You are so happy and bubbly that I'm expecting we're going to see enormous improvements in you.

Your daddy cried. "Glasses?" he said. "But she's so little. They are so little." He hasn't spent any time with you, and to see his little daughter in leg braces and glasses and the shunt and being quite undersized and almost two years old and not able to utter a distinguishable syllable—a lot to absorb. That doesn't change the fact that he loves you as much as a father can. He told me he's been drawing you pictures and writing you letters, hoping one day you'll understand that even though he was apart from you, it didn't change one iota how he felt about you.

We stayed there in the visiting area for a couple of hours. Cash ate some of the fudge, and we talked and held hands and drank coffee. Neither of us wanted family time to end. The word I'd put on it is *rosy*. I think we both felt a little *rosy*, you know, as in rose-colored glasses? Like we could sit there in that sterile, metallic-looking place and pretend for a bit that we were just one more normal family having just one more normal day together. The guard gave us plenty of space, and I didn't feel bad at all about anything. I didn't think of Grady Bell. Not once. Just felt happy to be with my husband and my little daughter. Cash got to feed you your blueberries and pumpkin. Now that choked me up. I asked the guard if I could go to the bathroom, leave you with your daddy. The visitor's bathroom door is right there, and I was only gone minutes, and I think Cash was nervous, but he needed to experience time with you. He needed to know how it felt to be a father holding his child, feeding his child. He tried to hide the fact that he was wiping tears when I came out of the restroom, but I saw it. I didn't say anything, but I know what I saw.

Time came when I had to hand you over to Mrs. Blessing. We made the arrangement that she would come for you after two hours. Her job was to take you back to the motel, feed you your bottle, and put you down for your nap. She said you cried when she took your glasses off! She had to put them back on and take them off before you got the idea that she wasn't taking them away for good. That tells me something. You know more about what's going on than you are being given credit for, and you'd better believe I am paying attention.

To get to the conjugal visit cottage, I had to go further inside the prison. I didn't care for the feeling, but they had a female guard escort me in. I had to go to this little cell of a room that looked like small clinic. Exam table and blood pressure cuff on a stand, that kind of thing. Here is something else a mother should not be telling her daughter, but I had to submit to a cavity search. What that means is that my parts had to be examined. I did not know this before your daddy went to prison, but women sometimes smuggle in drugs by stuffing a balloon inside their vagina or rectum. Isn't that awful? I knew it was coming. I'd been counseled on it plenty, but the humiliation I felt bending over for that female guard was not something I soon will let go of. It will be the same every time. The guard was very kind. She was very gentle and apologetic. But still.

Then I dressed and she walked me to the conjugal visit cottage. It was sort of cute, if you can picture joining the word cute with any element of a prison, but some attempt had been made. Paintings fastened to the wall—and I do mean fastened. They were bolted on. Ruffled calico curtains. A little table. A double bed. Nothing you could break off and break apart that might be smuggled back inside. The walls may have been painted (yellow), but it was still pretty austere.

Your dad, well, he fumbled a bit. They'd given us ninety minutes. Both the guard and the matron were waiting in what was set up to look like a little parlor outside the bedroom area. It had a sofa and a chair. They told us it was soundproof, but I doubt that. Cash and me, we're both pretty quiet about certain things, anyway. He was shy and embarrassed. I told him we could just talk if he wanted, but he said no. He wanted me. I had to be the one to bring the condoms, of course, and those were annoying. Every time he got excited, he'd lose it before we could get it on. Finally, we did manage to make it happen, but you know, the condom came off as he was pulling out. I went and tried to wash myself out quick in the sink. As I was doing that, your daddy came up from behind me and did naughty things to give me pleasure. He comforted me, and I cried. He cried in his hands as I put my clothes on and told the matron I was ready to leave.

October 22

I had to meet with the case worker this morning to talk about how the conjugal visit went. The next one is scheduled for thirty days out.

January 1, 1983

Two feet of snow on the ground Christmas Day. All gone and nearly forty degrees now. You are doing very well with the braces. Two more teeth.

March 30

Mrs. Blessing made you an Easter dress. Suzette and Burrell bought you black patent leathers.

April 10

That sound of a woman crying again. This time Mrs. Blessing heard it, too. We searched the house and the grounds over. But nothing.

September 17

Tough working two twelve-hour shifts a week at the hospital with all the u-pickers here at the house. We planted more end-of-season crops this year because of another expansion to the iris beds and also because it's hard to keep the goats penned up and out of the lettuce all the time. I hate having to turn on the electric fence. They never learn. They're always shocking themselves. But only when the lettuce is in. I talked to some folks over at 4-H and the county extension agent, all who say it's pretty strange behavior. Goats are stubborn, but generally they do learn.

You are getting bigger and bigger. Grady came over to service the boarding horses yesterday (I realize how far behind I am in writing in this; I did take in six boarding horses; Grady and Burrell built stalls inside the big barn) and talked about getting you a specialized saddle, but I think it's too dangerous and you're too small. He says he read about horseback riding helping kids with CP—that's what your diagnosis is now, EEC with mild cerebral palsy, and that last they based on your speech and motor delay. I guess when I realized you'd never read this is when I stopped writing. But today I decided again that maybe I'd one day want this for myself. We now know for certain that we won't get to keep you long. If you make ten we'll be lucky. I haven't told your daddy. I likely won't. It's just one more thing.

The issue with Grady passed. Do I wish I was available for him? Yes, I do. He's an interesting man. He talks about philosophy and Buddhism. I didn't know we had anything but Christians around here.

September 19

One thing that happened when I went for the conjugal visit this last time is that I ran into a woman who is a member of the Nez Perce tribe who happened to be one of the newly hired matrons at the prison. Now that conjugal visits are allowed, they have to have more women on staff. Her name was Diane Henry. She looked like she might be a tribal person, so I asked her. I felt kind of stupid about it later. But she was a really nice gal and seemed willing to tell me what she knew. I talked to her about the *Hell in Paradise* book I read and the reading I've been doing off and on about the Nez Perce and the war they fought with the Army and asked her if she knew anything about the woman's bones that were found a few years back. She said she's heard about the discovery, and most people believe her husband the fur trapper murdered her. Have I written about this? I can't remember. The old Indian bones that were found about the time your father got sentenced? Her name was Lah-tis-i-yet (I think I *did* already write about it, but no way in hell I'm going back through to make sure I'm not repeating myself— maybe the eighty-year-old version of me will appreciate the reminder), and the image of him burying her won't leave me. I think about her and think about her, her spirit wandering around the mountains all those years. Where did she go once her body was properly put to rest?

September 20

Well, I said no to the saddle. I can't see taking that kind of risk.

Many people came through today. The tomatoes have been plentiful, and they are still on, so people keep coming and coming. Zucchini I can't give away. I've got more orders for the last of the corn and the early potatoes than I can or want to fill. I have to save some for my own use. Mrs. Blessing has been putting up as much as she can as fast as she can. She brushed a little oil on some zucchini slices and salt and threw them in the dehydrator, just on a lark, and they turned out like potato chips! So now we're going to give away some samples and the recipe to try to get people to buy zucchini. The new student boarder tries to help, but she has to drive to La Grande four days a week for classes. Plus, the hospital has been busy, so I've had to do extra shifts. I hate to say it, but if you were a normal toddler, running around and tearing everything up, we'd be up a creek. We flat wouldn't have time for everything.

September 21

It's like my heart and soul are magnetic and the earth is one great big steel plate. If I don't keep moving, I'm afraid BOOM! I'll be sucked down and stuck so tight I'll never get loose. What did women like my great-great-grandmother Bethany do? How did they survive the pain and hardship of losing children? Sometimes I look at you sleeping at night and open my mouth and scream completely silent screams. Hard and so wide my jaw and neck muscles hurt the next morning. How did this happen? How did I get to this point? Shouldn't I be traipsing about Europe or climbing mountains? Shouldn't I be writing books or painting masterpieces or discovering cures for disease? A few times

I've let myself collapse to the floor in a heap of sobs and awakened the next day covered with a blanket. Mrs. Blessing never says a word.

January 2, 1980

A year already? Have I sleep-walked through another year? Can't be. I laughed when I put the new calendar up yesterday, because we were supposed to be annihilated by nuclear war by now.

The hospital job. Well. When you're on night shift, all you do in the daytime is sleep. Not to make a pun, but it is turning out to be as much of a blessing as Mrs. Blessing was when she arrived on the scene. Now I'm closer to her than I ever got to be to my own mother. She's taught me to look at tough things in a different way. She's asked me time and again to call her Doris, but I like being reminded of how lucky I am to have her, and that is the case every time I use her proper name. Plus, there's been all the church-going, and she is also the one who encouraged me to shop around, so to speak. I don't know why I think religion is the answer, but I've tried every single flavor. Mormons. Lutherans. Pentecostals. Bahá'í. Who even knew we had a Bahá'í meeting in La Grande? It sounds exotic, but they might be the most sensible people of all, except for the fact that they do have a prophet from the eighteen hundreds who was thought to be the second coming of Jesus. I don't care much about prophets, but the group in La Grande has taught me to be grateful for my creative gifts. That's what came from the few times I attended their meetings—which are basically potlucks—the realization that what I need is something creative to fill the gap. The sunflowers did that, too. I'll save that for later. I've got to sleep so I can go back and do another shift tonight.

January 11, 1980

Just like that—no warning, no nothing—and you were gone, Bethie. Heart attack in the middle of the night. Like an old man, you threw a huge clot. Not even two years old. All the meds and blips on all the machines weren't enough. None of us heard the alarm. Why? Because I forgot to set the damned alarm. It's supposed to go off if you don't move every so often. They told me not to feel guilty. It wouldn't have mattered. It was too big, the infarction. The my-o-car-di-al infarction. You were too little, too weak, and I was sleeping on the job. I went to get a razor blade to cut my wrist, but Mrs. Blessing stopped me, fought me, cut herself wrestling it away, then slapped me and told me to pull it together long enough to call the ambulance and the police. I want to say it right here and now: FUCKYOUFUCKYOUFUCKYOUGOD!!!!!!

It's enough to make a person bitter. It's enough to make you want to burn down your own house, fuck the preacher, impale yourself on a lightning rod, slit open the throat of a newborn foal and coat yourself in its steamy blood. I imagined all of it over and over. I thought about killing one of the horses, just to drown myself in its blood. I hate myself. I hate life. I hate the world. I hatehatehatehatehate Cash Dodge. I hope somebody does rape him in prison. I hate himhatehimhatehimhatehim. I hope somebody kills him with one of those shrifts or shrives or whatever they're called. I have all the modes of death for myself planned. I can drive off the same road that took my parents. I can drive to the top of Mount Emily, which is already deep in snow, and lay down in a snow drift. I can and will cut my wrists if it comes to that. I will not make myself live another day if I decide I can't endure this. Those are plans if I need them. I hate being tough. I hate being tough like a motherfucker.

Now I curse like a sailor, and I love it. I am in love with the filth of bad words. I curse my own soul with illegal words. Words my mother would have thrown a hissy fit over.

Goddamnfuckingsonofabitchingcuntlicker of a life anyway.

Why me? Why me? WHYWHYWHYWHY? Can't I go back and reset the clock? Can't I not have walked down the aisle with Cash? Can't I go on off to college in Portland or Seattle or San Francisco? Can I notnotnot be a woman of twenty-nine (or am I thirty yet? God! I'm thirty! I can't even think of how old I am!) who looks haggard enough to be eighty? Who has a DEAD BABY? "Oh no you don't, darlin'. You look superfine." This was my gay friend talking last week. Yes, my gay friend. So, sue me. I've gotten to be close with the cashier at the health food store who confides in me over wine dinners where we each show up with a little airplane bottle of brandy from the liquor store and a plate of food and sit on her porch and drink and talk and laugh until we fall asleep in her big hammock, and I wake up sometime around midnight and make my way back home. She's gay. I like that about her. To me it makes her more real. I wanted to fuck her. I didn't care about being married. I'm not married. How can you be married to a man who sets you up to have a dead baby? The night after you died Jen and I got drunk and talked about the best way to suck a dick. I laughed so hard I peed my pants and had to throw them in her washing machine. Apparently, she's had non-gay experiences, because she was pretty confident in her descriptions. She said, "Let's both take our clothes off and put them into the washing machine together. We'll be bonded by cleanliness." I couldn't stop laughing long enough to say yes or no. She stripped bare naked, helped me off with my shirt and bra, and there I stood on the moonlight overlooking her stand of pines and garden surrounded by deer fence. Naked as a jaybird. You aren't here to read this anymore, so I can say it. I lay with Jen. I lay with Jen, and I liked it, and I don't feel one iota guilty. Fuck you, Cash Dodge. Fuck you and your fucking kind. Men who make babies and abandon them. Men who can't see beyond the end of their dicks.

After it was over. we saw something. A woman. A figure. At first I thought it was just a deer. Then, she was walking toward me playing some kind of flute, which made me think of all the weird things that happen around our place. I wonder if this is the same woman I've heard crying. I know it is the same woman, but I can't prove it. At times I've wondered if the crying was a projection of me. Like maybe I held back my emotions too long, letting myself stay run over with work, just so I wouldn't have to feel anything. She was hard to make out, even in the full moon, but I could tell she was lost or looking for something, trying maybe to call something to her, so I yelled out, "It's okay! Can I help? What do you want? What do you need?" I reached toward her but she disappeared. Afterwards, I realized she might have been my mother.

February 12

Burrell said the other day that he thought the whole mess had worn me down but had not broke me. I said, "Burrell, it's made me crusty, and I like it. I can cuss good now. Beyond that, you know I don't want to talk about it."

He laughed and said, "A woman don't need to be so desensitized. A woman still ought to keep her soft side showing."

"Shit, Burrell," I said, patting my behind, "I got plenty of big soft side right here. If cursing is my way of coping, of keeping my stack of razors at bay, then let me curse."

He did his Burrell thing, rolling his eyes, shaking his head, and said, "Charlotte, there's not a soul in this valley with a complaint about your backside. But you don't survive the time you've had these past few years without figuring a place to put all the pain."

"I said, 'subject closed,' ain't that right?"

"Don't you go becoming no femi-nazi on us now. We see you hanging around Jen at the health mart."

"Burrell," I said, "don't you ever bring up Jen again. You want to talk about something, you talk to me about the way you raised Cash Dodge to be so stupid as to take up with an under-aged girl and to be so further stupid as to pick one who was going to be vengeful about it."

"Aw, Charlotte," he said. "I don't know. Squirrelly. Cash was always squirrelly that way. Always wanting approval of the women."

"Well," I said. "He sure blew that, now didn't he."

"Yes, ma'am," Burrell said. "You are right about that one. He sure did."

What I learned quick in your short, young, life, Bethie, is bringing up kids is the worst kind of job. You love it and hate it, and you don't see a paycheck. But you're stuck. You need it like it was heroin. I'm sitting here scratching this out in this notebook, and I would give anything to smell the sweet flower scent of your baby head again. Of course, that part of you didn't last long. Once you were sick with congestive heart failure, you started smelling like yeast dough. Something about that smell told me you weren't going to stay with me. I just didn't want to own up to it. Denial. By the end, your pretty hair got sparse and flaky. Don't know what that was. The dysrhythmia medication, maybe. Your funeral was about as big as I've ever seen. I didn't want it, but Cash insisted. I think he knew they'd let him come home. Even Pearl from Hill Street and Debbie Henry from the prison and a number of Hill Street staff made the trip. Burrell arranged bagpipes. The sound still haunts me.

Sometimes I want to go to that conjugal visit room with its cute little curtains and homey atmosphere and let Cash ram me 'til I'm bloody and dead. Then I wouldn't have to think. I wouldn't have to breathe the air where you used to be. I wouldn't have to remember that I am a woman who once had a fairly normal life with goals and hopes and almost no scars. When I met Cash, I still had my wisdom teeth. Now those spots are empty sockets still trying to fill in, even though the dentist yanked them out months ago. I'd been putting it off and putting it off and the first thing I did after your funeral was to make an appointment to get them cut out. I wanted to feel the pain. After every meal I have to irrigate the damn things with a syringe full of sterilized salt water, so it's just one more pain in the ass. The taste reminds me of Cash coming in my mouth. A thing he's started wanting. So we can spend the rest of the time cuddling, he says.

Why don't I just divorce him?

April 24

Sunflowers getting big in the new hot house. I love the hot house. It's a worthwhile distraction. Burrell and the hands build it out of reclaimed windows after Jen and I decided to launch the sunflower oil products. I didn't have any money. God no. Burrell had the suggestion of using reclaimed windows when I'd sat down with him and Suzette and showed them the business plan for 7Sunflower, a line of lotions, creams, lip balm, and massage oil. "What's the 7 for?" Suzette asked. Burrell and I looked at each other and looked at her. "Oh," she said. "Seven years."

"Seven years," I said.

"You realize how much of that is already gone by, don't you?" Burrell said. "You haven't let a mite of moss grow. You'll barely have time to get a crop in this year as it is, get the seeds down to oil and start working with formula. What happened to simply selling seed, like you've been doing? Are you going to set up your own cold press or have oil from your crop shipped back to you? That gets expensive, Charlotte. Seed is pure money without the trouble of creating a product. Where'd you get this know-how anyway? You get college while nobody was looking?"

"Burrell, you know damn good and well I've got plenty of college," I said. "I'm going to grow an extra crop and trade the seed heads for oil. We got land for it. I'll still make money off the original plot. I've been reading every book the library can order for me from University of Oregon, and I've been talking with a chemist at Eastern. Jen's already been sending letters to other health food stores in Oregon, looking for feedback. Nobody has a sunflower oil line. Not one brand. People use it in their products, along with another bunch of garbage, but nobody's doing what we're talking about doing. I've tried it in the blender with store-bought stuff. Jen and Mrs. Blessing and I stayed up all night one night. We tried different emulsifiers."

"Jen. That queer? Cash will have a fit."

What Burrell doesn't know is that Jen has kept me away from the razor blades. She's not easy to argue down from certain opinions, and it's her opinion that I will survive the loss of you, Bethie, so I hold on to her, and she stays upright for me. She's solid enough to do that. Solid in her body and her philosophies. Not in a man or woman way, but in a *person* way. She does a pair of Levi's and cowboy boots justice, and I have to admit some of my attraction is physical. She isn't prissy or fussy or dike-ish, she's just Jen. She's like a daddy and a Buddha and a mother and a best friend and a counselor and a lawyer and a walking encyclopedia rolled into one. She takes the place of so much I dare anybody to talk to me about "impropriety." Or *sin* or any of that other Jesus shit. It's 1980. My daughter is dead, my fucking husband in prison. I can do whatever fucking shit thing I have an urge to do.

"Not up for discussion, Burrell. She's my friend and business partner, and you can close your pie hole about it," I said, "and, frankly, I can't be bothered to give a shit what Cash Dodge thinks about anything."

It's hard to believe I told my father-in-law to shut up, but you know what? He hasn't said another word. He's been in on this from the ground floor, only asking for the same cut he gets out of everything else. He had the idea to build the hot house from salvage, and now all winter we'll enjoy greens and baby cauliflower grown in that hot house. Why none of us thought of it sooner. I get to craving a real vegetable in the winter like nobody's business, and nothing they sell at the grocery stores in town has any taste to it.

Burrell also built a production shed from salvage. Not very big, but enough to get us started. I don't know. Word's getting around. People are trying to help. If Cash ever does get out, he won't know the place. I think a lot about divorcing him, but Jen says I shouldn't make any big decisions until a year after your death. I'm still grieving, she says. Mostly I think she's worried what will happen if I do. I think she's worried I'll expect her to move in. Because, Bethie, if I do divorce Cash Dodge, I will be the one who keeps this farm, not the other way around.

I went up above Cove at Joshua's Bench and planted a tree for you and a bunch of bulbs. I took an old wrought-iron loveseat out of the shed, got some pints of exterior paint and restored it with raspberry with lemon-yellow highlights, and hauled it up there along with a couple of angel statues. That's all I'm going to do for now. When enough time passes, I'll think about a head stone for the cemetery, but as far as I'm concerned, I'd prefer to think of your spirit resting there with Mom and Dad. Sitting up there on that loveseat thinking about you and them? That's all of me so-called God is ever going to get again.

April 9, 1981

A year since I picked this up? Not much point in keeping track now, I suppose. Emptied out your room, finally, Bethie. The cherry hands are here, so I asked Jesus (they all came back once they heard Grady was no longer in charge) to repaint. I went to take him lunch and saw him on the floor crying. He hadn't done a lick of work. *"Por favor,"* he said. I completely forgot he'd lost his two little twins to the flu way back when. I told him to find the rest of the crew and help with the mowing. Later he came back and acted like he wanted to explain. I gave him a plate of cookies to share and told him not to worry. It's okay to keep that raspberry paint on the walls for a while. I'll redo that room in the fall when crops are done. Maybe I'll take in another boarder.

June 30

I don't know if I'll go and see Cash any more for conjugal. What he's doing to me isn't right.

March 5, 1982

Sunflowers in hot house about six inches high.

April 16

Damn. One of the new sows died. (Yes, Burrell talked me into trying hogs again.) Having to bottle feed. Six to the litter. Bad freeze. Cherry blossoms from here to Sunday. Raking them into bags, then I'll lay them out on sheets on the parlor floor. You can sell dried cherry blossoms.

June 20

Skinny-dipping in Jen's pond. I have come to love the feel of water on my naked skin. I love how it makes me feel clean and renewed. As we dried off, the woman appeared, seated on a boulder, and stared at us. Her hair was cut short, in a bob, and she was dressed in capris and a simple blouse, just what my mother was wearing when she and Dad died. "You forgot all about it, didn't you?" Jen said. "Seeing her before."

"Yes," I said. We were whispering. It had happened before. We would see her, then she'd disappear, and we'd forget about her until we saw her again. The air was always full of her presence, and it was magical. The essence extended toward us, and all around her, almost like a mist. We saw her the night we first slept together and then the night we dawned the idea for 7Sunflower and at three or four other times, always when I was with Jen. I tried to hang onto those memories, as I knew they would vanish when she did. I no sooner said to Jen, "I think she's my mother," than another woman appeared. This one in a deer-hide dress, dark-skinned, black hair, clearly a native woman. Immediately I thought of the woman in the book, the wife of the fur trapper. Indeed, her braids were woven with dark fur. She sat on the rock beside my mother, holding a spray of large feathers that looked to be tied with some sort of fluorescent ribbon. "What do they want?" Jen whispered. "What do you want?" Jen said aloud.

"What do you want?" the woman in capris said, as if an echo.

"Mom," I said. "Mommy, is that you?" At which point they both flickered for a few moments, or maybe an hour. It's impossible to know because it felt like Jen and I flickered, too, the way a candle flickers, brightening, then dimming, then fading from sight, just as music, like that of a flute, maybe wood, maybe bamboo, a hollow, reedy sound, some foreign, nether-world tune, drifted and spun around us, then *became us*, then came *from us*, then split and wafted upward, through the trees, almost but not quite corporeal. I could see the music as if a shadow of light. I could feel it as my skin, heavy yet weightless, draping me, surrounding me, bonding me to Jen, then lifting, again and again. Then a smell. Familiar, but I couldn't place it exactly. It too, shifted and transported itself, then ticked like time, like a newsreel, unfolding in front of us until we could *see* the smells: for one long second the scent of campfire, followed by that of spruce tip tea, then roses and lilies and watermelon, the air on the first sunny spring day, fresh-bucked hay, and hot cedar trees, then June dirt after a late snow, a plowed field, the untrod mountain snows of February. Underneath it all, something darker, something rotted and from the deep past, like things buried and never unearthed, decayed wood and autumn leaves, like ragged wounds and blackened blood, algae on stagnant creek water, like the underneath of pile upon pile upon pile upon pile of long-undisturbed stone.

ACKNOWLEDGMENTS

On the morning of December 5, 2015, the phone rang. It was my brother, delivering the terrible news that our father had been found nearly naked, covered in manure and mud, face down in a cow pasture, surrounded by forty head of cattle. The night had been the coldest of the year, the fog so thick and impenetrable that weeks down the road, auto insurance companies were writing checks without question because of the unprecedented number of claims, although our father's accident was the only one that resulted in loss of life.

Police detectives were unable to determine how long he struggled, but he managed to crawl several hundred feet. His coat was found ripped to shreds, caught as he tried to crawl under a barbed wire fence. His pants and underwear had been pushed off by force of friction as he clawed his way in search of safety, blind in the dark and the fog, trying to make purchase with anything other than mud. The doors of the cute pickup he had recently purchased, a little black four-wheel drive, were covered in his muddy handprints. Because none of the cattle had lain down beside him, the farmer who owned the pasture and the police thought Daddy had not lingered long. Apparently, cattle, just like dogs, will instinctively lie beside an ailing human in an attempt to keep the body warm.

My father was neither smoker nor drinker, and, as a rule, he did not drive at night. For reasons no one understands, however, he left the house at about eight o'clock that evening, obsessed over a bill that needed paid that still hadn't shown up in the mail. Mom went on to bed. He drove to the post office. Stopped to pick up a sandwich at the quick stop in the little Southern Indiana village near where he and my mother lived on four acres of hardwoods and scrub cedar. Less than two hours later, he was dead.

The grief was, as grief is, immeasurable for all of us, but for me, my father had been my best friend, my confidant, my advisor, my fellow junk store junky. We spent hours on the phone every week. On occasions when he was ill, we talked as often as several times a day. I had feared losing him since the day in January of 1977 when I drove away from Indiana and our Kentucky past and my long family history of women being owned and over-lorded by their men, angry men who committed rape and molested children. I did not want that fate for myself, and so, at twenty-one, moved out West just to spend the next twenty years making the same mistakes my grandmothers made. This collection is my attempt to exorcise all that, to take my family history and create from it stories about women who own themselves, women who are victors, not victims.

The path has been rocky, painful, and difficult, and many times in that past three years I determined to give up writing altogether. I learned that despite my family's mixed heritage, I, as a person who visibly is white, cannot claim to know what it is to live as a brown-skinned person. I cannot write from the point of view of my grandmothers, for example, despite what they might have suffered for the way they looked, or my mother, or my father's brother, all of whom bore the darker complexions of their melting-pot ancestry. Their experience is not my lived experience. I can write from the point of view of an overweight white girl with bushy hair, or maybe even from that of a fair-skinned boy with bushy hair, but that is as far as it goes. I have learned to recognize racial appropriation, racial micro-aggression, racial profiling, and I am glad, because I would hate it if I were doing anything to perpetuate racism in our culture. I have tried to handle the backgrounds of my characters as truthfully yet delicately as possible so that I depict them wholly without offending anyone else, so that I don't make myself into a wannabe or stereotype, and so that I at the same time still honor my origins. During the final revision of the book, after the second well-respected author pointed out the racist tone of the stories, I literally held a private funeral for the generations of my people, so that I could put to rest the incredible disconnect I have lived with as someone who looks one way, but whose genetics are in reality something quite distinct, and went about, as much as possible, erasing, as much as possible, every mention of race or skin color from these stories, relying instead on craft to carry the ball, which is as it should be. The lesson to be learned for myself, is just how wrong it is to judge *anyone* by his or her physicality.

As with all my previous books, I have many people to thank for the tremendous help and support required to get me through the joys and pains of the creative process. I am a big baby, and am constantly wanting to give it all up—in favor of what, I don't know—so I have to thank those who kept me going during the dark times and who had faith in me when I did not.

First of all, Phil, who sustains me in all ways. He cooks, he cleans, he pays the bills, he supports me financially, emotionally, spiritually, creatively, makes me take vacations, holds my feet to the fire when I am being stupid or insecure. I see him as my reward for having suffered through and survived a trail of misogynistic, clueless men, all of whom constituted my life's learning tree, and as such, I have to honor them, too—despite the fact that, in truth, I want to tell them all to go to hell.

Also, my sons, their incredible wives, and my grandchildren. I see them doing what I could not do, and that is, thriving as functional families.

Ruth and Jim May, owners of Reflections Inn in the mountains of north central Idaho, where I have, for seventeen years now, gone to work on writing projects. Jim keeps me laughing and Ruth has become my most trusted confidant. She has strict orders never to let me quit.

Tiffany Midge, for saving me from making a fool of myself, as well as Laura Pritchett and Kristen Sundberg Lundstrum, who were the first ones to note that something about the collection just wasn't setting right, and Kim Barnes who has read every single book of prose I have written, and has lent her name to them with such kindness and generosity.

Debra Heironymous, who looked at drafts of some of the stories.

Jodi Thompson, who opened an entire publishing house to rescue my books and those of several other writers way back in 2016, when my previous publisher closed up shop, and who continues to support me for reasons I can't understand. She definitely is not getting rich off of me. Also, TwylaBeth Lambert, the editor for this book, who asked just the right questions at just the right moments. Seeing the book through her eyes made all the difference. The entire team at Fawkes Press deserves thanks, as well, for the hard work and exquisite talent that translates into beautiful books.

Lance and Andi Olsen, my eternal teachers, wherever you are.

All of the wonderful women who have attended our series of retreats at Reflections Inn, but in particular Melinda Artz, Matti Sand, Susan Ross, Rachel Clark, and Elizabeth Sloan. We all just keep on inspiring each other, which is as it should be, but, in particular, you all listened to drafts of these stories. Your feedback made all the difference.

My brother David and his wife Deborah, who continue to endure incredible hardship brought on by their having taken on the care of Mom in the wake of Daddy's death. I should have done things differently, and I didn't.

Mom, whose lessons have always been the hardest.

Lastly, the generations of women in my family, whose lives in the hills of Adair County, Kentucky, were numbingly labor intensive, fraught with prejudice, disease, children lost in infancy, mean men with indecent proclivities, isolation, and hardscrabble subsistence. Next time you feel inclined to make fun of a hillbilly woman, don't. Give her a bouquet of flowers instead.

Did you find an error in this book?

Fawkes Press strives to present a perfect product, but being staffed by mere humans, mistakes happen. If you find something we missed, please visit www.FawkesPress.com and click on "bounty program," to submit your find and enter to win our quarterly bounty.